Rebecca,
Born in the Maelstrom

ALSO BY MARIE-CLAIRE BLAIS

FICTION

The Angel of Solitude
Anna's World
David Sterne
Deaf to the City
The Fugitive
A Literary Affair
Mad Shadows
The Manuscripts of Pauline Archange
Nights in the Underground
A Season in the Life of Emmanuel
Tête Blanche
These Festive Nights
The Wolf
Thunder and Light
Augustino and the Choir of Destruction

NONFICTION

American Notebooks: A Writer's Journey

Rebecca,
Born in the Maelstrom

MARIE-CLAIRE BLAIS

Translated by Nigel Spencer

ANANSI

This edition published in 2009 by
House of Anansi Press Inc.
110 Spadina Avenue, Suite 801
Toronto, ON, M5V 2K4
Tel. 416-363-4343
Fax 416-363-1017
www.anansi.ca

Distributed in Canada by
HarperCollins Canada Ltd.
1995 Markham Road
Scarborough, ON, M1B 5M8
Toll free tel. 1-800-387-0117

Distributed in the United States by
Publishers Group West
1700 Fourth Street
Berkeley, CA 94710
Toll free tel. 1-800-788-3123

House of Anansi Press is committed to protecting our natural environment.
As part of our efforts, this book is printed on paper that contains 100%
post-consumer recycled fibres, is acid-free, and is processed chlorine-free.

13 12 11 10 09   1 2 3 4 5

Library and Archives Canada Cataloging in Publication

Blais, Marie-Claire, 1939–
[Naissance de Rebecca à l'ère des tourments. English]
    Rebecca, born in the maelstrom / Marie-Claire Blais ;
translator, Nigel Spencer.

Translation of: Naissance de Rebecca à l'ère des tourments.
ISBN 978-0-88784-825-4

I. Spencer, Nigel, 1945–   II. Title.   III. Title: Naissance de Rebecca à l'ère des
tourments. English.

PS8503.L33N3413 2009   C843'.54   C2009-903509-X

Library of Congress Control Number: 2009932088

Cover design: Bill Douglas at The Bang

Canada Council Conseil des Arts
for the Arts du Canada

ONTARIO ARTS COUNCIL
CONSEIL DES ARTS DE L'ONTARIO

*We acknowledge for their financial support of our publishing program the Canada
Council for the Arts, the Ontario Arts Council, and the Government of Canada
through the Book Publishing Industry Development Program (BPIDP).*

Printed and bound in Canada

For François-Étienne.

And Vénus remembered the words they spoke, the lamentations of her forebears just decades before, crying out, bent double under their yokes and in huts with rotted planks, crying out, where will you spend eternity, you horsemen and women, whips to our backs all over your lovely plantations — yet tomorrow and forever, where will you be, and we never knew where they lay beneath those carved tombstones, amid the luxuriant and silent plantations transformed into golf courses: so many souls shuddering beneath the woven green of cropped grass, thought Vénus, skulls cracked, then lynched, returning to earth well watered by sprinklers in the daytime, and the thundering voice of Pastor Jérémy, now punctured with brief, muted echoes, trumpeting for a rest and a pardon forever denied them, no rest at all, answer this, you base slavers, where, tell me where, you will spend eternity, and Vénus held her daughter Rebecca by the hand saying we must walk faster or you'll be late for the Christmas concert, and don't forget to sing high as I showed you, Rebecca could hear the jangle of her mother's bracelets, this would be her first recital, he'll arrive by boat to surprise us with all kinds of Santa Clauses, little and small ones, all by boat as a surprise, Rebecca said, but they won't be for our kind said Vénus, yes they're here for all of us Mamma, all the kids in our class, Rebecca answered, even if they glide through the water in flotillas with strings of lights and masts lit up too, that's not for us replied Vénus, and the parade's at six o'clock, Rebecca went on, I told you it's nothing to do with us, repeated Vénus, boats and rowboats will all be there, they told us, Rebecca continued, they told us so at school, and we'll see them lining the canal along Seventh Street, they'll all pass close to port where the lighthouse is, Rebecca said and Vénus shook her rattling her bracelets, you talk too much, she said, chattering away like a magpie, when you should be concentrating on your recital, don't go and embarrass me, Vénus shot back, her voice hard and bitter, you hear me, and why am I telling you this anyway, you're too young to understand, Mamma just wants you to work more on your singing, she continued gently, though she still looked angry, and what strange anger her mother had, Rebecca thought, and the click-clack of her bracelets and anklets annoyed her, I could have got up this morning and played with my iguana, she said in a still-sleepy voice, well I have to get up early as well, said Vénus, we'll see the parade go by across from the bay, said Rebecca, and there's going to be prizes and presents for the kids in my class, you know I used to sing in the Temple of the City of Coral, Vénus told her, the twins weren't born yet; Carlos and Lazaro would box each other, and shame hadn't befallen us in those days, shame of the blood Carlos shed when he attacked his friend, Carlos wasn't in prison charged with criminal negligence then, and I sang every Sunday in the Temple of the City of Coral, then the twins were born — Mama called them Deandra and Tiffany — and now they sing in the temple every Sunday, where Pastor Jérémy your grandfather preaches, I get up this early in the morning to study, Vénus said, and so you're ready, washed, dressed, and your hair brushed, because I want you always to be the best groomed in your class, see, now don't pull your hand away, do as I say and walk faster, why can't you just be like the other kids, eh, why, I can't do everything at once, study like Perdue Baltimore, be on time for the first breakfast service at the hotel, and bring you up in Pastor Jérémy's faith, no I can't do everything at once, now don't let go of Mamma's hand when she holds hers out for you, really, why are you so stubborn, what have I ever done to you, but Vénus thought, oh I know, I know what I've done to Rebecca, and what he did to me, the manager of my husband's estate, and if I kept a gun under my pillow, he'd take it, oh yes, I know all about Rebecca, everything she doesn't know, poor child, give me your hand and we'll go see the parade, Vénus told her, I remember I sang too in the Temple of the City of Coral, you said I could have humming-birds and passerines, Rebecca said, yes, Vénus said, and they'll come taste the honey and the sugar in the flowers, like before when my husband the Captain was here, we'll have humming-birds and passerines and snakes and iguanas sleeping on the stones by the water, said Rebecca, that was in the paradise days when I lived with the Captain, Vénus answered, long before I was born, Rebecca said, you weren't ever sad then, and why would I be sad with a little girl like you who sings so well at her concert, Vénus replied, why, it's because you get up too early, Rebecca stated, you can't get up when it's still night time, he's twenty-one now and he'll go to trial when I get my diploma, Vénus mused, then she fell silent and took Rebecca's hand in hers, at the hotel I meet important people, she said, but I don't want you to bring them here, said Rebecca, no Mamma, I don't, be quiet now, said Vénus, do be quiet, I'll do what I have to, and past twenty he'll be tried as an adult; who, asked Rebecca, if we walk by the lighthouse we'll see them from Seventh Street, we'll get presents and prizes, that's what they said at school, and Rosalie, the young lieutenant, and I we'll both be twenty-five, thought Vénus, she sleeps in the downs at the foot of a hill as it slopes to the Hudson River with so many graduates from these past two centuries who've been just as unfortunate and fallen among the trees, fine young people from a well-known military academy, but Rosalie would be the first woman graduate, the first admitted with a scholarship in medicine, an athlete, the star of the academy, admitted and pushed out in a soldier's uniform, months later under the trees on a hill at twenty-five, she might have been Vénus marching to school, holding her little girl's hand, covered in honours, but Rosalie had no little girl to hold by the hand, for it must be remembered she was a leader of men, and that day she would have left for the South with the men of her section, at the head of a convoy, confidence in her carriage and so much hope for the future in her smile, no little girl in hand, but a sabre, the star of her class, her smile a little like Vénus's, why not, telling herself she wasn't driving twelve hours to study law for nothing, smiling as few people smiled, with self-confidence, Rosalie the lieutenant was one of those toughened women, Rosalie was drawn to self-improvement, but Vénus, too sensual, was not, she remained unworthy of such comparison with Rosalie, on whom so many different honours had been bestowed, yes, they might be the same age, Rosalie and Vénus, the unfortunate thing was that Carlos had fled, he had seen Lazaro's knee bleeding in the sun and run away, fear or stupor under the midday sun, this need to take flight, on the stroke of the bell at Trinity College, the Cuban cook's gun fallen at his feet, he had run, and that's how he found out the gun he'd only meant to scare Lazaro with was loaded, a scare, that's all he wanted, okay, the bitterness between rival gangs had something to do with it too . . . and Vénus recalled that other boy, sixteen and going into the county's high-security detention centre because he'd also fled the scene, not used to piloting his father's boat, deadly mistake, surely not a crime, just a childish prank at the outset, how could he know racing across the water with the noise of the engine, they were only four and six, and he didn't see them diving and splashing around, just their father crying, oh God, my boys, and a halo of blond hair adrift on the water, my boys, my boys, they've been hit, he'd heard it of course, but like Carlos he wondered what had happened, I've got to get out of here, get away and never come back, I'm always going to be seeing that wash of blond hair and that devastated father, I mustn't, I mustn't see them, go go go far, breathing fast, he spotted a marina, he left the sea and the boat far behind, Hallowe'en, that's it, he'd disguise himself so no one would recognize him as the fugitive, maybe he just thought he saw the halo of blond hair in the reflection of the water, because of this special day, the kids would be going from house to house looking for candlelit pumpkins, paper skeletons shuddering in the wind, they'd just forget about him, had he really slit both their throats with his boat, on the run in a mask and a new disguise, and having had his first drink, got drunk, would he still remember, would he forever see that blond hair spread in the water, he lied non-stop to the interrogators, to his parents, he may not have lied and run away, but Carlos, brother of Vénus, had, a deadly mistake, from accident to crime, and at his trial, bewildered, he asked the boys' father, what did I do, stole two lives came the answer, my children's lives, tore them away from their mother and me, ripped out of our guts by your carelessness and your father's $45,000 powerboat, you've sent two little ones into darkness, and their mother no longer sleeps, she hears them calling and she wakes up but they aren't there, those cries coming from the water, the hellish tear of your boat over the sea, and she asks where they are, when will I see them, both families had cried at the trial, helplessly damning God in their hearts for allowing this hellish mistake, and the mother of the boys could no longer sleep, and the father saw again the eyes of the boy who had taken them, offended eyes that asked what he had done, tell me what have I done, then thrust into the prison bus, what have I done, I just wanted to have fun with my dad's boat, his fate for having taken flight out on the water after taking those lives would indeed be harsh, thought Vénus, but he'd be better defended and looked after than Carlos the dark-skinned boy who'd also fled his own crime, better brought up, he'd had everything he wanted and stolen his father's luxury boat, had believed in the supremacy of the objects he owned, as though they gave him the right to kill with indifference, from atop a wave of arrogant superiority, even the powerboat was his at age sixteen, and if he'd been free, he'd have driven his own Chrysler, travelled with his father, hiding his face beneath the same shades, wearing the same gold watch, insignia of unlimited purchasing and consuming power, all that had suddenly been swallowed up by the sea, dragging him down to a level with Carlos . . . no more Emerald Coast for him, just a filthy cell where he'd likely be raped, and Vénus felt Rebecca's fingers touching hers as she asked her mother if Trevor really was her father, she liked that, Prince Trevor they called him when he played double bass, Vénus said, why ask so many questions, we're going to be late for the concert, thinking then it might be better if she lied to her daughter, um, yes, he is, Trevor's your dad, that's why you look like him, you notice his skin's lighter than mine, he is my daddy Rebecca said, I wish he'd come and see us more often, and Vénus replied his jazz group is all he has on his mind, that intense pallor, not brown or black, in Rebecca's skin, this was him, the other man, though the features belonged to Vénus, just enough of her in the child, she thought, to forget the one who had forced her daughter into being, though he was not wanted, nor she for that matter, not being the longed-for child of the Captain, the only man that mattered, she should not have loved him but love often comes on its own, whether we want it to or not, looking at the girl she could not refuse, and Rebecca seemed reborn and would be splendid, like Rosalie the young graduate of an elite military academy, though not buried in a uniform on a hill and soon to be forgotten by all, tomorrow, in Rebecca's day, children would shine and have what Vénus never did, freedom of their bodies, recognition: that is how she thought of her daughter, someone through whom she herself could become invincible. You'll soon be inside my church, sweetheart, Reverend Ézéchielle said to Petites Cendres, you're running away from someone, aren't you, so what are you afraid of gangsta brother, help me cut these lilies to give to the Lord, I do this every morning, is your soul light Petites Cendres, I came here to pray came the answer, head between hands and resting on the Reverend's corpulence, she had danced over to him singing, hey son, now what have you done, nothing Reverend, where would I be without you, I was hungry and along you came giving out food for Hallowe'en, a man can't pray on an empty stomach replied the Reverend, and why is your soul heavy, what swamp have you come crawling out of, sweet pea, nothing, I've done nothing said Petites Cendres, Timo's the one who stole the customer's Sonata, it's wrong to sell your body the way your friend Timo does, the Reverend said, for a Sonata — that's not good, and you sweetie have a heavy conscience for being with him; vicar, Reverend Sister, thanks for the fine meal, it really warms my stomach, like I say, a hungry man can't turn his eyes to heaven, can he, it's the church and the community that's given this food to you and all these other poor unfortunates, poolside pot-smokers on Bahama Street, a shame before the Lord, but charity does begin with a good meal and a shower said the Reverend — we've had them put in all along the beach, so gather up your self-respect sweetheart, then you can pray, when your conscience is as clear as a running brook and your soul no longer heavy, fall on your knees and pray; what have you been up to all night anyway my sweet rakehell, head as empty as your stomach, get moving, where have you been dragging around, pray God to light your way through those clouds in your mind brother, pray sweet pea, and don't think I don't know what goes on in this town son, the sheriff's got his detectives out looking for a Hispanic boy, maybe your friend Timo, when he went into the store to buy a bottle of Bacardi, he said now see what I've got in my belt, I don't want to hurt no one, so just give me everything in the cash or I'll, I'll . . . he had on a striped polo shirt and a baseball cap . . . see what's in my belt, yeah well move it, I don't want to hurt no one but I'm running out of time, and they gave up the money, and he took off in a stolen car, yup, that's Timo alright said Reverend Ézéchielle folding her arms over the ample bosom where she held the lilies, warm, so warm, thought Petites Cendres, can't be Timo he said, he never wears a baseball cap or a polo shirt, brother you just come and help me cut these stems, can't be Timo, he dresses like a fashion model, can't be him, anyway I don't rat on my brothers, nope that sketch in the paper isn't him, it's just a drawing somebody dreamed up, no way he wears a cap and a striped shirt ever — just ain't him pastor; well what are you doing in my church so early if you're not on the run from the law, just praying like you see, Reverend Ézéchielle, just praying and waiting for your sermon, well it's gonna be strong stuff for those puny ears of yours she said, because I can feel some real anger coming on, now Jesus He chased the money-changers out of the temple, didn't he . . . well he should have seen the ones we've got peddling the Theology of Wealth, that's what it is, oh woe to those Protestant evangelists who've turned God into a lucrative business opportunity, for theirs is not the Kingdom of Heaven, not bearing the cross and misery you do Petites Cendres, or the humble joy in your heart, oh no, the religion of Health and Abundance as they call themselves, Theology According to Gain that reconciles Jesus and the acquisition of possessions, oh shameless graspers, and they go right on buying up farms and livestock, too smug and self-assured in their wealth and false knowledge of God, and instead of sending their kids out to get an education they build schools for them on their vast properties to teach them, you know what, to get more and more my son, in ignorance and contempt of love my son, oh my son, Jesus was just like you are, homeless, and in his poverty would He have wanted a six-figure income for every Christian, oh what a shameful creed my son, the creed of a Business God pawning a bit of Paradise for fabulous wealth, that place in Heaven we have dreamed up that can't be bought or sold, you hear me son, and my sermon of fury will ring in your poor ears, she then stopped to remind Petites Cendres that Christmas was coming and he was invited, along with all the pot-smokers on Bahama Street, unemployed good-for-nothings whose wives do all the work, to a Christmas feast at the Community Church, you hear me, it'll be one more reason to thank the Lord for His bounty, and Petites Cendres saw she was once more erupting in anger and the rhetorical flight of her daily sermon, then Reverend Ézéchielle got back on track: now Jesus didn't say you can go get a Mercedes and all those other high-tech gadgets of our century and Heaven as well, no, He never did say that, but our wayward preachers do, don't they: why not get all the worldly riches you can plus the salvation of your soul on the side they say, but Jesus he says no way, put aside the plea- sures of this world that call to you and take up your cross, and therein lies the nobility of our race my son, for we have borne our cross and prayed without expecting either salary or reward, and those preachers, preachers of lies, book-writing charlatans that sell by the millions, they are heretics my son, the Church of the Merchants in the Temple — the most pop- ular in all the world, as full of believers as China has people; the true preachers do like our pastors in the Community Church, real Christians, they go to Rwanda to help the suffer- ing, but the Theologians of Wealth have been so busy gather- ing up riches for themselves that they have forgotten about the poor, oh you my son, with your head as empty as any basket, you know you can get arrested on Bahama Street for just a few grams of cocaine in your shoe, you know it; so you're going away again said Petites Cendres, sensing how lonely he would feel after Reverend Ézéchielle was gone, rejected by less tolerant churches for the "black sin" of prostitution this ragged transvestite represented, why go off to some dangerous country said Petites Cendres; this world is not the only kingdom open to us, she replied, and you have to learn to be a man; what are we going to do without you at the Community Church; oh there are plenty of chatterbox preachers in the congregations around here, she said, just listen to the temple merchants waiting to tiptoe into paradise in their crocodile shoes and flannel suits, listen to me Petites Cendres, the kingdom is not of this world, learn to be a man, you can't always be sheltered within the walls of my church, and Petites Cendres thought of those generous arms of hers always ready to enfold him in bunches of fresh-cut white lilies, under the wooden lintels of this church or the one in Africa, she would always hold him near, he thought, even if her pacifism might be useless in such hostile regions, and I don't want to see you on TV, he said, not talking with the governor or the congressman or any of those leaders with granite consciences, can't move 'em, can't change 'em, yup he said, that sure would make me feel bad, time to be on your way son, she said, there's going to be a Christmas feast for you and your friends, New Year's too, now get going before those thugs show up and put you in handcuffs like that poor kid Carlos, they'll be here any time now, is that what you want, I told him to beat it too, and they didn't respect the sanctuary, I told him to go to his sister Vénus's by the canal, and he took off, now get out of here poor boy, do you really want to spend the night in jail for a few grams in your shoe, eh Petites Cendres; just let me wait here with you until the parades and all are over, okay, Pastor, just a while longer, it's been a long night he thought as she sweetly danced her way around the church arranging the bouquets of flowers, she'd forget he was there, and the lily smell, not quite a smell so much as a greedy perfume rising from the pinkish corollas, he thought maybe he'd just pretend he was praying and nap for a bit, so at least he'd get some rest until it was sermon time, then he saw the old black man still sitting on a bench with his cane, the same as he had been when Petites Cendres opened the door, very old and frail, he'd said hi Brother, what you doing up so early, then he spat on the floor, and you Old Brother, what are you doing sitting out in front of the church so early; oh I'm waiting on the nice lady to take me to my reading and writing lesson said the old man, comes every morning and off we go to school, he spat on the ground again; so Brother, you can't read nor write said Petites Cendres, nope can't do it . . . if only I could get rid of this bronchitis, he spat again, don't blow your nose into your hand said Petites Cendres, what's your teacher going to think if she sees you doing all that, she's no teacher, she's just a nice Christian lady doing it out of charity, not many of them, just then Petites Cendres saw a beautiful lady step out her car and say, come friend let's go, and the old man and his cane disappeared into the shiny new car under the first rays of the sun, and Petites Cendres thought, well one of those ancient aristocratic ladies out of our past piously doing her duty by us before her servants are up and seeing nothing wrong with having modern-day leftover slaves, then while he was daydreaming and pretending to pray, he fell asleep, and the reason Ari was here in Guatemala and one of the most over-populated cities in Central America, drooping with fever, seated near Asoka in a jolting bus, some bumpy, not-so-meditative adventure the orange-robed pilgrim monk had dragged him on, far from his quiet artistic life to witness his completely unmanageable spiritual life, yes unmanageable was definitely the word for it, or maybe this was his own initiation of some sort, him the ordinary man whose Buddhist spirituality often flickered, really just questing for inner silence with not too much of an outer mess, although the sordid invasions of the everyday already defeated him like a spiderweb wound around his brain with at least one demon of political carnage cancelling out all his most joyous moments, even when he had his daughter Lou in his arms and kissed her, all these nasty little hominids squeezed his mental space chuckling and ridiculing, as if to say we're the worst ones, the liars, the sneaks, and and we always come out on top, so your happiness is always going to be shaky at best, and the best he could do was push them away with the gradual torpor of silence and yoga practice, but even with every ounce of will and the considerable strength in his body, Ari knew he could never match Asoka in his metaphysical search soaring ever higher with each action, his friend scraping ground-level and even taking root like the brute matter he used for his sculpture, as massive as a monument that might crush him in transit to some park or garden; cultivate the inner flowers of patience and acceptance in yourself, Asoka said as he had before, acquire the perseverance of the tea tree or the flu, thought Ari, why this feverishness, he examined Asoka in profile and dared not say a thing, Don't let me down, sang a man on the radio, and a Spanish western played on a screen as they shook their way towards the mountains, then the bus braked, and Ari felt as though he'd run headlong into a crowd of kids in their Sunday best and the almond cakes sold at each stop in clear viscous paper, then a bloodless creature like the starving dogs he'd seen climbed on the bus and brushed past Ari wearing a brilliantly white beach towel around his neck, red shorts stretched over his long, hollow body, all bone like the dogs too, sunken eyes like a living corpse, Ari thought, and least bearable of all for him in this otherworldly creature like an incurable convalescent, the open smile of a child, Asoka had mentioned he'd known this man or teenager or what was left of him with AIDS for a long time, he'd enjoy hanging out at the station each day and climbing the steps onto the bus with his towel around him, occasionally putting it to his mouth and coughing up a star of blood, Asoka told Ari one had to bow before a man who stood upright like this to the very end, you complain of the slightest fever, but how would you deal with this my friend, Asoka asked, though his sense of smell may not have equalled Ari's, it was not only the effluvia from the dying man with the towel that oppressed Ari but also the weight of that unknown misery described by Asoka as the other three-quarters of humanity most of us never see, never want to see, of course it's true you don't have to be rich to be happy, otherwise how come this poor fellow is smiling with such limitless candour and confidence with only maybe a few weeks to live; Ari was thinking he should never have followed Asoka on this trip instead of just stretching out on the beach in Mexico in between working on his article about the paintings of Marcel Duchamp . . . a little narcissistic jubilation there, sure, for he'd love to have painted like the French master, and what art there was in those sculptures rising and descending like *Nude Descending a Staircase*, and art to him was the world in disintegration, and Asoka said it had become useless, unlike the beds and medicines needed in the clinics where he worked, Ari's charcoal outlines and his thoughts on art, however gifted, no longer mattered, but maybe in addition to a sense of smell, Ari thought, Asoka lacked feeling, his wide-ranging restless and busy pilgrimage prevented it, like when he learned the death of his two young sisters and mentioned only the name of Matupali the survivor, because life is such a short-lived guest in this body, and the faces of his sisters gave way to Mongolian orphans, for these he mourned, along with the monks of Tu Aimag and the ghostly trucks piled with bodies in northeastern Sri Lanka, then a softer image of a coat someone had given him in Moscow, no, thought Ari, Asoka no longer had time or room to feel the way he did, second by second, most of all when he thought about his daughter Lou, Marie-Louise, he should never have left her with her mother who would force Roman Catholicism on her and deform her mind, what an atrocious thought, a profane heart now afflicted by ideas of good and evil, his wild little girl, he never should have left her an instant, but he was glad that at least he'd convinced Ingrid to send her to a non-denominational school and get a better education, though her mother had fiercely held out against private lessons, well once she'd grown a little more, her father would see about that, and Ingrid was her mother and had to have some say, compromises were inevitable in a divorce; unable to smell, Asoka sensed only the emanations of mute, unspectacular pain that surrounded him, adored by the oppressed for his extreme simplicity and transparency, seeming to say to each and every one, those who offend you also offend me, though it appeared to Ari there was nothing sentimental or indiscreet about it, quite the reverse in fact, he made a beeline for wherever the emergency was, no the usefulness of art never crossed his mind, nor its sovereign role in the most demeaned of lives, as it did Ari's, but Asoka just went right on strong-arming individuals and aid organizations to get beds and medicines for destitute hospitals, precise and rigorous was his determination, and whether in Mali or Guatemala, always his was the un-glossy universe of inexpressible pain, panting and silent as the smile on a dying young man on a bus in red shorts who brushed up against Ari with his ravaged body, or of the ceilings and walls and courtyards of hospitals, clinics, maternity wards, dim but for a sickly paint the colour of their patients, stretched out and bunched together on smelly mattresses or on floors, he just cries on and on said the father, and how's his chest, crying and crying in the restricted space of the little hospital and its dumb dull walls coloured like the patients, Asoka, leaning towards the baby and his father calling for the doctor or perhaps praying as Ari thought, had no answer to give, like those on the Marine Promenade in a Mumbai port at dawn, performing their graceful ritual of

homage and exercise to the opening pink flowers of sky, the
fingers of Asoka the monk gently settled on the baby's temple
as he sat panting and crying his dismay on his father's knees,
and will I lose him and his mother as well, the man seemed
to think, but the lacklustre walls had no more answer than
Asoka did, suddenly overcautious and saying nothing, his
confused senses, so freely and regularly exposed to this, no
longer detecting any odour at all, not the damp smell of ran-
cid or mouldy clothes unwashed for several days, no longer
could he tell or hope, with his open hand on the anemic
baby's temple, oh let him stop crying, just let him stop, he
waited and perhaps prayed quietly or moaning like an animal,
or if he no longer found words, just let this mute pain of father
and child be over, Ari could not imagine that he could be this
silent and desolate father holding Lou to him, this nameless
baby here in a Guatemala dispensary, Lou, why not Lou,
Marie-Louise didn't seem inappropriate, aloof as though Ari's
daughter seemed from this crying and embattled baby in
another universe, a society that perverts children by overspoil-
ing them and destines them to sordid privilege, for to Ari,
how could one contemplate what was beyond imagining . . .
elsewhere, that was all one could say about her birthplace,
this baby had as good a father as any — as Ingrid or Ari — this
father's fate was simply different, hostile to him and his sickly
newborn in this otherwhere, hostile to Ari in its deprivation
and poverty: Lou was simply fortunate not to have entered
the world by this gate where her parents would have to pick
through garbage for food; no avenue of the imagination could
do anything but disturb him deeply, and he never should have
followed Asoka here to this desolate spot forgotten of god and
man, the doctor saying we'll save him as she took the child
from its father, lots of liquids, lots . . . a woman as delicate as
a butterfly in Ari's eyes, delicate as the mosquito that did this
perhaps, or was it fragile from a difficult birth, torn and tear-
ing, the unnamed and unnameable except in the father's

burning eyes and silence, fever oozing from the child like tears, a fever in Ari's eyes too, glancing hesitantly, sure of nothing at all — think, better think about Picasso's *Guernica* and its shattering dislocations, yes, better that than this contagious fear from father and whimpering child, the gangrene of bodies on the ground, some missing a hand or leg, *Guernica*, oh if it weren't for this fever, and he'd say to Lou when he got back, oh there really are kids who aren't this lucky, and she'd whistle nonchalantly just to let him know she wasn't listening, eat your soup he'd say, and stop playing with your bread, still not listening she'd leave the meal they'd ordered to go play on the beach, only swooping back from time to time for the morsels her father held out to her, come and have something, he'd hear her singing as she played in the sand or chased off the family of plovers at the water's edge in a rush and a dance; all this would be later of course, when Ari's fever was long forgotten and perhaps with it the father and child in the village hospital where the consuming pity of Asoka had dragged him, and Petites Cendres saw Timo just as he'd been back when he danced on tables in the Porte du Baiser Saloon with his gleaming wide smile a slash across his dark skin, as he unbuttoned his skin-tight jeans and wound up a solo tango naked from his leather jacket down, laughing as he said to Petites Cendres, see how I pull in the customers, look at them lining up at the door, and Timo would end up in the watery caverns and neon green of the sauna, Petites Cendres marvelling: look at all those dollar bills, you're a banker, a regular banker, but this night Timo said, yes I'm the bank now and I say we've got to get dolled up for Christmas, what do you say, strolling out of the store with my bottle of Bacardi I thought, hey why not the Bank of the Americas, seeing as how my picture's in all the banks anyway, have you noticed Petites Cendres, and they're never going to catch me because I changed the Sonata's plates, they can try and get me for Internet fraud and I'm still going to spend the night in a motel, whaddya say Petites

Cendres, I mean you're the one who stole the keys while I
distracted the owner, you're the one . . . and Timo danced on
tables at the Porte du Baiser Saloon and had a good insolent
laugh at Petites Cendres who woke up to find him gone, nope
it was Reverend Ézéchielle who was laying hands on an old
man: O hundred-year-old man, she said as though singing in
a whisper, welcome to the Community Church, and may God
relieve you of your overzealous memory, oh yes, he trembled
on his cane, after a hundred years I've heard and seen everything . . . Milwaukee I remember, oh my son, may you forget
what you have seen and heard, she said . . . I was on the run
Reverend Sister, because I staged a robbery with two other
hoods and a man got killed, yes on the run, unhappy thief
she said, it was 1930 or '31, no trial, they hung the other two
and it was my turn at the tree, maple it was, and the leaves
were autumn yellow, and I could smell the hay and the apples,
they had an apple tree there too, and some of the apples were
ready to fall at the same time as me, then one of the village
folks hollered out, it wasn't him, he didn't do it, and there I
was Reverend Sister, noose tightening around my neck and
someone yelling, not him, not him, and now I've been in your
church near a hundred years, come all this way to tell my
story, blessed be you my son and may God spare you from
an overzealous memory, and now I can go back home he
said, yes, for now heaven awaits you along with the other two
she said, for forget we must, and Petites Cendres shook himself thinking he heard Timo's laughter in his ear, and Asoka
knew he'd seen this father and baby before, somewhere in a
famine in Ethiopia or the Sudan or the Niger, they said "food
crisis" so as not to pronounce the devastating word *famine*,
crops devastated by locusts, harvests intended for the months
to come, everywhere attacking lives by the thousands, and
Asoka again saw those skeletal babies in the nurses' arms,
ageless skin already stretched tight over their bones, trans-
fused when it was already too late, wondering if it was too

late for that anemic baby as well, impossibly born into hunger, impossibly born at once to die, impossible yet every day it happened, barely anchored to life by a transfusion line, throwaway babies weren't they after all, like the Buenos Aires kids sleeping pell-mell in the streets at night with their dogs guarding them, both of them starving, both throwaways, faces lined with hunger, all this and more Asoka knew and it shook his faith, he wondered how the leaders could go home at night to dinner with their wives and think about comfort and sleep when they too knew all this — below their own roofs a dying population of children and babies, and above the silent, throwaway masses — they lay down to sleep at night fully satisfied and disgustingly free of thought for those beneath; for what ignominy had these men and women been created, thought Asoka, not shame that they themselves felt of course, but which he felt for them with a faith that could have wavered but did not, such was the mysterious courage that ruled his life, Augustino, only twenty years old and writing books, stubborn and unfathomable, thought Daniel, so recently a sweet child and now suddenly a frail and lanky man, still as curly-haired as ever, not as attractive as his brother Samuel, nose perhaps a little too prominent for his liking, but those curls so thick and silky his hands were always combing through them with pens, pencils, anything, and perhaps growing up too fast had taken away from his looks or, thought his father, his beauty lay elsewhere, still he should never have published *Letter to the Young with No Future*, unworthy of his father to have a son writing a book of such desperation, misunderstood, yes, but to have a son so different and still a writer like his father was infuriating, and Daniel could find no way to describe what he felt towards this son he no longer recognized; so far off was the time of proud fatherhood when they'd left New York for a sheltered Caribbean island close to the sea where he thought the air would be better for them, bursting with fatherly joy as they strolled beneath palm trees

along the jasmine-scented edges of the Cemetery of Roses,
hoary leaves covering the graves and cocks wandering everywhere, the youthfulness of the eight-year-old Samuel walking
straight-backed by his mother's side, and Augustino, his second, precocious and gentle, whom he taught to walk and who
soon asked his father all sorts of questions that intrigued him:
has the January war begun, Dad, and if it has, why bother
brushing our teeth if we're only going to die in an explosion
tomorrow and we don't have a house or a dog to protect us
any more, already a boy unlike any other, but to think he'd
one day be a writer and one with this unexpected hit *Letter to
the Young with No Future*, that the time was already gone
when he'd be up at night talking about literature or a healthy
environment with Chuan and Olivier (a rare black senator)
and their son Jermaine with the slant eyes of his mother, only
eight himself and sleeping in a hammock with Samuel; Daniel,
come to this island to write, would often turn out to be less a
dramaturge than an ecologist with Chuan and Olivier, a sam-
urai ecologist, his father said, trying desperately to clean up
the waters off the Coral Coast, no his dramas would not be
written in peace, how could they with so many outside social
and political dramas haunting him, and it was for Augustino
that he'd given up the refuge of writing, for the peace and the
future of those slender and graceful child's legs scampering
awkwardly through the Cemetery of Roses, asking his father,
why, why, why, and now at twenty he dared write that this
future was unlikely, killing his mother and father as he did so,
no, something had to be done, talk to the boy, set him straight,
but how exactly, at fifty did Daniel even know what he himself was, maybe he should have been like Jermaine, sports-
minded, car-loving, womanizing, Augustino, who was this
Augustino . . . did Daniel even remember his own wild youth,
that's the way it was, youth had to spit out its venom, and for
Augustino, steering clear of alcohol and drugs, more upright
than his father at this age, the venom was outraged pessimism,

a turn of mind so dark, a doctrine so black it lacked even the philosopher Schopenhauer's leavening of light, believing as he ultimately did in the future of the human race, Daniel thought there was no trusting human virtue; observing Modern Man led one to believe he was essentially evil, but this child Augustino was no philosopher-prophet contemplating the world and its inhabitants from a hammock next to Jermaine, or playing ball with his father on the beach at sundown, this was the little boy Daniel had lost who-knows-how, and as he grew up his father had seen him through successive dreams that did honour to him: Augustino first in a science faculty, Augustino a research chair in biophysics, Augustino inventor of a new biological tool, surely university would be an incubator of invention for him, a cure for Alzheimer's perhaps: this was the flattering lens through which Daniel saw him, then, as though born under a bad sign, here he was writing to tell young people of his generation, the time, my friends, is coming when we'll be nothing more than PINs, microchips in us to let the Great Masters of all nations identify us, we won't be the first of course, they'll start with convicts and the stateless with almost no rights, then all of us, faceless, nameless victims wiped out by a technological age . . . Daniel looked up from reading Augustino's book, how had he brought up his son for him to think this way, as though he saw himself as some sort of computerized implant, where, at what crossing-point had the human given way? Timo wasn't the only one, thought Petites Cendres, and why do people come after you even in your dreams, and he remembered the drunk hanging onto him with his bundle of belongings at the Porte du Baiser Saloon, then going from one barfly to another, morose or enjoying their drinks, asking, d'you like me, d'you think you could like me, and the more he clung to Petites Cendres, unable to get loose from that drooling, foam-flecked face of permanent drunkenness that turned his stomach, the more everyone laughed, till a boy in a skirt and red feathers in his hair gripped him with one hand and dragged him out into the street, saying, go on home (where's that) and don't forget your things, a few steps and he fell in the street, then Petites Cendres rushed over to him, stopping the cars, and the old guy cried, him, Petites Cendres, he loves me, Petites Cendres, and the Porte du Baiser Saloon filled with laughter, the Lord is in everyone and we must love Him said Petites Cendres, He told us that, even if they're stinking and downtrodden, you've got real patience said the boy, it wasn't you he wanted, it was your powder, he even had his hand in your pocket, yeah, yeah, I know said Petites Cendres, but that's what the Lord said, and heat invaded the bar, consumed the men and lulled Petites Cendres as he tapped his feet on the stool, for the loud music pouring out into the street lulled him too: oh lonely young men, I've seen it all, people blind to disaster, flag-draped bodies in the streets, the city sinking into ruin like a boat in the fog, and woe is us who saw nothing, draped in the flags of our desolation, our terror, drowned bodies face downward in black, chemical-waste water, bodies in bloated shirts under a lake of black, men, women, and children, we'll never know who, uprooted trees and wind tipping boats as they try to flee, flames beneath the sky, water lapping at windows, skies darkly mirroring the poor Whites and Blacks whipped and struck down by the wind among gardens set adrift, shredded like the trees and flowers, buried under wrecked boards, sometimes the forbidding fury of the skies arriving soundless, snatching flotsam from the water, an old folks' home, an infirmary, hands hanging on, losing one another, oh my son, I have seen my city go down like a boat in a fog of smoke and all those about to die, leaving their houses at gunpoint, go on, get out of there, but what about the poor with no place to evacuate to, thugs, thieves, pitiful plunder on the waves of the deluge, down under the waves to surface no more, grandmothers, sons, brothers, in rags, refusing to leave, or dying on the roof with a dog, or in the shadows of fire and water, locked in an embrace among electrical wires and debris that never let go, and I saw O my son that we were alone, a landscape contaminated and fetid, a ghost ship of a city, fading into the grey fog and trailing smoke, and through all this story, Reverend Ézéchielle and Petites Cendres thought they heard a fanfare of desolation — a soundtrack laid on the bodies and winding like balm around trees and over swamps, made from the music of Louis Armstrong, Sydney Bechet and King Oliver, he'd danced to it, shared the hope, while Reverend Ézéchielle called up all the hurricanes and tornadoes that raked the island, often more than once or twice a year, as Petites Cendres again saw himself wading through the streets while winds whipped up the sea and he took refuge in church basements, everyone fighting off the putrid water, men and sharks side by side, the sea engulfing all, the speed and violence of the wind allowing nothing to close in the condemned town, not bathroom doors, not windows, and threatening E. coli epidemics and exploding gas cylinders under the bellowing black sky, terrified and soaked, Petites Cendres had seen the blue of the sky return, months go by, erosion diminish, and like a Christmas miracle, a magical wish come true, the houses on Bahama Street emerge from the waters and reach for the sun, their inhabitants seated as before on galleries and balconies, palms bent up against walls brownish green, chickens and roosters on the flooded lawns, the Community Church in all its modest splendour, and Reverend Ézéchielle beckoning him to a row of wooden pews smelling of wax, her arms filled with lilies, and in every church singing and praying, he thought, for peace on earth among men, and he too prayed and danced to the jazz, the jazz that comforted the living and the dead as it did in Louisiana, on his feet, clapping and praying, and soon in the B'nai Zion Congregation they'd be lighting the first candle, as they'd done for a hundred years, rising out of the water like the Community Church, out of the fire and the hurricanes that struck so often in these times of the shortest days, the longest nights, a candle every day for eight days, and surely, thought Petites Cendres, with all this light we bear we can overcome the violence of the dark, after all these hurricanes and tornadoes the sky again was blue, the heat of the sun caressing his body, yes singing in every church, yes who was this Augustino, Daniel wondered, as if he'd come from an altogether different sphere, and they no longer talked late into the night with Chuan and Olivier about the environment, for Olivier, in a state of high anxiety these days, felt that all was lost, for how could the idea of a pollution-free world survive if the reality of it no longer existed, he said, as Daniel observed his face so hollowed by his recent depression, so different from the exultant and joyous faces of Chuan and their son Jermaine, though his parents never wondered who he really was, this Jermaine, little Jermaine rushing off to school on his skates with Samuel laughing behind him, he too had changed so much, now such an avid reader of scripts for the films he produced in California, a likeable and serious boy, with so much foresight his father said, recalling how he'd driven along the coast: let me drive Dad, he'd said, you're so tired, time for your big boy to think of you, yes still Olivier's child as he remembered him, coming in from his writing pavilion in the morning by the hibiscus path and springing towards his father saying I love you Dad, oh how radiant Olivier was visiting his son in California; so when exactly was it this gloomy cloud of anxiety descended, when was it Chuan said he thought the military draft would be reintroduced to swallow up Jermaine forever, and at once he was convinced so that even his psychoanalyst couldn't convince him, a true nightmare, but you, dear Daniel, you never change, do you, so exuberant, and of course you're right, Chuan's joy subsiding all of a sudden, my dear Olivier, my dear sweet Olivier sleeps no more than two hours a night, so sure he is of the very worst beyond imagining that I can't even console him, and I've got to be off to

Hong Kong, please watch over him, he saw that young man Lazaro in a dream and is convinced he's a terrorist, always has been, and I should never have let him into the house that day with the tray of seafood I'd ordered; this anxiety gives him abominable, uncontrollable thoughts, but the analyst told me to look at it differently, he said I know the road he's on, and even if it leads down into the abyss, yawning glaciers, he sees things we don't, fresh tracks under a starlit night, for him brightly lit, so much so that even in the farthest depths he knows he can't get lost, and you'll see he'll find his way back to us, and of course nothing had really changed, like that night we celebrated Mère's eightieth birthday and Daniel smelled the African lilies, their flowers sensuous and pendulous in the trees, nearby a red chair next to the pool inserted immutably into the décor Chuan had created for the Cuban architecture of the house and the hot, sunny yellows and oranges of the walls, young Lazaro in a black apron that day, just as her husband sees him in dreams, frightful ones from which he wakes and refuses to go back to, dear Olivier, she says, please keep an eye on him while I'm away, Daniel listening to her and thinking of the warm welcome he'd received coming back south, everyone leaning interestedly in to the young author he was then, you are my family, he told her, shuddering at the word and thinking of Augustino and how suddenly our children can become strangers, then he hugged her and realized he was now the protector of those who so recently were once his, a sign of his mature subconscious, for there could be one fruit and one fruit only to a tree, he hadn't felt himself maturing, a few strands of his hair turning salt-and-pepper, or at least that's what the children said, still it seemed odd that they didn't realize how their father's early-morning exercises, his relay run by the sea, were headed for firm all around rejuvenation, and he had certainly not bequeathed to Augustino the congenital misanthropy that seemed like his own, and Mai certainly worried him, but not

Augustino, and why had he made Samuel and Augustino too responsible for the deplorable state of the planet by saying, it's up to you to set the world straight again, you have your duties as I do, probably a lot of boring speeches that just wore them down, how exactly was the father to blame for what the son did; yet Augustino's thoughts went to the lower depths, and Samuel's art was unattainably transcendental, transfiguring the world; from birth, one son was more in harmony than the other, while Augustino was alone and angry, Samuel had been shown love early on by Veronica and was in turn showing her choreography, thinking that women artists never got the respect they deserved, one following his mother's brand of feminism and the other in denial of anything learned from his father and grandmother, even dismaying the latter with his remoteness, never or hardly ever going to see her, better to keep his mind on Samuel and his success in New York, a captivating piece of choreography owing much to his training with the deceased master Arnie Graal whose final, monstrous *Rite of Spring* propelled Samuel as a dancer into a wall of flame, too true to life, paralleling Samuel's version of Stravinsky's ballet to the omen of Nijinsky's own dancing and to the troubled and troubling present as Samuel perceived it, the sacrifice of the virgin, dying and Dionysian, shadowed the genocide of a dying Earth, not the primitive, invented, or prehistoric Russian, but today's man, battling with an exhausted Earth, like other choreographers before him celebrating the cosmic force and flowering of love and sexuality, the tableaux though emerging from another kind of tumult, swimming amid dying fish between layers of Alaska mercury, monstrous, yes, perhaps, still the audience had eyes only for Samuel in his aquatic abyss, even forgetting the subject, seeing just the fluid agility of the dancer, or in another sense, a disturbing and shocking continuation of the controversial tradition of Arnie Graal, swimming ever downward to a metaphoric drowning in blue ether with the whales and white bears where the ice barriers and snow had given way, and the unforgettable drop of mercury hanging over the head of every living thing, plant, animal, and human: a hundred and seventy-five species consumed by its burned and pulverized metallic particles melting into the sky from factory vapours as world leaders approved and bats, panthers, dolphins, eagles, and alligators fed off it on land and water, became sterile, birds lost their song — all this was part of Samuel's choreography, the birdsong modified by intermittent silence that shocked, even scandalized audiences not ready to admit that the satanic reign of mercury on Earth had already begun, earlier than expected, Samuel the son of his ecologist father, and who were these children of ours walking alone among Guatemalan cities still torrid from the day's burning heat, on one of these nights perhaps, Ari had felt so awful and had seen a baby in a hut by candlelight, possibly a brothel with men and women going in and out in a din of voices and yells, less than a year old and sitting on the dirt floor, with grownup legs overhead and crying eyes, he had looked at Ari, who wondered why he was so alone in his soiled diaper, bony dog sniffing nearby and where was the mother of these crying eyes searching the night through a broken-down door, Asoka really thought happiness was possible in these conditions, in the privations of misery was the opprobrium of the world, and how could any of us, even the holy Asoka, know Nirvana or any other form of beatitude when one of these little ones was crying from hunger on the dirt floor of a dingy grotto filled with shadows and exhaling alcohol fumes, with only a dog to watch over it, both of them starving, prayer was not an ethic, meditation had no meaning faced with a child such as this, Ari thought, then remembered his visits to hospitals and village clinics with Asoka where he could not define the unalterable smiles on so many faces, smiles he compared with that of the man in red shorts on the bus with a beach towel around his neck, or those of heavily pregnant thirteen-year-olds in cotton dresses, they too had

smiled that same free assent, apparently impervious to everything, all discomfort in the precarious life ahead for both
mother and child, and on another day, it was a young girl
stretched out, as though on sand, next to the crib where her
healing baby fidgeted, raising her head to Ari and offering a
sweet, luminous smile that surely made her an angel in flight
and removed from these sordid surroundings and seeming to
say in Asoka's words, come closer, Ari, don't be afraid, for in
this heart there is only joy, beatitude, Nirvana, look my son is
better now and tonight I'll take him home, and for hours at a
time I'll carry him along the screaming highways with the
schoolchildren in the navy blue uniforms and white shirts
their mothers have embroidered, and at sundown, little by
little, the dogs and horses and donkeys will wind their heavy
way up the mountain beside us, forever hungry and thirsty
like us, Ari how can you not know that in these simple hearts
there will always be joy, it is all we have while you have it all,
and the young mother's seraphic smile reminded him of Ingrid
back when he still loved her, oh Ingrid and Lou with her
computer and her piano, Lou who never should be brought
to this place, never would be pregnant at thirteen, how could
he imagine it, now so small and yet even at thirteen not pregnant like these teens, here, only here could this be, and yet
they smiled as though without memories, or was it the pro-
miscuity and abandonment in which they lived, fatherless and
motherless, but not Lou, loved and protected, guided by her
parents through a perfectly balanced childhood and coming
adolescence, studying in the best colleges and universities,
no, Ari's child, treasure and princess, never pregnant at thirteen, and in the garden pavilion with one door open to the
smell of jasmine wafting in from the rain-soaked garden, Mère
wrote in her diary, what willed and unwilled connections that
word *Mother* carries, the word everyone uses for her, even
people she isn't close to, her daughters-in-law, how could
they call her that with the same tone as her daughter Mélanie

or Daniel, Samuel, and others in the lineage headed by her white and well-coiffed crown, falling in light strands onto her cheeks just like Mélanie's, though her right hand, and occasionally even her left, were betrayed by intense, irregular trembling, what was the point, she thought, in finding a medical term for each and every nervous ailment, even if her daughter took her to the doctor once a week to be told incessantly what she suffered from, and upright she stood, enthralled by the bougainvilleas and frangipanis flowering in the garden, thinking each day had its special essence and beauty, Mère, once her children were born, the word was heavy and imposing, perhaps something of a caricature, Mère, tell me Mère, with all your experience, everyone seems to want what she could no longer give, wisdom, advice, too little time left not to spend it on her diary, all the things she still wanted to write with her barely tameable right hand, they had told her what she would rather not know, that this thing would follow its course, and the spasms, the rhythmic oscillations that shook her entire body when she wrote or listened to music or slept were nothing to be concerned about, she hardly knew where they would lead, so why bring it up, especially since she was the most lucid of them all, savouring every instant, every second as she did, and they all wasted so much of it without even realizing that if life had only one destination, death, why did her sons, daughters-in-law, everyone latch onto that handle of hers, Mother, and fight amongst themselves, wrangle for possessions, divide the inheritance well before it was time, less of it anyway after Augustino's education, faced with such deference she would rather leave everything to Julio, Marie-Sylvie de la Toussaint, or Jenny doctoring in Africa: would she be the object of her sons' contempt to the end, even though they pretended to love her, bringing gifts and calling her Mama, our mother, Mère, but once, as she wrote, decried and caricatured with the memory of all the women who had struggled before her, lightening her spirits, our children, their

children were not the only ones we had on this earth, for a
woman like her, wanting to find a meaning in life beyond
maternity and the duties that went with it, the almost debasing
humility it required, and the spiritual lineages as well, those
little-known women fighting for an art, a science and triumph-
ing like Marie Curie in her daily confrontation with doubt,
doubts never ceasing, even as she discovered polonium and
radium, was the first full female professor at La Sorbonne,
harassed by doubt as women are, doubt, she wrote in her
own diary, even in victory and conquest, as never a man
would know, for surely it lies in all of us forever, in solidarity
with women whose intelligence had been long subjugated by
a power as extensive as it was secular, and Mère, writing in
her ancient, flawless hand, just as she had before her mar-
riage, with that same schoolgirl concentration, had the feeling
of entering into the secret of destinies like Marie Curie's as she
discovered radium, or the writer and self-taught ethnologist
Ella Maillant's as she described her triple voyage through Asia,
though still perhaps a woman without a vote, a non-person,
a nonentity growing up rebellious in Switzerland and dreaming of being a navigator-explorer, or more than just dreaming,
had with no permission but her own heeded destiny's call,
and what she must have undergone on her boat *Atalante*, and
her first all-girl crew on the way to the Gulf of Biscayne, yet
still a dream that would take her to the lofty solitude of Asia,
perhaps joining the caravan of a Mongol prince on horseback
in Kuku-Nor with the teeth of icy winds in faces, crossing bare
spaces on skis, then later in Tehran on the way to Afghanistan
with cholera in the villages, a woman virtually alone in desert
places with camels, sheep, Mère thought, what did someone
as free as Ella Maillant feel, this is what Mère, called Mama,
Grandmother by one and all, would like to know, how does
it feel to be born with this gift, this infinite gift of freedom,
and still be a woman like Marie Curie or Ella Maillant, and how
would they end their lives, in serenity or regret that scientific

experiment, a nomadic life, were such short interludes, or would they be like Mère, contemplating the meaning of life alone in a room with one door open onto a rainy garden, gratefully breathing in the scent of jasmine and listening to the cascade on the roof, the chant of the grasshoppers; for the writer-traveller did finally have to forswear her Asian steppes, returning to Europe to care for an ageing, possibly cantankerous mother, never letting go of her travels to the unknown, the teachings of India, contact with the master Atmananda which had given her a perception of her much-loved, much-travelled world, an approach almost frivolous, for it too was frivolous: its people, their passions and appetites fading before the thought of a Supreme Consciousness swallowing and obliterating all we have, what, Mère thought, was left to these women, or to Mère herself, but to bow to the unknown, whether death would surpass life in beauty, surely not, for no end to life can be beautiful or lofty being made of nothing, a weakening under the irresistible hostility of our annihilation, for the wise it was vain, and for the moral it was bad, and who would leave this world without violence and tears? This Mère knew deep down, and let none of her children or grandchildren say otherwise she thought, always wheedling consolation around her, even though she was perfectly at peace, heart inconsolable at the thought of never seeing them again, just as Marie Curie's must have been at living apart from her daughters, though she had calmly conferred on Irène the continuation of her research and the burdensome weight of her knowledge of atomic physics, death would come for her as for anyone, with its disconnects and sombre dissolution of cells, be they by a trembling right hand or a palpitating heart, wouldn't it? Mère thought she knew the despair of youth facing death, her grandson Augustino's, who no longer came into her room in the morning, his budgie on his shoulder, smothering her with kisses, as he did not so very long ago. She'd once had a dream foreshadowing how her ebbing life would

affect Augustino more than any of her offspring, one presag-
ing the slide of life into death, when the budgie had flown
off, where's she going, oh, don't let her get away Grandmother,
she's going to break something, he seemed to shout, she
doesn't know where she's going, and why are the palm leaves
in the garden bent back like that, why is there frost on the
grass in summer, oh, of course she had often called him to
task for his manners, though he rebuffed her; this conformity
to a code of social class repelled him, just as his torn jeans
and sloppy hygiene displeased her, but the birth of a writer
in this scruffy boy attending the College of Science and
Mathematics didn't really upset her, it was natural for him to
despair at her impending demise, and this youthful desperation had taken root in him as the shadows wove themselves
around our Earth, of course it was natural, she thought, calling
death natural was unnatural to him, and she was thankful to
him for being who he was, ill-fitted to thoughts of death, so
imbued with life force, and for his rebellious writing, so full
of anger and so void of pity for his generation, like other
poets who had written before him but had not had to face the
ghosts of nuclear war, Augustino, Mère's grandson was perhaps right to express himself as he did in his first book, though
she confessed to being less learned than he, less prescient
of the future of technology, as in the dream the budgie had
flown from his shoulder into the wintry air of dreams with
summer grass bending under the frost, she had forgotten
how to fly just as death trims our wings, and it had changed
Augustino, hardened and fortified him, with the birth of his
first book came the first trauma of loss, she wrote proudly in
her diary that he would be a writer, yes that is what she must
write about, his first childhood despair; Augustino, her grandson, proudly she wrote, will be a writer or a philosopher, oh
how she'd love to share that with him and so many projects,
if only she had another twenty years ahead of her, and thinking of his youthful rebellion, she thought back to Franz who

sometimes visited her in this very pavilion, there too an inflamed, erratic youth commandeering the soul of the elderly musician, always such inexhaustible energy, she thought, his Britten *Requiem* so well received in Vienna, London, and Mexico City, he would have loved it to be taken up with the same perspicacity and urgency he had drawn on to conduct it everywhere, as if to say, listen to these sounds of the very last hour, and tomorrow when all your children are killed, will you still hear them, why so passive and indifferent, these voices and sounds are the very last alarm, somewhere on a plane he had written his *Sonata for Clarinet and Piano* and the opera commissioned in Germany, his family procession before him wherever he went, his musician-sister to look after him or rather his extravagances, a maid, his children, and his grandson, much bigger now, all of them with him as though wrapped in his sheet music and within the air he carried as though ready to conduct at any moment, his shirt collar open under his black tuxedo, the hour of the deer, the deer descending from their forests and mountains to search for food in the city streets, oh they're not listening, whenever will they start listening to me, he said to Mère, who replied the critics were right to say your *Requiem* unfurls like waves on the ocean, dear friend, and how good it is to see you, you, your sister Lilia and your children and grandson, not so long ago you were rocking him to sleep, and now he's nearly five, ah many cradles will be broken, he replied, and many more grandsons unborn, as she listened she found him as wild as ever, but so very gifted, do you remember, he went on, I was like that concert pianist in New York, Leonid Hambro, what a superhuman memory, I too was a quick study for complex, difficult works like him when he learned Paul Hindemith in a day, and Hambro stunned the audience, as I have done and could do again tomorrow, Mère thought he noticed the trembling in her right hand and her unsteady gait, suddenly the emotion-filled face held her too close to its large body, which arched towards her and said, dear friend, who knows what will have become of us ten years from now, but my dear, what are you thinking, you've forgotten to serve me my glass of whisky, you know I can't live without it, oh goodness, the whisky, she cried, how could I have forgotten it, I don't see enough of you, that's what it is, or perhaps I'm just too accustomed to being alone here, every day I wait for Augustino and of course he drinks absolutely no alcohol at all, certainly not as voraciously as Franz always drank, a second, then a third, there, he said, now I can compose, I'll tell you more about the opera, my dear, oh and what's going to happen to us if there's no one to listen, Mère couldn't help thinking that he was about to start in declaiming Blake and Milton, as he did in his seamen's bars, gripping and kissing her hands, here's to us, the *Songs of Experience*, I love you as I always have, Esther, and now I must go, my sister Lilia's waiting in her car to take the little one to school, and you know how she watches over me, it wasn't what she was meant to do, she too was a concert pianist, how unfortunate that her brother turned out to be me, Esther, I won't say farewell, because I'm coming back, poor Lilia keeping an eye on an old man writing a requiem of his own, poor Lilia, and the anarchist-musician was off again to London, Vienna, and Mexico, with Mère thinking about the sister, once a pianist, and Franz's wife, the new one, the young one who would no doubt wilt rapidly from such a despotic and capricious husband, and all of them trooping after him from concert to concert, even Yehudi the grandson, named for the great violinist so as to develop his human qualities later on in life, regardless of whether or not he became a violinist, a soloist, or a conductor; I want Yehudi to be a man of character, a fervent humanist like Menuhin, a thinker and musician spreading joy before him, we never know what God has in store for our children in these times when any number of monsters and demons can walk into a kindergarten, once sacrosanct but no longer so, she wanted to say, will I see you again, my friend, but she didn't dare speak it, instead she affirmed, I'll be seeing you again Franz, soon, yes, soon, and what a blessing it was he didn't complain like the other old people she saw regularly, not because she really wanted to, but because they always hung around querulously at tea time, there was some reason she couldn't be with them, what else, their lips, thinly creased by meanness, spouted nonsense and banalities she couldn't abide, and those complaints, however justified, of ailments, defective glands, or irregular insomnia, that was old age wasn't it, they said, complacent in their physical decline which was not all bad, since it got people at last to listen to them, boring though they were, no, Mère preferred this monotony, this ennui in the face of the inevitable, Augustino's anger, she read the pages where he had written about the talismans that soldiers took with them into the desert for protection, the deployment of poetry was surely a sign of life, hope for resurrection, a psalm printed on a scarf beneath the beige sweat-stained undershirt to ward off bullets, a grandmother's Bible to give a black corporal strength, a bit of dog's leash in the pocket would stun the enemy, a ring, a medallion, pictures of Jesus or Saint Paul, a woman's underwear, all of this worn to rags next to overexposed flesh, would be allies in vain battles lost and won under a sky where doves and turtledoves still took flight between gunshots, these young people, leaving behind family and fiancées, needed these charms, toys almost, within reach of fingers paralyzed by fear, yes, thought Mère, better to read Augustino with his finger on the pulse of terror than listen to the mortifying old people forever knocking at her door, saying, dear friend, Mère, you know everything, do you have a minute, ah, we all have to go through it, I can barely hear or see any more, and my liver, oh, if only you knew, digestion is really a problem and constipation, you know so much, dear Esther, tell me, will all this soon be over, my how good you are looking, what is your secret, no secret at all, she thought, if only to radiate joy or

be radiant in sadness, like the musician Yehudi Menuhin, as
Franz said, himself one of the most sombre and contradictory
beings she had ever known, and what would become of
grandson Yehudi, she wondered, like the young recruits in
the desert, would he ever come home to his parents and
grandparents, a bloodstained talisman stitched to his clothes,
a psalm printed on a scarf, his grandmother's Bible, the leather
fragment of a dog's leash, a ring, a medallion, pictures of Jesus
and Saint Paul, would all these fetishes ward off bullets or
would a mother, a sister, a grandmother have to recognize his
remains only by the image of Jesus or Saint Paul still imprinted
in the cloth and stigmatizing their dead, unrecognizable flesh,
oh yes, that is my child, they would say touching the Bible or
scarf or picture of Jesus, the only things they could identify,
stained with a purplish red, the last trace of life, though its last
struggle was over, for they had clutched these things to the
end, a bit of sand, sweat, still seeming to flow, then possibly
Yehudi would turn out like Patty, a young officer who'd vol-
unteered for the navy, once a seafarer and captain, headed
for one more adventure, though here the training was so
tough, the daily routine too, and killing was part of both,
photographed in boots, head practically shaved under a beige
cap, beige like everything around her, the men, the desert, the
endless sand-filled daylight, pointing her gun to the ground
and thinking I'm in charge of this camp, and what I do, I do
well, my kid brother's here too, determined and proud, that's
me, boy a hamburger's gonna taste good when I get some
leave, nope, no regrets — guts, decision, bringing my kid
brother an adventure, a career — and she too had a medallion
on her chest, and what swollen purplish red might it be tomorrow, under what heat would it melt, under what sun, thought
Mère as she read Augustino's book, perhaps, as her grandson
wrote, it might be better never to have been born into this
world, but since we are, she would tell him that all lives must
radiate joyfulness, and you with it Augustino, remember that,

my over-lucid boy who has known bitterness so early on, and why must this be, the bus bounced over mountain roads and Ari's fingers combed the hair away from his fevered brow, his temples burning, but the impenetrable profile of Asoka next to him did not seem ready to admit fatigue, surely he too was human, perhaps praying, and if only it would turn towards him Ari would say, I don't feel well, I really don't, but said nothing, just muttering a few ill-tempered words beneath his breath that no one in the noisy bus could hear, then pretending to sleep, though both head and stomach felt heavy despite not having eaten for several hours, be grateful if someone offers you a handful of rice, Asoka had quoted a Sri Lankan saying that now came back to sustain him, though in his fever he wasn't sure about that, still the fistful of rice might be the happiness Ari searched for everywhere when he sensed the acknowledgement of the poor towards the masters of the universe, God, Buddha, whichever, he flashed back to himself and Asoka on a beach, a sea inlet he had discovered from a groaning old truck, the sky suddenly the gentlest of blues, the white sands, the tide withdrawing to the sky, black families, escapees from ancestral slavery no doubt, serene and laughing, five little boys tipping their boat in the waves, laughing and joking, fish served under a beach shelter in the humid smell of smoke, maybe this was the unexpected escape to a world more his than Asoka's, stretched out on a hammock with a book, Ari felt what might have been the recognition of a handful of salt his friend talked about, saved from wasting away, feverish no longer but febrile with liveliness, he would paint all he'd seen today, and what would Asoka be looking at getting up off his knees in his orange pilgrim's garb, ready to walk, there on the sandbank, he saw five black boys' heads and heard their melodious laughter as they snorted in the waves which rose and battered the boat, then ran for the shore, gasping for breath, their skinny bums dumping bright-coloured swimsuits and underpants onto the sand like leaves from roughly blown trees, then running back into the water slapping their naked bodies, farther off, Asoka too watched, almost smiling — Ari could see the sun reflected on the enamel of his teeth, there was a centenarian grandmother surrounded by her entire clan, over a dozen of them, also on her way into the water in a nightdress and a slip underneath right down to her feet, shoes to pebbles, she moved carefully forward to the waves sheltered by arched arms and steered by other hands, almost blind under her cotton hat, and who, thought Ari, could feel a more earth-bound tribute to life, sea, ocean up over the ankles, then feet, her progeny around her as though letting herself be immersed in this water, sea, and ocean she was intermingling with her original and eternal maternal sources, she was the incarnation of all life fixing its gaze on the harmonious group, and Asoka trembled as though about to rush over and hold the grandmother up on top of the waves; he was thinking what . . . perhaps that he would never marry, never father one of these little ones, chaste to the end, and what gift to this vast universe forever giving birth and blossoming could his unfailing purity make, how to resist, was virginity not something rigid, or did he liken himself to one of those chicks inside the egg he had talked about in his book *The Evolution of Consciousness*, for back in his childhood village his mother, out of respect for life, had never boiled eggs for fear of damaging the shell or a hatchling, devotion to life meant asceticism and renunciation for the pilgrim monk, a love forbidden to live, maybe though all this was just how Ari saw it through his ignorance of Asoka's outlook, judging it by his own voracious quest for pleasure, but the laughter of the five boys flipping their boat and standing on the upturned bottom must have reassured him that if he never actually fathered a child, the world, in fleeting images of overwhelming pleasure, would lend him all of its sons and daughters, whether as disciples, like these who would forget all about him the moment their mothers called to them, just as he had parents before whom he had knelt in thanks for the handful of rice that was their blessing with the recognition that was still with him today under this gentle blue sky by the sea, for who are we if we cannot be humble before all, this Asoka thought, a man like the rest after all though he had based his life on the absolute good virtually devoid of subtlety, for evil too was good without distinction between them, as when a father brings up his daughter Ari thought, this ambiguous question of good and evil was not to be pushed away, it was no simple thing to inculcate the basic respect for life in a child like Lou who saw flowers only as something to pull petals off, ants to be crushed underfoot, the cat's whiskers to be harmed, everything she laid eyes on from the earliest age to be dissected, though her father was always after her to stop and to respect all that lived: plants, flowers, everything, but I picked them to give to you Daddy, she seemed to say, and they appeared to be repeating the same disputes he had with her mother Ingrid, minor conflicts that soon built up and spoiled both relationships; when he had said, no Ingrid, I don't want to be with you any more, and I can't stand your son Julien coming into the house with his skates on my wood floors, then playing the flute at night, but he knew these pretexts stood in for a love that was dwindling because he was one of those people who could not live with someone else, and this was why he accused her of faults that weren't hers, sometimes right in front of Lou whose broad forehead, perfect lashes lowered towards her cheeks, and straight-across fringe made him think, especially when she slept, that she was as much her mother as herself, and this annoyed him when he needed to discipline Lou and she didn't listen to him any more than her mother had, preferring at the drop of a hat to say, Mummy, I want my Mummy, you be nice to me or I'm going back to my Mummy, and lately he'd been having dreams in which he looked for her in some Nordic country in a mountain chalet where he couldn't make the electricity work and it was dark,

except when he opened the blinds and saw men sliding down
the snowy slopes speaking some rough language he didn't
understand, hunters maybe, all of them indifferent to Ari who
was calling his daughter in vain, where he wondered are my
yellow-flowered frangipanis, my palms, the sandlot where
Lou played cook, complete with casseroles in the cupboard,
her school friend Alexandra, is she here too, I wonder what
time it is, why am I here in this chalet shivering cold, where
is she, where is Lou, and he'd wake up to Lou still taking her
afternoon nap next to him, still sulking from their argument
even in her sleep, and of course she'd threatened to go to her
mother's after Ari scolded her for taking Alexandra's beach
hat, not nice, and besides what would Alexandra's mother say
if her sun hat was missing, eh, what would she say, Mummy,
I want Mummy she'd whimpered, and Ari was as sad as when
he fought with Ingrid, so where was Lou, his morning sunlight? Since then he'd of course met children lonelier and
more abandoned than Lou sleeping in a pile together in the
Brazilian night, a little Guatemalan Indian girl whose face he
couldn't forget and whom he first noticed apparently washing
dishes in a roadside café, first mistaking her employers for her
parents, so how could she be working in this unwholesome
café, as young and fragile as Lou in her dress, not sky blue
but a greyish dark blue like those in a hospital corridor, her
face creased and prematurely aged beneath a mass of dark
hair, then putting the plates on a greasy table and walking
towards the street like the bone-flanked dog sniffing leftover
pancakes in the street and begging from passersby, puppy-
like, rubbing against their legs to be noticed, take me home
with you she said, please take me home, I have no mummy
or daddy, imploring words that cut miserably through the
night and the city and Ari's heart, how was this possible, and
how could he not save her and take her home with him, and
how was it this little Indian girl did not have a right to the
same fate reserved for his daughter, so much like her but for

the poverty and misery, and sure to fall prey this evening or tonight to unscrupulous licence, the most devastating thing of all was his powerlessness to help this innocent whose eyes seemed to say, I know what is waiting for me, and when I've been debased they'll toss me in the garbage, blue-grey dress and all, still smiling at Ari and free of reproach, as teen prostitutes in white shirts and black trousers emerged from the bushes begging in silence, not playing for pity, just ready to be scooped up by unseen drivers, and others along the sidewalks lying on their backs in an alcoholic cloud, curly-haired young addicts, eyes closed and collapsed against the trunks of trees redolent with the night's perfumes and lit by passing headlights or the shimmer of street lamps, but amid all this confusion, Ari had eyes only for the little Indian girl, had she already fallen prey to someone and been gone in an instant, in any case, she was no longer there, and another child had already taken her place washing and drying glasses in the café with a dirty rag, but the child born for rape and defilement so much like and unlike Lou, her words still hanging in the air, take me with you mister, I have nowhere to go, no one to go to, don't leave me alone here, and time and again Ari would hear the plaintive little Indian voice in his nightmares, not always the same child exactly, perhaps older, still her cries might turn into a newborn's, his conscience stirred as he went to console her, then suddenly she'd be gagged and choking from cotton wool blocking her throat, he wanted to free her but he couldn't, and the dreams of helplessness seemed to confront him with his own stagnation, a battalion of guilt-ridden men and fathers sowing rape and strangulation in girls and women, unscrupulously beating and killing them wherever they were, in the Sudan and in Asia, men, even the best of them, might have to pay for these crimes, or would they forever get off scot-free as so many did now; hearing the shrill cries of newborns, even in the muffled sound of dreams, yet still clear and standing out against the silence,

echoing out of limbo, going to sleep at night with the crimes
of others on his own shoulders, crushed and broken in a pit,
indistinctly aware of the abandonment and morbidity of the
crazed Texas mother who had drowned her five children in
the bathtub and would end her days in a psychiatric institute,
all of it caused, her lawyers said, by postpartum depression,
though one of the prosecutors had doubts; the woman had
all her reason when she pushed her little children one by
one into the cold bathwater, better to have killed herself like
Lady Macbeth haunted by innocent blood, but here death
was bloodless, water stifling their starved lungs, this is how
their mother remembered them and the voice of God telling
her to drown them each and every one, and the strength of
hands and arms did as they were commanded, it was so
ordained, and then the painful assignment carried out as she
thought, she carefully wiped the fine moisture from her
glasses, sighed with satisfaction, then took some time to settle
her spirits and remembered the laundry not yet finished in the
basement, the shopping to do after that and her husband's
breakfast to prepare, and echoes of silent limbo settled over
the house, where on earth could the kids be, it would soon
be time to wake them up and dress them, where could they
be, now she gradually forgot the little bodies on the bottom
of the icy bathtub, God had come back for his offering, God
who commanded her delirious mind, after her glass of milk
she set the table for them, at each place a bowl of cereal as
usual, such a good mother, what then had happened to bring
her before these judges, then to prison, and finally to this
psychiatric hospital where everyone stared her down, where
she was medicated daily, becoming heavier and heavier as
though all her children were back in the womb, she would
have wished to die had she been strong enough in her tortured stupor of self-hatred, forever the silent limbo where the
children's arms were folded, their legs finally at rest, where
were they all, their lost, amnesic mother wanted to know, lost

further and further in her maze where no therapy could ever absolve her of what she'd done, Ari thought, and if Lady Macbeth had been motivated by family vengeance or thirst for power, misty sleepwalking bore her nightly towards her children's ghosts, she the mother could remember no real reason other than a vapid existence, without purpose, including her children, and if these motives were still anchored in her embroiled subconscious, she could not tell where, and who could get to the very bottom of it, perhaps being deflowered in childhood, something long since hidden, but as a criminal perhaps her abysmal subconscious interested no one, like many suffering mothers left unanalyzed, a thirst for death untreated, incurable, only this psychiatric condemnation that helped her avoid that of the judges who would not have pardoned her in her black-framed glasses, heavy, so heavy with her five children, no real existence, no verdict but to while away her days of captivity in an institution still not knowing why or what she had done, what was evil and what was good thought Ari, a few months ago smiling and celebrating Christmas with her children as the video showed, then the mental thread broken under irreparable tension, and the five children gone from presents under the tree to drowning under a surface more troubled than the thought of murder, no, Ari thought, good can't be accomplished as Asoka believes, and yet he was glad his friend had at least taken time to relax on a beach, though still remaining at a distance to meditate, though the group of boys distracted him, five of them too and very much alive, and their mother walked towards them with a laundry basket under her arm calling, come on, boys, come on, and they slipped their colourful swimsuits back on and ran to the ridge of dunes then disappeared under the gentle blue sky, the century-old grandmother still floating beneath the sheltering arms and resting on supporting hands, Ari noticed, and in a single day he had received several handfuls of that rice the wise man in Sri Lanka had described, something to be grateful for, yes, Asoka must be right about that: tomorrow is unfathomable, he thought, breathing in the salty air. This was thorny overgrown ground, thought Vénus as she gripped Rebecca's hand, when they're sixteen or seventeen I'll warn her about hanging around in overgrown lots, schoolyards, I'll tell her and she'll have to listen, even if she pulls at the red ribbons in her hair with those pink-varnished nails of hers, she'll just have to hear me out: they are men not children and you're not to play with them, 'specially whites, watch out, and do stop staring at me with those big attractive eyes girl, just stop I'll say and she'll understand, it's thick thorny brush and if you fall or someone pushes you and . . . you could see where the poor had hung their washing out to dry on the metal ladders among the weeds that crunched underfoot in summer, it was June 7 and one of their motorcycle helmets was metal too, turned up a bit at the edges, you couldn't see their eyes, both of them had jeans with braces, nothing underneath, dirty blond hair falling over their shoulders and chests, I told him no, they weren't the White Horsemen but they looked like it, galloping faceless, eyeless in their white robes with the flaming crosses they left on our land, no not them, they jumped off their motorbikes and said, hey we've come to see you and play with you Vénus, they say you have your own tree around here and the flowers are yours too, acacias and mimosas, the acacia tree is mine and I come to see it every day, I'm seven years old and this tree and the flowers are mine and today is June 7, isn't this a lonely spot for such a little girl, what are you up to anyway, I told you I've come to see my acacias, my tree and my mimosas, it's a surprise for my mummy, well now why don't we talk about the flowers Vénus, hey why not just stretch out on the grass and let us cover you with flowers, want to, then the insults, dirty little black bitch, I won't tell you the rest, you mustn't know about that and it's all in the past, the White Horsemen too, your school's integrated now, and things have even changed in Atlanta, you're a child of this fervent revolution, yours and mine, freed in blood, you are you know, smell those acacias of mine, the fragrances of the past in our nostrils here and now as we walk this street, it's not my fault if I can't erase their shameless genitals and their insults, such insults, from my memory, though I never told my mamma and your grandfather Pastor Jérémy, they would have told me to forget and I didn't want to, they would have forbidden vengeance and I wanted it, they would have said wish no evil on them but when they got squashed on the highway I rejoiced in a cry of vengeance, mine, going so fast on the Miami-bound highway what supreme hand of heavenly vengeance slammed them and sent the metal helmet rolling across the bridge, God in his great mercy hammered them as He should, okay I won't think about their mothers and fathers, just about the righteous vengeance of Heaven, maybe not the kind of thoughts fit for a pastor's daughter, but they're mine, Rebecca, and not yours to think, not yours, not Trevor's, none of you, the insults were the most devastating but no one will ever know about that, worse than the estate manager, worse than anything, little girls' bodies are still not formed, and if they come up to you, get far away and don't talk to them, a real nasty revenge and there was no water around the lot to wash up the blood, so I had to hide, where were my tree and my flowers, I can still smell them as we walk by here, hey give a proud look to your mother for having drawn down the wrath of Heaven on those two young men who had no right to live, one June 7 in the Temple of the City of Coral, my father the pastor suggested everyone read the Gospel According to Saint Matthew, and the faithful prayed and sang in that church, I remember it, and some others were playing ball in the yards, the smell of grilled meat drifted in from the sidewalks where men stood over their grills, and what would Mama say when she saw my soiled dress, the acacias and my tree, no I'd never come back to see them any more in that overgrown lot with thorns everywhere

and the grills behind where the laundry was hung out to dry
in a lazy breeze, houses pale green in the sunlight, kind of
like these huts, I didn't want to see any of it any more, never,
not even the roosters on the reddened grass, and my father
would say to one and all, have you read the Gospel According
to Saint Matthew, let's stand now and sing these psalms, and
up they got one and all and you could hear the stamping of
their Sunday shoes because there was always a bit of a hop
and a waltz in those feet, all of them to the same rhythm, and
I said to myself I'm never gonna pray like those people, 'cause
God doesn't love little children, but I will sing there right next
to Uncle Cornélius, you know he was in Korea once, well him
or Papa, and he said for the longest time they weren't allowed
on public beaches, and whites, 'specially the women with
tulle hats to keep off the mosquitoes, would watch them from
their verandas to make sure Papa and Uncle Cornélius didn't
go there, long time ago, was it true what Papa said, that her
musician uncle promised to take her on one of his many
trips to New Orleans, and he told Mama how well she sang
already at seven years old, no we're never coming back to this
thorny jungle with its rocks hiding poisonous snakes in summer and its scorpions, never, but the acacia smell, you can't
ever forget that, I'd think about it all while they were all in
church, and why did Mama say Carlos would never do what
he was told, going off to those farms in Atlanta where they
beat him up, going to juvenile hall for stealing a bicycle, I
never wanted him to be punished, nor my brother Le Toqué
with his one leg shorter than the other, but those big brutes
under their metal helmets, them I wanted punished with all
my heart and God granted my wish, punished they were and
just right because the whole world was getting even with them
too, but not my brothers, no, I didn't want that, my father's
voice would ring out when he said, what have you done now
you unrepentant good-for-nothing Carlos, padlocks, wheels,
bike chains, aren't you ashamed, it's not me Papa, it's Lazaro,

he told my father later when they'd both grown, because I was seven and they were even smaller, but Carlos had started off stealing fruit from the teacher's garden, he was bed-ridden and couldn't get up or do anything, he just had to watch from his window across from our place, my father would visit him and say, dear friend, please read the Gospel According to Saint Matthew, I think it will give you strength, but the teacher said no, I can't, besides the lemons and bananas will all wilt if he doesn't pick them, he's not stealing, I told him to come and get them, I'm afraid said my father, he's a born thief, I'm truly sorry for it, but there it is, no, no, said the teacher, he's done nothing he should be punished for pastor, but Carlos, you mustn't eat the green fruit from the giant lime tree, definitely not, Le Toqué and Carlos, both of them born thieves said Pastor Jérémy to the teacher who never left his room, what a pity Papa said to Mama that evening, pity for him and all of us, we have enough young people like him around as it is hanging around the Cemetery of Roses, we'll have to pray for him in the temple ourselves because the professor doesn't seem too pious, and we need prayer to enter the Kingdom of Heaven, oh yes indeed, said my mother, and look at these unrepentant good-for-nothings Carlos and Le Toqué, sure Mama would slap them around a bit but it didn't seem to do any good, now where has Vénus got to again, she's out on the swing, my father said, and that dress of hers is way too short, my how quickly she grows said mother, we aren't so rich we can buy a new dress every year, you can see her knees and her thighs and it gets the boys coming around, Papa said, that was a June 7 and nobody knew where I was, and they'd never know a thing, nothing, I thought about going to sing in Uncle Cornélius's club when I was big, and I'd live in a trailer like him with cats and dogs and birds, he complained he never got his pension for being in Korea, but his music earned him a good living when he wasn't drunk Mama said, see that in the paper, all those black boys shot in Chicago,

see, mailman told me when he delivered the paper, see, but
Papa said it was better to pray than read the papers the mailman brought, it was on Warm Breeze and Astronaut streets,
Mama said, and they talked like that after the meal and a long
time after that June 7 too, I was singing at the Baptist church
and Uncle Cornélius's club both, but Mama said he wasn't a
good influence, still I wanted to get by on my own and I had
nothing to say to anyone, there were always shows going on
at the club, sometimes girls danced naked at the private tables,
they served pizza and alcohol, and couples were welcome
any hour of the day or night, lots of men, and Mama asked
why I came in so late and what I was doing at night, because
a minor should be at home with her parents, where were you
anyway, and there were completely naked dancing girls waiting on tables just like it said outside, but I only sang just like
Uncle Cornélius taught me, this was long after that one June 7,
and I often thought about those two bikers never making it
across the bridge, I was avenged and the truck wheels had
squashed their necks and never would they set foot on my
thorny overgrown lot with my tree and acacias again, it was
all in ruins now anyway, just the lingering smell of flowers
and here we are again Rebecca and me as we walk down this
street, but she must never know, not about the guys, nor her
father the estate manager Richard, nothing, nobody, because
sometimes a lie makes life liveable, yesterday there was a
Santa Claus in the store with a boy in sandals on his knee and
the boy's hand on his beard, they both had red Santa hats on,
but he didn't look too pleased to be on Santa's knee, Rebecca
said, he told his mother he wanted to go, but I wouldn't be
afraid Rebecca said, that's for three-year-olds, I want to go and
see him Mamma, I'm not scared like that little boy, not even
in the dark, because I'm here with you said Vénus, but you
aren't always Mamma, and even then I'm not afraid, Rebecca
twisted the ribbons in her hair, don't undo those said her
mother, how many times have I told you, but Rebecca knew

this would blow over and her words disappear into thin air, she was used to hearing her grumble when they walked along the boulevards that ran parallel to the sea like this in the morning, saying things she didn't mean and clicking her necklaces and bracelets, it wouldn't last, with the rising sun heating up the sky she'd soften up and pull Rebecca closer to her, maybe hearing Trevor playing with the Groupe de Jazz Collectif and a woman singing into the mike, eyes closed as she remembered one of the melodies, our heritage, thought Rebecca as she longed to be on her father Trevor's lap just like the boy on Santa's with his red cap trimmed in white plush the same as Santa's beard, there were herons and gulls flying over the jetty, and farther off doves circled before landing on the wires, the world was in love the way Mamma was in love with Trevor, his brown body and long thick woolly hair like some sort of nest on his head Mamma said, just one weakness, he was dreamy and lazy, she said, putting out one joint after another on the steps, that made her mad, he said he had to relax after playing all night, not here, Mamma said, not here, and besides I've seen you sniffing other things with your friends, not in my house she shouted, and there was no way to keep her quiet though she loved Trevor and spent as much time as she could between working at the hotel and studying in his arms after telling Rebecca to take her book and her colouring book and play outside, everyone was in love the way she was with Trevor, the doves and other birds gathered on the jetty far from the cars streaking through the streets and the boulevard, and I knew Mamma wouldn't be annoyed or irritated or angry with me for long, it would just be the short rain before a beautiful rainbow and you would wonder if it had even rained at all, so there were all these cigarette burns on the steps and sometimes the sweet sharp smell of smoke, and those marks were always there, part of the wood, and when I saw them I always knew I was home, even if no one was with me, sometimes Trevor played afternoons and

all through the night emptying bottles of rum with his friends
Mamma said, that was not good, they said he had the blues
in his blood, and he played double bass and guitar, his hair
stood straight up on end, it was eclectic music Mamma said,
and it wasn't good getting numb on tequila as well as the
sounds in the tropical night, it amused him to tease Mamma,
playing over and over the same Miles Davis piece, "So What,"
for her, and so what, can't I do what I want, or he'd play Frank
Sinatra's "Fly Me to the Moon" as an acoustic bass solo,
Mamma would shudder in the night when he played under
the palms by the sea, his fingers tumbling through the Cajun
rhythms of New Orleans the way Uncle Cornélius had done
in his own club before him, that's what Mamma said, and she
said the past was also the present, and even if Great-Uncle
Cornélius was long gone, he was the one who taught me
to sing out for freedom Mamma said, so what, eh, so what,
Trevor said, we won't give in to nobody, he never got rewarded
for his victories in Korea, one morning in his trailer on a vacant
lot by the ocean he just never woke up, rum or tequila Mamma
said, that's what takes our men, never-ending injustice grinds
them down, squeezes the dignity out of them, I always had
my iguana, though I couldn't take him to school, he was tame
the same way the snake was that Uncle Cornélius kept for a
long time in his trailer with his birds and his cats, it used to
wind itself around his arm or his neck, heavy creature with
a piercing look, and we also had hummingbirds, budgies, a
toad, and my aunts Deandra and Tiffany went on Sundays to
the Marine Rehabilitation Center to see the thousand-pound
whale they have there, and they worked as volunteers helping
to move the whale to a bay in the national park if they could,
but it was so dehydrated and didn't survive, Deandra and
Tiffany told me all about it, the whales got disoriented when
they got in the shallow water near the shore, and so we had
no more whales in the parks, I sing in the school choir and
sometimes I even solo like Mamma, and I get free piano lessons

in a room the choir director calls the music lab, and we can play every instrument on the computer just like Trevor, he says it'll be mine later on — you can mix the voices of the Bible Song Choir, the students in preparatory class, the younger ones playing violin and cello the best they can, and play with the drums — I get to sing into the mike in my white silk dress and gold cross and chain, and Mamma says to everyone look, that's Rebecca, my daughter, you just wait and see where she goes my girl Rebecca, Vénus clearly recalled the professor in the window too weak to stand, blue eyes staring out at the sea from over the hollow curve of his cheeks, beyond the military beach where children and dogs ran, the pastor told them all not to make any noise and to be respectful when they passed the house, once, when he could still stand, he used to walk all the way out to the sea with his cane amid the kids and dogs swirling around him, before the visits by his sister the nurse, or was it some stranger in a big black car, and when he could still get out, she would take him for drives around town settled in cushions on the back seat and waving to friends; that was before things went horribly wrong and people only saw him in the window, his gaze lost in the distance of that unattainable beach, the turquoise water, Papa said he listened to the same sacred music over and over again in earphones that made his face look smaller: the cantata of David the Penitent, Mozart's Mass in C-Sharp Minor that his devoted friends Luc and Paul put on for him until the earphones would suddenly give way to fatigue, apparently deaf and blind at the window in the light of day dying on the water, on the flowers in his garden, the mango and orange trees, a cat leaping into the foliage would make him start, thirsty, he said he was always thirsty, and his sister would press the ice-water carafe to his forehead, saying drink slowly, very slowly, sometimes she would cry without a sound, and Papa would say, children you mustn't make any noise, and he was the one who thought of the yellow hibiscus, wondering if it would be too late, hey Le Toqué, why don't you take some to him, thus it was the professor saw Le Toqué limping towards him with yellow hibiscus in his arms, was it too late though, I don't remember if it was, if he had time to see it as Papa said, the oil lamp had burned low, perhaps he never did see it or hear Le Toqué clopping, too many young people like him in the Cemetery of Roses Papa said to Mama over and over, that's what we called it, Cemetery of Roses, because every day some- one came and put red roses on the graves, and I wondered if at nightfall on full moons young people lifted their rigid coffin lids to dance and sing on the grass with roses between their teeth, why not, yes why not I thought, I'm sure they come out of their dingy crypts and return to their unstained youth to dance and sing unobserved, sometimes I'd actually go there to watch them, sure their shapes would be airy and barely visible, and I thought I heard them whispering, Papa said we should pray for them, I didn't though, I just said to them come and look at the sky and the sea, they're yours, come dance with me; maybe the yellow hibiscus came too late for the professor at the end of his short life, neither he nor my father knew my vengeful spirit, nothing but fire and vengeance, all they knew about me was that I sat next to the white people in church and sang with a pure voice and, thought Vénus, although Rebecca's the child of a revolution whose anger has cooled, I long for more vengeance against those arsonists who burned our temples and churches in Alabama, and so long after killing our kids, even when they're caught, the sadists-turned-contemptible-old-men get off again, just as they did back then, cursed fire-starters, let their work turn back on them, capital punishment is what they deserve for this if it exists for anything at all, a cycle of unending curses on them and their families till the end of time, now sons of doctors and businessmen carry on their dirty deeds, a crop of new suspects and conspirators in the destruction of our race, like father like son, once deer hunters, now school- and church-burners, and I don't believe it's going to end, the only thing that hasn't changed in Alabama is pain, ours, our children's, mine; my daughter Rebecca staring at me with her loving eyes doesn't know, nor do I want her to know that nameless ancient sorrow, mine in that overgrown thorny lot, in his sermons my father says vengeance is a sin, he's a spotless man who dreams of nothing but goodness among humans, but I'm not like him, why should I be even if he's my father, my vengeance is straight like a road I have to follow and not lose sight of for Rebecca and for me, this is a time of progress for Alabama and everywhere, everything has changed but the pain and sorrow, thought Vénus, feeling the tiny warm hand of Rebecca in hers and the ribboned hair brushing against her elbow, no capital punishment or any other kind for them, she thought, and my brother Carlos, God knows what they'll do to him in prison, when she'd sold everything for him — the Captain's house by the canal, his paintings, his villa, his wealth and house, all gone forever — so much given up or snatched away so Carlos could be free because he was innocent of attempted murder, so many doubts weighing on her spirit, even if Perdue Baltimore had written to the Parole Board, serious doubts that she might not be able to keep Carlos out of adult prison in Louisiana, that all her efforts might be brushed off by the justice system as though her brother's life were just dust in the wind, she thought, not an actual life, just nothing at all as it always was, and Perdue Baltimore and Vénus's struggle was for nothing, just as it always was; Samuel opened the door of his apartment and saw the planes landing on his kitchen table, though of course he never told anyone about it, they were on his dresser too and criss-crossed the walls with no pilots and no orders, imprisoned by acts of terror, attacks taking place within his living space no longer wracked his entire being with tension as it used to, he was getting used to it as so many others did, even though he was happy to be young and sensual, he was open to the fact that

all facets of his present being could be rapidly wiped out on
a subway platform by an odourless gas just as the doors
opened, whose target would he be, perhaps young people as
healthy and strong as himself and hating him so that he captured their despair, and if the struggle was between him and
them, they might explain the reasons for this mutual hatred,
making it clear, he thought, but those who had built this
hatred, however armed and fearsome, were not the same as
the ones who stood behind them, urging on the attacks,
respectable people whose faces Samuel knew well, not really
faces so much as masks of complacent hypocrisy, on one side
people, on the other the indoctrinated, both of them enemies,
the instant cyanide gas is absorbed, the hectic race for trains
at the platform stops cold, but Samuel had never shared with
his mother this dismaying ease with which erasure and simple
disappearance could be accomplished, or the increasing natu-
ralness of it to him, this was a reality he couldn't sidestep,
nothing he could do, the colourless gas tried out in the Nazi
camps was insidious, parasitical and treacherous, and before
long anyone could get it and release it into a ventilation system, and workers in the confined space of a train or sitting on
a seat reading the papers, breathing in poison without smelling it or knowing its name, even that had been translated into
code by a clever terrorist as Honey, Honey Jar, agent of eutha-
nasia to many, ready or not to succumb, in the flower of one's
life or at its start, regardless of our will, thought Samuel, food
for violence, why not feel prepared for it to devour us alive
and in the full bloom of health, as it did those carrying out
suicide missions every day, the meaning of that word *life* had
perhaps changed since Samuel's birth, though true glory came
only through the acquiescence of a long and serene life, like
those of his parents and grandparents, despite the upsets and
agitations just below the surface; he had the feeling, as he
walked the streets of New York, enraptured by the musical
and visual marvels plus his habitual iconic objects (cellphone,

Mac, iPod), of being free but wandering towards a future that would be violently cut short through no fault of his own, wrapped in predictions of an odourless gas, loving and dancing while it lasted as though precariously carrying his own oxygen tank, not that he put down Augustino's *Letter to the Young with No Future* the way his own father had, but he'd often felt unable to show the negative and withdrawn Augustino his tender side, though Samuel probably found another family, other siblings, in Julio with whom he'd set up the Shelter for Refugee Artists, maybe one day that's what we'll all be, he thought, in fact everyone performing in Samuel's choreographies was from somewhere else, political refugees and artists once imprisoned at home for having practised their art and thus become dissidents: Russians, Cubans, whatever, they had galvanized the dance world like the young Venezuelan Rolando whom Samuel compared to Rudolf Nureyev, small like him, and who danced in his *Rite of Spring* to a wild rhythm and savage orchestration, teaching Samuel the bold audacity to treat the various art forms as a fusion, modernity without limits, and Samuel's choreography with its fractured ice shelves, its dispossessed and heteroclite animals, resembled Robert Rauschenberg prints showing combined objects mired in red paint to announce the coming society made up of victims of our waste, and to show us that artists can often initiate us into truths, Rauschenberg's truths long ago anticipating what Samuel wanted to say today, a perennial vision of fraternity was worth every bit as much as a longer life without it, now being the time to fulfil promises for the future, his life seeming a joyous, endless temporality he'd so love to inculcate in his brother Augustino and set against the dark opaqueness that seemed to tell his brother to keep his distance and not try in vain to rupture the crystal of solitude, because life's meaning had altered since their birth and nothing, thought Samuel, nothing; Mère asked Augustino if he sometimes listened to *The Art of the Fugue*, as Franz had suggested,

listen to the transparency of the work, the artful description
of joy and exultation in faith that are never apart in the mas-
terful work of Johann Sebastian Bach, the balance and joy
were a daily battle for him against the shadows of blindness
that would overtake him at the end; then he was admired
as a virtuoso, but sadly it took time and the brilliance of
Mendelssohn to show Germans the composer in him, had he
only felt through the silence of death on that hot day in July,
and after so much pain, the hand of young Mendelssohn
reach out to him; forever onward and beyond said Franz, past
these fields and hills of silence where soon he would sleep
without memories, not *The Art of the Fugue* or the sumptuous
Passions, and so it took another musician, Mendelssohn or
Schumann, a thinker-poet in love with his work like Hegel,
and thus is our slow march across this Earth, we need one
another beyond this borrowed time, and Mère wrote to ask
Augustino if he sometimes listened to *The Art of the Fugue*,
for she was enraptured and transformed by it and by the rain
on the roof, for we never know who we are composing and
writing for if not for generations unknown Franz said, as the
Italian romance writer Goliarda Sapienza had done in his long
cantata, the story of a lifetime, *Arte della gioia*, the art of joy,
an autobiographical account or an autobiographical dream
conjured up by magical spirits from a rigorous uncensored
vision, unfairly contemned by the critics for decades, thus
writing only for the future, readers from another plateau, less
formal, less withered, launching towards them his adventuring
characters and grand themes, unravelling the tangles of consciousness as Virginia Woolf had done, where closed wounds
go to hide, to make life's heart beat again through the multitude of characters in periods of history marked by war, fas-
cism, total collapse and ruin, to raise the tableaux of men and
women valiant in revolt, their courage, their dignity, and did
Augustino listen to *The Art of the Fugue* sometimes, and perhaps, just perhaps, he too would be transformed and come to

see her soon, oh she could wait, and she requested it so discreetly, for she knew he had to put his studies, his books, and his friends first, did he even have friends, was he alone too much, well his answer didn't surprise her: Dear Grandmother, through all your passionate reading, your love of music, and your thirst for learning, you seem to have forgotten that presidents and prime ministers put up with and even encourage the worst kinds of abuse on their citizens, can't you hear the crumbling beneath your feet and mine, while whole villages burn they say nothing, 40,000 already forced from their homes, women gagged with cotton, raped, and killed, militiamen disappeared, swallowed up in the desert sand, black gangrene blossoms, lifeless fingers, or else raped and burned to death by the barbarians while you listen to your music in raptures, a horde of starving monkeys, primate anthropoids so advanced they crawl every which way through traffic with their little ones on their backs, in Delhi animals which once inspired respect wandering aimlessly through the Indian capital among the cars and taxis, uprooted from their jungle, beaten and wounded, stretching up to windows in desperate hunger and thirst, sometimes in hopeless, threatening packs or herds, once the gods of devotion and wisdom to the locals, nothing now without their forests and habitat, sanctuaries gone, at the mercy of any and all, caged in prisons on the outskirts of town for lack of anything else, you'll see dear Grandmother, they too will soon be extinct, like anything else destroyed every day while you read all those books and listen to that exalted music, you'll see, this is just the wrenching start of all the genocides, then tell me once again that a boy like me has a future; his grandmother could only agree, all he had written was true, the spectacle of Earth's disintegration was hard to face, and what he felt was not, as his father said, threatening or destructive, but a truth wholly believable, but how to explain to Augustino, Mère wondered, that she, alone or with him, could not let herself be deafened by this day and night,

her days and tears being counted as they were, of course I
think of those noble creatures thrown into prison like convicts
in cells, she wrote him, I hear them whimper and protest at
the atrocities inflicted on them, and the picture of beleaguered
monkeys seeped into every thought as she read or listened to
The Art of the Fugue, still these few words she must add for
Augustino as though impelled by some irresistible force,
when we listen to this music we forget the price its composer
paid, he could barely see, how could he ever manage to
compose with such deteriorating health, and did he really
spend all his time dwelling on those who owed him something, inferiors who had employed him, every possible worry
and humiliation can come only from the men and women
who surround us, though this music born of heaven could not,
in spite of everything, allow him to escape from all his worries
such as the obsession with his health, composing even as
thickest night fell on his eyelids, Mère didn't know, and perhaps never would, whether Augustino was even listening to
her during this furtive exchange, rumbling along in the bus,
Ari intently observed Asoka in profile and wondered, as he
smelled the cinnamon cookies the squirming, ever-so-tidy
kids were hungrily biting into as they looked out of the windows, if Asoka was at all interested in art, which Ari would
have loved to discuss with him, or was he plain indifferent to
something so close to Ari's heart, did he even know that the
most contemporary of North American painting flowed directly
from Picasso, that art was as durable as life itself, just being
Lou's father meant nothing if it could not be attached to some
form of artistic longevity as Picasso had done, and what
enraged progeny he now had among a vanguard he continued to lead, unclassifiable, the puzzle of his art still intact
despite so many imitators, Asoka's concerned look meant he
was again going to beg nurses for his clinics and infirmaries
in Champerico and Cobàn, no point in getting involved in a
discussion of art; he wasn't someone like Ari who sometimes

took comfort in letting his mind wander, his theories on Picasso now evaporating into the stale and cinnamoned air of the bus, American Abstract Impressionists certainly had as much imagination as Picasso, their originality being precisely in turning away from him, as though physically unscrewed and doing it all again differently, not restricting themselves even to their own models, Picasso, Kandinsky, and the rest had all shattered what they once revered, leaving us thunderstruck again and again, as though the destruction of our gods would automatically give birth to the new, one of them saying, maybe I could paint my studio over and over the way Picasso did around 1928, another doing it as a challenge with distorted shapes in oil on wood, yet a completely different imagery from Picasso, bursting forth from the painted studio in forms possibly human or disfigured as humans, later titled *Pink Angels* or *The Pink Angels*, a strangely vivid exploration of colour and shape, Ari thought, so that even space seemed to be reinvented, but would this interest Asoka in any way at all as his thoughts centred on the meeting with hospital nurses he wanted to incorporate into his mission's order, a strict one, there were no random thoughts for him as there were for Ari, except for randomness itself which could slide in between the meanders of his mind at any moment, like that apparition of the not-to-be-forgotten boy with AIDS and a towel around his neck, now even thinking about Picasso, he was also distracted by the Mexican poet he heard one student reading to another behind him: *muerte sin fin, muerte sin fin* — unending death, as though Gorostiza's words suddenly determined his actions, and he wondered when he would see his studio and his sculpture again, maybe I should be sculpting and painting right here and now beside Asoka, this man so utterly impervious to art, *muerte sin fin, muerte sin fin* the poet wrote in words that pounded at his temples, one sentence: where was Lou, and why had her mother still not written when he forced himself into sleazy Internet cafés hoping for a message, nothing, he'd been forgotten, fatherhood was what exactly, making sure of Lou's life, what was that longevity that he no longer painted or sculpted, had it become the anxiety of a pointless existence, art the only source of life-giving self-sufficiency which Asoka had surely sought in the stability of prayer and meditation ever since his ordination as a monk at twenty-one, wandering from village to village, monastery to monastery along the world's byways, like Russian ascetics, barefoot or dragging chains, as they escaped servitude and dependence on the lords' lands or the iron hand of a pitiless imperial court and offering solace to souls in torment, preaching poverty and penance, having nothing themselves and living from the alms of peasants and monks they encountered, Asoka had no fear of the elements or loneliness, an Indian guru obeying no one but the fluidity of divine commandments that demanded nothing of the poor but to be poorer still without wanting to avoid the fleeting karma which is the common fate of all, as Asoka said, for whom karmic existence was a test of any destiny, this too Ari would have liked to discuss with him, was hell a Machiavellian invention of Catholics, and what about the multiple hells scattered through everyone's life, did Asoka really believe in the places he called Brahman worlds where one could live in peace and harmony with nature for more than a century, and who were these beings so psychically developed and invincible to chaos and suffering, how could Ari go and live with them at the end of his journey, for they too would die before attaining another birth, Asoka said, as if meaning that, suddenly cut loose from beatitude, one goes from a country of complete contentment to another, quite unknown, constantly changing course, barely able to change clothes or habits, a series of Brahman worlds to elevate oneself by degrees, unless an unfortunate birth (bad or in the wrong place, as often happened) sends one reeling to the multiple hells known as *apayas*, and even this will come to an end Asoka said, life being a ceaseless journey of fresh beginnings as infinite as flowers in a boundless field, every one of his images and gently persuasive techniques was intended by Asoka to sound out Ari's beliefs or tip him over into a world of faith where all at once he would question no more, but simply say Lou, Ingrid, and I are mere flowers blossoming and fading as the summer morning is reborn and the day embalms, serene he would be in these plant-like preoccupations, his soul no longer irritated and inquiring, no longer harrowing him; one thing, however, was sure in Ari's mind, that the pilgrim monk could no more give up his happy solitude or his freedom to travel or spread his green leaves to the free air than he himself could, and in this at least they were true friends, even if Ari had never had any such illusions that the famous "journey of life" could be longer than the stars had foretold at his birth, and Mélanie watched as her daughter left the group of schoolgirls and skipped towards the Jeep, all thin legs under the fringes of her pleated skirt, and how could she let her daughter leave for school like this in the morning, still, at a private school she'd have had to wear a uniform and Mai had absolutely refused, butting heads with any class privilege in her favour as if under the influence of Augustino, the most defiant and asocial of her children, for although they rarely saw one another, Mai and Augustino corresponded almost every day, Mélanie, disconcerted by her daughter's attitude, the thin impertinent face about to press up to her for a kiss, knew she was going to ask about the boy I saw you talking to yesterday in his car after school, who was he, oh you mean the Mustang convertible Mai would respond innocently, nice eh Mum, not exactly a boy Mélanie would say, a man twice your age, you're too young to hang out with people like that, and your father saw you going to the beach with him yesterday, oh yes to see the boats all decorated with Christmas trees tied to the masts what's wrong with that, we could take you and Dad to see them but you'd never have time being in Washington or somewhere all the time, what's that on your tongue and your navel, Mélanie would knowingly pester her, jewellery Mum, little metal balls, how ugly her mother would say, aren't you afraid of injuring yourself or getting an infection, no Mum, why, Mai of course being the only schoolgirl to carry sandals in her hand instead of books, a female soprano scratched from the radio, c'mon dear, Mélanie hugged her daughter, let's go for a quick lunch, why the rush, are you taking off again this afternoon Mum, just a few days her mother replied, so who's the guy in the Mustang you were talking to, just a friend said Mai, another one who's too old for you, you know we're going to worry when you're talking to strange men, I told you he's a friend, she sounded impatient but felt like laughing at her mother's interrogation, then seductively putting her hand on her mother's knee, I'd be so unhappy if you didn't trust me, oh don't worry about me Mum, you've got your hands full with Vincent, actually he's doing fine she said, thinking it's just one of those crises, puberty, I'd still like to know who that man is, you told us you had a tennis lesson but your father told me you missed it, so where were you, with my friends came the answer, washing cars at the garage, Saturdays it's a dollar a car, now we told you that wasn't a good idea, if you need money just say so, you'd be better off going to your tennis lesson on Saturdays like Vincent, yes Mum you're right, I won't go to the car wash any more, happy now, now give me a nicer kiss, I already did Mélanie replied, and you're not getting another one until you tell me why you were talking to the man in the Mustang, nice car shot back Mai unruffled, why and what did you have to say to him Mélanie persisted, nothing Mai laughed, and the woman's voice scratched its way through the speakers, let's get some rap was Mai's answer as she switched cassettes, I want my own music, of course thought Mélanie a woman president has to be flawless, a mother and grandmother brought up to be polite and refined, demands that women senators already faced, if she's liberal, she mustn't go too far, moderation in all things, never take sides, with all this was there any coherence left to her for a purely pacifist, progressive, inventive, intuitive, and humanitarian ideology, and could she put forward rival positions, if so how to support them, their family had a black chauffeur, so where are we going to eat Mum, Mai was asking, now what are you thinking about, her mother's thoughts melted into burning air, often confused and stressed whenever she came to pick up Mai from school, as though her daughter forbade her to think clearly, everything had to be right there for Mai in the Jeep, in the hollow of her mother's shoulder . . . her music, the voice of the stuntman-doctor singing rap that Mai kept time to with her nodding head, that's love I'm tellin' ya, that's it that's all at the end, the Jeep was a boxful of sounds filled with acoustic acrobatics just for her pleasure and to keep her mother quiet and mindless, which didn't keep Mai from being a delicious kid, if you could still call her one, breasts budding already under her tight swimsuit, though she wore next to nothing and it cost a fortune to clothe her in what didn't really seem to cover her, and why did that uncomfortable thought clutter Mélanie's reflections on women and politics, women leaders and their roles, things Mère had conscientiously discussed since childhood, Eleanor Roosevelt's courage, and closer to home, the tolerance and boundless energy of women governors, of course Mélanie had listened to her mother, yes Mama, I know, I know, but most of us do bring up our own children, we think of nothing but that and your political heroines, jealous of them when we can't live all of our dreams, as well you know, that's how you thought of us growing up, wasn't it, yes but you Mélanie, you and I were meant for very different things Esther replied, when all of a sudden there was Mai, everything for you Mum, and for Mai, 'cause you wanted a daughter and here I am, and now I've got to be at the airport by late this afternoon said her mother, Mai was incredulous: you're off again so soon, and Dad spends all day writing, boy you two are boring, still she was laughing, and she'd already moved on to music or something else, and there was the nightmare right in front of her mother's eyes, the palms, the streets, and the houses along them all misted together, first she was on the plane in Reno, all the windows filled with faces as they watched officers rolling a coffin towards the baggage hold beneath them, Samuel was inside it and Mélanie could hear him breathing so loudly they pulled away the flag and said, hear that, he's alive, hear him breathing, someone was saying the young ones all do that because of the lack of ventilation, his lungs are affected, no air going through them, and could they, could they just believe he was still alive, he's going to have to be quiet said one officer, they were all gentle and ceremonious, let's just allow him to breathe and mourn any way he can and he'll stop, another one said, they bent over his body, what'll we do if he doesn't, Mélanie's forehead was pressed to the window, nine of them in separate compartments, nine faces raised and crowding into the windows to see the funereal tableau, too bad his breathing was so loud and wheezy as though he'd just climbed a hill, too bad no one would ever see the little lieutenant they called James or Samuel ever again, he'd just vanish along with the passengers whose hearts at that moment beat to bursting at the thought of him and his murky destination, what exactly was he like under there, did he have all his parts, and why was he complaining so much, Mai remonstrated to her mother, but it's my own dollar I earn washing cars on Saturday, Mum, that's the thing, mine and only mine, I'll pay my own way through college and you'll be so proud, anyway you still haven't told me where we're going to eat, someplace by the sea said Mélanie, near where you used to play the Cuban football team, you know, Mai said, I may not have worked all that hard but I'm top of my class, first in everything, even if you're always telling me I don't study enough, and Mélanie felt like saying that's exactly why I was thinking about a private school, but she just repeated mechanically, that's fine, that's just fine, you'll have to tell Dad tonight, I just don't understand, that's all, I never see you in your books, her voice sounded dry and distant in response to Mai's joyful success, the nightmare of the shrouded young lieutenant was still present as James, with Samuel gone forever beneath his features, Samuel or James both born to mothers, Mélanie held back her tears, Ari's sleep was feverish and shook with the wheels of the bus, then following Asoka into a hospital, he encountered a young white-clad male nurse on one leg and crutches coming towards them, dangling a heavy key ring from his fingertips, this is the infirmary he said as he opened the door to a dark, dusty room with empty shelves, no medicine but a few musty Aspirins, he smiled at Asoka, that same unfailing smile he'd seen on the AIDS boy that said we haven't a thing, Ari would love to know how he'd lost his leg and stood so straight on the other, I'm in charge he said with pride, but we're short of everything, this way's the laundry, we're out of sheets and nurses' shirts so we wash them as we go and hand them to one another, several of the washing machines were broken and a cloud of soapy disinfectant smell rose over them, watching the young man so agile in his infirmity, Ari thought of a little one-legged girl making her way through the crumpled corrugated-metal village in Kashmir after an earthquake, it was cold under the snow-capped mountains for the little refugee with a hooded raincoat moving alone on one black boot and steel crutches through the ruins of her house, and she seemed alone at the summit of the world, snow piling up on the granite above her, somewhere farther off there might be some tents for the refugees, some dilapidated temporary camp with cooking fires, she probably had no idea though in her desolation that she and the nurse were one in this enigma of misfortune, try as Ari might to explain it, and this is the delivery room, the nurse opened yet another door with his massive ring of keys, female nurses in green caps welcomed him beside empty beds and one plunged a plastic doll into a basin

with barely a trickle of water to show how they bathed the
newborns, it was the pink plasticity of the doll that jolted Ari,
Lou had had one like it then tired of it, knocking it gradually
to bits as she played with it carelessly, then abandoned like
many others, then fished out again and recycled into one of
her paintings, embedded in the gouache for a second chance
at life with a drumstick and some pebbles, beach sand made
its way into the paintings and crayon drawings her father had
pinned on her wall too, still feeling the torpor of just waking
up in the bus as it climbed the mountain roads, Ari thought
for a bit about his daughter's garbage-art, drawn and painted
from material saturation, the end of an exacerbated civilization signalled by the outcast malleable pink doll, just as in his
dream of the infirmary that same doll meant the exact oppo-
site, total deprivation of even the water needed to bathe a
newborn whose delivery itself was so uncertain that it had to
be replaced by a pink plastic doll, the baby, thought Ari,
would then have to be docile enough for all to handle as they
wished, he was also amazed that Lou had understood the ideas
that guided Rauschenberg without being told, the vigorous
condensing of objects onto a single canvas, he should have
let her spread out as extravagantly as that, buckets of paint
layer on layer, letters cut from the headlines, a sock, a leftover
shirt, a goat sculpture covered in angora, every possible com-
bination crowding into her fancy regardless of logic or meaning, giant canvases, a chicken portrait, a metal sculpture with
wings that seemed to flutter, but that was a game to Lou, just
piling up cubes of colour with no real balance between them
and the disparate objects, Rauschenberg's assaults on us sprang
from long reflection, thus the goat was swollen and crushed
by the car tire so fused into its middle it first seemed outra-
geous and insanely deliberate, then perhaps not, the investi-
gator and accuser of these mediocre times was there, the artist's
eye like a yellow sun in the middle of his paintings, judging
through the bizarre tapestry that this world, wherever one

looked, was both furious and sombre, inflicting violence on us through pitiless forces often beyond our control, so was Lou's garbage-art then a child's confession that, having received so much from her civilization, she like it was completely disillusioned? Mai slammed the Jeep door behind her as she rushed to the beach, Mum, remember when I drew a circle around Emilio in the sand she cried into the wind, remember, but Mélanie was already on the restaurant terrace with her face bent over a book on her knee and didn't reply, six white egrets left a line of tracks by the water as Mai got quietly closer to watch them, that was before, she thought, before he went to the Spanish Catholic School, I used to see him every day, the very first time was by the volleyball net and his teeth gleamed in the sun, that was a while ago, I don't see him at all any more, like those things from the past that Dad writes about, I mean they'll never know whether I'm actually first or last in my class, they've got all kinds of other things to think about, for Dad it's the past, what's not there any more, even Emilio, he's in the past, there are lots of other immigrants in my non-confessional school, why isn't he there, and I thought that circle in the sand would keep him here forever, but the past just disappears, no one but Dad thinks about it, he says it's for his books, at two we're going to see the psychologist Mum says, yeah like I'm going to tell all my secrets to some-one I don't even know, a guy who says the past is important just like Dad and asks me all kinds of personal questions, like why do I hate Marie-Sylvie de la Toussaint the nanny, why, why, why, and whatever happened with the fisherman on The-Island-Nobody-Owns the day they buried that poet Jean-Mathieu, I remember Dad carrying me on his shoulders back to the boat and saying where were you, what were you doing, and I leaned on him and slept, dear Dad, he was my friend then and he wasn't always trying to decode my soul like they're doing now, hmmm so what did happen that day, I remember the grande dame Caroline who'd lost her bag, that was history too because they said she's dead now, why do they do that, why do they all die, Jean-Mathieu the poet, Caroline, why, and I'd brought some shells back for Vincent, that's past too, and I'm not saying anything, 'specially to some-one who thinks she's so smart because people bring kids to her office, then she says now tell me, what happened that day, what day, the day at the stadium Mai, you know what I mean, that day at the stadium, who was waiting for you there, I dunno, that's a long time ago, there were the shells, a bitter smell, and Mum said Vincent couldn't go out because he might suffocate out in the water, but Marie-Sylvie didn't do what Mum told her and took him to see Samuel's boat *Southern Light*, that's past too because they're refugees my parents were sheltering, so Mum forgave them everything, even Marie-Sylvie de la Toussaint, but it was her fault Vincent didn't get better, Marie-Sylvie de la Toussaint, he's the only one she loves, she calls my brother her son, Mum ought to tell her he's hers too, but she lets everyone off except me, she's way too easy on people and they abuse it but she doesn't even notice anything, you want to know what happened the day they buried Jean-Mathieu at sea, I'll tell you, everyone was crying and carrying on because he was just a pot of ashes, it was awful and I wondered what it was all for, so I went off to get away from them and have some fun, then just as I was leaving Caroline came up in her wide-brimmed hat and asked me if I'd seen her little purse because Jean-Mathieu had given it to her, she said they're all on the platform, even Isaac the oldest one, and they're talking about my friend as though he's not there, now isn't that strange, I mean he's still in Italy she said, I've got a mirror and powder in the bag, I didn't want to tell this lady I was off somewhere else for the rest of the day, besides she didn't try to stop me, in fact she said when I was your age I didn't want to have anything to do with my parents or my nanny, I liked being alone, though I had lots of toys like you, one day my mother's boyfriend, oh no, I'd better not tell you that, go little girl, go and live your life and quickly, it's all we have, then we're soon enough fixated on the past, and she just let me run off without a word, and already I could hear Mum calling, Mai, Mai, where are you, I know I could have told Caroline anything, the tide was out and there was a guy in a boat standing upright, he was the one who was going to scatter Jean-Mathieu's ashes on the ocean, the past, yes, we'd never see him again unless Caroline was right and he was still in Italy, he was a family friend and he often came over, I remember sitting on his lap and I loved him, why this pot of ashes, it was wrong, he wasn't the poet who loved kids any more, loving and loved by everyone, a sailor who had a tough childhood in Halifax and had been a seafarer's apprentice and kept going back to the sea, my father was saying on the dais, but why was he just a pot of ashes and Caroline didn't believe it either, his bags were arriving from Venice any day now with the unfinished manuscript of his poems and his scarf and hat she said, all of it, an elegant man she said, oh you're so much like me Mai, remember me when I'm no longer here, have you seen my bag, my compact and mirror are in it, which one I don't know, where can it be she said, oh this business about Jean-Mathieu has got me rattled, we've been such friends, insepa-rable for a lifetime, that circle around Emilio and his teeth shining in the sun, over, we never see each other any more, there are kids from the Bahamas, Cuba, all over in our class, but I'm the only one with light skin except for little Max, and he's too young for me, though I could teach him to write better but I don't want to, Mum didn't want me to go to the Spanish Catholic School, so I'll probably never see Emilio again, just like Jean-Mathieu who's gone, past, all past, imagine yourself in a jar of ashes tossed into the sea, the awful things they do and now they want to know all my secrets, a boy on skates slid off the bicycle path, as if on a rink, with a Labrador pup in his arms, Mai smiled at him, thinking she'd like to follow him onto the wharf then disappear far out on the end where her mother couldn't see her, just a faint hint of the shadow she saw now as she leaned towards a flock of egrets, a silhouette ready to take flight like the birds, barely moving in the glare of the sun, but how to get away when she had to get in her mum's Jeep and meet the psychologist at two . . . to say nothing, raising her head from her book, Mélanie signalled Mai, and don't forget your sandals she said, so she put them on and went towards the terrace, noticing the hibiscus in vases on the tables, coming Mum, relax, as her gaze wandered to the boy on skates with his beige puppy winding his way from the bike path to the wharf, Mai could see herself running towards him and with him, overtaking him, she was used to running every day, and whatever happened, her mother would lose sight of her and call out to her and run after her to the very last plank of the wharf, out of breath where sun and sky met and grasp her in an embrace, kiss her and say, my crazy kid, come back here, where on earth were you going, but that is not what happened, past already thought Mai, in a few months she'd live by her own rules, besides Mélanie was wary of too much tenderness towards her daughter and way too busy thought Mai, Vincent was going to need more treatment, he was the fearless athlete in the family, and never complained provided his nose didn't bleed, so Mum couldn't really stop him from windsurfing, he was less frail, more muscular than he used to be, so it was out of pity that he refrained from brushing Marie-Sylvie aside, though she did get in the way, Mélanie watched her daughter, her egret, thin legs below her pleated, fringed dress skipping bird-like towards her, okay now let's go eat, come sit by me, as Mai snuggled for a moment against the hollow of Mélanie's shoulder, Mum why don't we skip this appointment at two, why don't you forget about the airport at five, why, it's so nice out, this, Mélanie replied, this is where you used to met Emilio, right here on this beach, that's back in the past Mum, Mai said, why don't we forget about it, I don't want anything, just ice cream, please don't order me anything, yes, right here on this beach, Dear Augustino wrote Mère to her grandson, I can't, as you say, deny the things men do wrong or women's passive assent, cowardly and powerless as we often are, not the irreparable, unpardonable mistakes of generations before yours, which won't leave their mark on you because I know you and others born after you will forever bear the burden, but don't you see that we women take up every challenge in this time of torment, that we're reaching for a time of justice and triumphal metamorphosis, and have you thought of all the female leaders in new styles of government, seeing, thinking, applying justice, and fighting oppression and poverty, these women are strong and majestic, be they president of Chile, Jamaica, or Liberia, head of our own country or chancellor of Germany, survivors of military dictatorships, tortured and raped for anti-government books, even vice-presidents reunifying separated or hostile countries, at last listened to and joined by the mass, voices united in calling for an end to war, wives, mothers, and even clergy alongside men, now Episcopal bishops railing against bigotry, a social mission most of all, earthly more than Heaven-bound, first feed the hungry they say, heal those afflicted by tuberculosis and malaria, there's the real connection between science and religion, development not backsliding, I know how discouraged you feel Augustino, but perhaps in some way this can console you a little, your mother has all the qualities of such a leader, ardent and devoted to the defence of women and children, and she loves you, your brothers and sister more than all, she and I share the same weakness for renunciation, she is too ready to step aside, so devastating and irreparable the mistakes made, the time of torment will give way to another time, the intelligence of mothers and daughters, the frangipanis are in flower as I write this, and there are so many reasons to think of hope dear Augustino, the offering of nature is a miracle in itself, may it always rejoice my senses, but in writing to Augustino would she hit a wall of ice, he either didn't really care or didn't take her and such conventional ideas about the future seriously, yet above all she wanted to prevent Augustino and others from distancing themselves too far, to bring about some kind of convergence, that she not be at complete opposites with him, and though shaky, that they have some future meeting ground, this was life as it really is, the risk in the encounter between generations, each of us being a little of everything, the excesses of one secretly being those of the other as well, unconfessed and inadmissible, sheltered and untouched by the experience of life, Franz had said to Mère that in his dreams life lasted as long as a cigarette, slowly, gradually dissipating all by itself, its smell engulfed his house by the sea, the dense odour impregnating his clothes, and sometimes the cigarette sat there in the ashtray consuming itself, seeing the short cylinder of tobacco and paper he also saw his life as it relentlessly shortened, he found it so frightening and dizzying that he would wake up to a thumping heart, wondering if anyone was still around, his musician sister, little Yehudi, where were they all, during his frequent visits he'd tell Mère, you'll see my dear, an incorrigible smoker and unrepentant and joyous drunk like me will end his days in the smoke of a single cigarette savoured to the end, or a fourth whisky, one too many, and so it goes this life of ours, punishing and cruel, and I never get tired of it, whatever premonitions I dream up, oh by the way dear Esther, you've forgotten my whisky once again, never let it be said I'm as virtuous as you are, the virtuous going to paradise, well, I'm not so sure about that, Mère kept the reproduction of an engraving by Albrecht Dürer, *The Knight, Death, and the Devil*, in which a scrawny dog runs under the belly of a horse with a knight in armour, rickety but ready, the procession was filled out with devilish figures and death, but he had no intention of backing down and urged his horse onward into the forest, this is how Mère saw herself, full of resistance, and though the forest was still a haven of life and fertility, what was not as obvious was the symbolic richness which drew us into a lush and serious mythology inhabited by both life and death, though the knight held a lance to his shoulder, he did not deign to use it, his resistance and fight being those of a man who had compacted for peace with the world, but the poor thin dog with trembling ears beneath the horse, where was he going, and where would he ever go in this blind charge of horse and rider, this was the German Renaissance painter, engraver, and theoretician's call to Mère to reflect on her life, though the light was slow to dawn and the symbols remained buried as in the painting, she knew from the knight, the hysterical dog, and the demon death, one by one, the outline of her race across time, if the cigarette burned itself out like Franz dreaming of how fleeting his desires were, Mère found life, like the engraving, as hard to read as a mystic book, so fascinated was she by the range of epochs and images, as well as their staggering secrets, and thus thinking about the time of her childhood, she wondered at the mystery of recovering from the sorrow of losing her French governess, her parents' lies when they got back from Europe about how she had disappeared, as though this were not enough to break her heart, the way any child could encounter sadness and at once be done with it, the terrible secret of absence, the wrench of separation always lay within us as preparation for the very last one, the only one we cannot be there to see whether it has healed or not, Augustino wrote to his grandmother that nothing survives except by the evil triumph of arms, when we were kids, the same day Dad let us play in his library and writing room, like Vincent and later on Mai, I rolled myself up in a ball at his feet or on his lap, and it was as though he couldn't write without us, without touching our foreheads or kissing us while he worked, it was a study that smelled of the past, the antechamber to so much, the past with only victories in battle or death, I opened albums of ruins and asked him why, why, why keep these photos and documents in his boxes, and he said you'll understand later, what it came down to was men of the past wanted supreme victory in everything, victory always and everywhere, and they still do, I contemplated the horrible images of Saint Paul's Cathedral in London amid the smoke and bombing of the Battle of Britain, buildings everywhere destroyed, Stalingrad too, boats set ablaze, what had they become these young men in trenches and bunkers amid the rising inferno that melted leaden statues in churches and cathedrals, a bronze angel crowned and transformed into a weapon, nothing sacred or forever, nothing, the young enemies would die, surrendered under a white flag of pity, the pictures of an incensed crowd hanging fascists in Milan, Mussolini and his mistress united in treason, everywhere only putting to death and dying, where would I have stood in those years of hatred my father shows me in his books, with the young resistance fighters of the White Rose maybe, a student indoctrinated to face up to a regime of terror and shame, would I have been brave enough, been guillotined in a schoolyard in Munich for my pamphlets or anti-Hitler graffiti, roses white as our necks or heads lopped off, Hans Scholl maybe or his sister Sophie, woe to whoever betrayed us at the University of Munich, did he hear the knell of our falling heads, or might I be Hannie Schaft the red-headed law student tortured and shot on March 21, so many white roses whose names won't survive either, resistance groups and newspapers now as forgotten as soldiers waiting for the enemy veiled in snow, unknowingly digging their own graves in the forests, an entire infantry on alert among the pines and spruce, France, Belgium, elsewhere young German soldiers seeming to sleep, half-opened lips on the snow which likewise moulds itself to their boots and helmets, every one of them forever forgotten, dying for what or whom in these ice fields, oblivion or Hitler, even those still breathing on stretchers, statues of ice, petrified flesh outfitted in frost, this is the story of winter glory, cold and misery, men and horses finished off in the frigid fog, the young in uniform, hands raised and crying, I give up, enough, enough, I'm sixteen, he'd just run across a bridge as it was to be bombed, arms in the air and crying enough, enough, when pity ignored him, a teenager like so many ran towards the raised rifles, one more white rose blown and bent in that dark night of victory, victory or defeat no one could tell, the liberators no longer gathered up men from the winter camps, just bones whose shadow remained standing, dark and endless winter had devoured them all, men, women, children, Captain Krämer who had placidly watched seventeen thousand men die of hunger, where was his hideout, what salving battle of conscience had he waged thinking of the bodies undressed by their comrades to keep warm under the snow-filled pine trees, branches and patched shirts going up to heaven in smoke, yes where was this Captain Krämer while the survivors carved up the dead, eating hearts and livers, one day this man and his carnage, the placid eye he cast over them, he too would meet a phlegmatic death, in the heartbroken light of his last glance, would we see what he already had, feet piled in the gas furnace, just the feet and an occasional head, a few skulls perhaps in the piled multitude at Buchenwald, crowded with furnaces and hammering at the captain's memory as though in the trance of his nightmare he wondered, where have I seen that before, where did we get this extraordinary supply of feet and who dares punish me with such filthy images, I acted according to my convictions, though my submission to orders may have been abject, I really knew nothing, could we see from that hideous eye what it had seen when every setting sun was extinguished, ghosts of men in their huts, above all their feet, their legs bursting through skin stretched to the last, huts, open furnaces, as a man of duty did he revisit this with outrage and indignation, or the humiliation of his own SS women obliged by English soldiers to gather up those buried alive to give them funeral services and grabbing hands and feet first, and

the snow endured in frozen drifts near the sepulchre, what
had these women endured, no telling, disgust at the cold and
the wracked bodies, amid such atrophy what did the war
mean all of a sudden, victor or vanquished, he'd felt shame
for these women promoted to putridness, and what else, his
chief patting children's cheeks the same as Papa Stalin and
saying good boys, that's it my fine boys, one of them still
remembered being patted by the calamity-master, bravo my
fine lad, the last caress he ever knew, his last link to the world,
and ten days later the calamity-master was no more; in a
spring garden the master's bare hand had touched the boy's
cheek as if to say, see I'm not dangerous, he was decorated for
bravery that spring day and he felt the breeze of that bizarre
and bloody spring which always felt so cold, and a sudden
caress on the cheek to single him out from the others so surprised and standing beside him, he remembered the hand
trembling like an old man's that day, an old man with loose
skin and lined eyes he'd remember stroking his face in that
post-winter garden breeze, he'd also remember the battalion
of sixteen-year-olds massacred a few days later, as though the
tap had signalled the suicide mission of young men against
the Russians that Krämer had watched with his hideous eye,
that's it my fine lads, and it had seen the candid messenger
smiling and glad to serve, a messenger with a creamy com-
plexion underground, discovering corpses in a bunker as he
brought in a tray of fruit, sandwiches, and mineral water, and
he too was sixteen, so many deaths in the neatly divided
underground galleries where a few days before a blonde
woman had also been patted on the cheek and more, the
honour of dying with the master in a final embrace and quick
release, she had a kind and gracious smile for the messenger,
you have to eat some fruit and sandwiches too, you needn't
be polite young man, the messenger remembered her smile
in the closeness of that subterranean hell from which she'd
never emerge, rather descending every possible step with her

demonic friend, for an instant perhaps she'd seen in this boy
her own son, and from this flowed the generosity of her smile,
also noticed by Krämer's hideous eye, as though the blonde
woman with a cursed lover said as she closed her eyes, you
too are my son, one mother to pardon all though the captain
was sure he was right, and yet he still gave a shudder when
he saw all those unearthly feet from the furnace where they
still seemed to be moving, would they hang him by the heels
like Mussolini with his mistress on his right, surely the real
terror was to feel one's blood ebbing all the way to one's ears,
a mob would applaud the tying of his feet, but under his hood
Krämer would be impassive, shivering fear is for women,
justice, he thought, would belong to future generations of
liberators who would be no better with trials and hangings
of their own, the same indecency, the same executions at
dawn, playing the same bloodlust games as their parents and
springing the trap on themselves, still in that victorious winter
without end when one life counted as little as another, and
the horrible eye of Krämer saw a degenerate world that was
his unable to rise from its ashes, thus was my succession and
my heritage, a world dissolving into violence, that was how
Augustino described it to his grandmother, this I learned in
my father's study reading his manuscript of *Strange Years*, as
though all that interested him was this antechamber of all
shames and agonies, mine to inherit from my father and
grandfather and great-uncle Samuel who was shot, another
white rose lost in the snow, and that was how I understood
so quickly that all was disintegrated and dissolved, that my
generation would be crushed under a complex of catastro-
phes, conflagrations of perverse clashes, and you my dear
Grandmother, listening to *The Art of the Fugue* all this time, as
you say, and breathing the perfume of jasmine at night, and
that is how it is, she wrote back to him, I would love to share
with you what I see and hear that still gives life such a rare
sweetness, the mango trees blossom and never so plentifully

as after a storm, it's rained a lot on my hibiscus, my hybrids, and my orchids, resplendent with colour and opulent with flowers, from the terrace I can see mourning doves drinking at the fountain, you used to be the one that knew the names of all the flowers, not long ago when I still had you near, and I can still hear your child's voice declaiming it all, this fruit is edible, this tree grows in Asia, we tasted the juicy orange pulp together, the mangoes you held out to me, I feel you here as it used to be, now Vincent is the one who helps me in the garden when those awful allergies aren't bothering him, why should someone so young be so short of breath, mind you he never complains, you know he's very brave, and everything arouses wonder and surprise in him, the latest penicillin treatments have done him a bit of good, but he's still prone to lung infections, with the strong health you have Augustino, you don't know what it's like not to be able to breathe properly, the smell of jasmine, the nearness of Vincent — when he's not in emergency — are the rare sweetnesses, the miracle that life still offers me, this is what I so want to share with you my dear Augustino, you know Vincent's going to be a doctor later on, oh now the rain's begun again, kisses to you my dear, and I hope to see you soon, you did write something about Sunday, what a joy that would be, she wasn't mentioning Vincent's hope too, for if Augustino in his taciturn and defeatist turn of mind was burdened by a life that overflowed, Vincent wanted more from a limited one, albeit marked by crises of breathlessness, he loved life more than anyone else and never gave up hope through frequent hospital visits, oxygen tanks, and all the drama around him, such a frequent ritual, leaving Daniel's boat in an ambulance, college classrooms, Vincent avoided thinking of his body, except the part close to the heart where the cunning evil sat as it did in conquerors, Vincent attacked it relentlessly, wishing himself in the body of his heroes, and so it was that his health constantly rebounded ahead of him like a tiger, he had only to turn on his computer

and it overflowed with athletic bodies of swimmers and foot-
ballers, the highest waves and balls overreached by his arms
belonged to him, a dream that went straight to his heart and
restarted the rhythm of life, though pale with blood leaving
his cheeks in the seconds when his bronchial tubes clogged
up, he pictured the triumph of Allen Iverson who gave him
his tiger leaps, possibly wearing the same winged red and
white shoes, the same vest with a number three on it; if not,
then he would be melancholy in victory, as Iverson was, bow-
ing his head to success as though a bit blasé, holding the
generous offering of thirty-six roses in his large hands as they
spilled over onto his black shorts with a red stripe, Vincent
even appropriated his skin colour, a burning brown, not the
sickly white of Vincent's spasms, a hockey player whose skates
slashed the ice in his controlled headlong dash, all these bodies at the height of their strength revived Vincent, who felt
borne up just like them by water and air, when two of them
attacked the ball, they formed a star shape, celestial and magic
for Vincent, who felt he had been given an incomplete body
at birth, breath that was fleeting, just a bubble he always had
to recapture like an athlete chasing a ball in sporadic and
desperate spurts, how awkward he would have been with a
real oval ball over the goal line with his breath holding back
every move, as his chest dilated he one by one became these
players, skiers, Marquis Estill and Mike Dunleavy raising the
ball on the crowd's roaring, rising as he spun, racket in hand,
Jennifer Capriati, Venus and Serena Williams, all of them on
the wall in Mai's room, and most of all the leopard leap of
Atrews Bell in satiny white tights and matching cap, the
miracle he alone believed in to the point that he continually
moved like those palpable silhouettes in the stadiums, even
on his cushion-covered bed over which his mother or Marie-
Sylvie de la Toussaint leaned, saying do you feel a little better
now, you can get up and go outside to play again now, if you
want, it seems to be over, let's just not think about, let's just

not think about it, okay, he said in his natural good humour, let me take you out for a ride along the ocean said Marie-Sylvie de la Toussaint, you need the real sea air that cures everything, and at every attack his mother's eyes misted, tears hesitating as though they really shouldn't be there, Marie-Sylvie's forehead was bathed in sweat, and his father worked even harder writing and broadcasting to protect the town and the Coral Coast from the pollution invasion, yet Vincent some-how thought he was the cause of all these worries, Marie-Sylvie his Haitian nanny hadn't moved out of the house and had founded a refugee shelter in town with Julio and Jenny, who had gone to Africa and China with Doctors Without Borders, Vincent so wanted to join her later, yes, Marie-Sylvie was still there like an immutable rock wall lashed by waves of memory, a fortress of bitterness to those who had banished her brother from a Cité Soleil she'd never see again, she and her lunatic, wandering brother He-Who-Never-Sleeps, for he never really had since they'd tortured him, and she herself feared even to see his shadow in the cemetery or in the alley-ways, though she'd been very strict out of a jealous love for Vincent that shut out even his own mother, Marie-Sylvie the somewhat slippery and fault-lined rock was always there for him, thought Vincent, holding him close in her watchfulness, this poor and incomparable white child to whom she had given what remained of her shipwrecked life brought all the way to Daniel and Mélanie's house, there to be welcomed, nevermore to be set adrift on a raft as she once had been, and so it was that Vincent thought of himself as having more than one mother and perhaps even more than one life, though it shocked her that he read books and magazines he probably shouldn't have with pictures of naked women, it just wasn't proper she thought, but Augustino thought what set her apart from teenagers now was her going to elementary school with the priests, making her inward and unexpressive, and if Augustino was attracted to girls, he wasn't very certain they were drawn to him, he took yoga and tennis lessons with them on the dock surrounded by the glittering water of a long twilight, but they had eyes only for their own slow movements, the lifting of their arms accompanied by the slow rise of the waves, of the gulls and the pelicans, never seeming to notice him, even when he wore a mauve scarf like André Agassi in a tennis competition in Australia, if the waistband of his underpants rose above his Bermudas showing the word *Love* in red, Marie-Sylvie de la Toussaint disapproved of such unseemly attire as this of Augustino's, who avoided conflict as though he had no time for such futility, Vincent simply closed the door to his spirit and walked alone with his dogs on the beach, emerging from his dreams alone, but Vincent, whatever his trials, was a happy boy: this is what Mère would have loved to write to Augustino, and that life would pass by so quickly that not a minute should be lost in pointless reproaches and bitterness, she remembered visiting Caroline one afternoon after a long trip without Mélanie through the Pyrenees she could never forget, would she see the communicant struck down by the side of the road, in what twists among these snow-covered mountains would she search for scenes from the past without consolation, long and hard the voyage in the same bus as long ago, but it wasn't the same, just a dream which was missing Mélanie, then she briskly got out to answer an invitation from Caroline, who was living in a modest rooming house nestled in among some trees, and in a room more modest still, come, come and let's chat a while, Caroline said in the silky pyjamas she'd once worn to welcome Jean-Mathieu, come my dear, we have so much to talk about, this room and this bed are all I have here, come and sit with me, but what do you do here with all your time Caroline, Mère asked sitting on the bed next to her, well you see, I use those penknives I loved so much as a child to sharpen my pencils and draw all the faces I've photographed, but why do you draw the blade towards you, asked Mère, aren't you afraid you'll hurt yourself, oh nothing hurts you here, came the answer, here nothing can threaten us any more, with admiration Mère observed how elegantly she still kept herself, even in this remote spot, sociable she had once been, where was all her wealth, the furniture and paintings she once had, and above all, wasn't it strange that she now had the sad activity of reading, not photography, and of sharpening her pencils like this with a child's penknife with the blade towards her, this is something I have to learn she said, until I tire of it, you see dear Esther, for the longest time I turned the blade against myself, and that was my mistake, everything had to be about me and me alone, even Jean-Mathieu, I'd say even Charly, I wanted it all, she smiled amiably at Mère as though back in her salon with her friends all around: Charles, Frédéric, Adrien, and all the others she'd adored, laughing and enjoying herself, Mère was about to ask about her well-being when Caroline said abruptly, my dear friend, I know I've brought you here to this out-of-the-way place, but it's to tell you this is where my modest eternity will be spent, in this unassuming house, and I also wanted to warn you that your children are lying to you, constantly lying, remember Charly, Mère was jolted to attention, frightened by this last sentence, modest eternity, and the thought that one's children could betray one by lying, it was like waking from an uneasy dream with a cold shudder of deep uncertainty, during her short nap in the lounge chair in the garden, Mère had forgotten that Franz was there, pouring his own whisky, how many was it even before she fell asleep, four, dear Esther, he laughed, imagine Carlo Menotti, the people's composer, likeable and popular, a glorious man who lived to be ninety-five, ninety-five, now that's something for a man to celebrate when he loves life, isn't it, that's how I'm going to be, you'll see, now don't look at me like that, I'm not drunk yet, Gian Carlo Menotti, now there was a life with time to explore and experience everything in music, renew composition, make it available to all audiences, though the

critics said he wasn't intellectual enough, that didn't stop him
from writing masterpieces, comic operas, to insert irony into
the least pretentious of music, do you think I could have written a radio or TV opera and still be so limpid, no, he involved
all the other arts as well: dance, song, and he even invented
a rather complex art, but still within everyone's grasp — still
not intellectual enough said the critics, and am I myself, why
don't we go for a walk in the garden, you and I Esther, I don't
walk nearly enough, Mère listened to Franz, thinking that he
had saved her from a dream where the words "modest eternity" still penetrated, and why couldn't she accept that words
in dreams might be senseless, mean nothing, and that where
Caroline lived she neither sharpened pencils nor lived in such
a small room with one bed and silky blue pyjamas, that's how
she always dressed, the same long neck and swept-up hair,
her grey eyes still piercing, yes, however reticent, one could
not help but listen to her with respect, for she was a sage,
though she'd never been that earlier in life, a sage from another
world, or perhaps the same one seen differently, a modest
eternity in this world where Caroline had been a sovereign
woman, often proud and hard when it seemed right to her,
Mère thought, a concupiscent being as was right in her milieu,
how long had Franz been so stoop-shouldered, she wondered, leaning on his arm as he led her into the densest part
of the garden where the corollas of yellow African lilies had
opened, look at those voluptuous flowers, so languid in the
air in the moisture after the storm, he said, but Mère still felt
riveted by the piercing grey eyes of Caroline on her, Caroline
saying I've come to warn you that your children are lying to
you, do you smell that Mère said to Franz, oh I know that, it's
the smell of cannabis, he said, I know it well, it's coming from
the street that one, and through an alley flanked by palms one
could see the ocean, Mère could hear Mai being driven home
from school by a friend, she couldn't see the friend or the car,
but she heard his voice along with Mai's, a mature man's voice

and a smell . . . of . . . Franz, do you think someone in that car is smoking, my granddaughter's in a car with a man, she nearly said fearfully, but she said nothing, thinking the dream about Caroline had troubled her, distorted her perceptions, that's all, after all, Mai was too young for, she, well, Mélanie had talked to her about a young man in a Mercedes, and how are all your poet and musician friends, she asked suddenly, tormented by the smell coming from the street, yes, how are they, she asked Franz, oh for them nothing is simple, he said, they don't even answer their phones, and cellphones, well, they hate those, sometimes they're so solitary they end up in psychiatric hospitals, not because they've lost touch with their muses, but because claustrophobia weighs too heavy on them, or because they're obsessively meticulous in their work and madness creeps in unobserved, it's usually a wife or a daughter who notices it first, they've avoided public life and become too inward, often it's a matter of alcohol when they wander off the track, like mine dear Esther — he still had his whisky glass in his hand — I'm telling you my dear, better to be voluptuous in life like these flowers than be as decadent as you can only as long as you take no risk of consequences for yourself or others, which doesn't always happen, errors we'd like to avoid but it's too late, that smell Mère said, do you know that these African lilies can outdo wine in getting you drunk, Franz said with a mocking glance, after all, what did the future of her children and grandchildren matter to him, she thought, he's got his hands full with his own, far too many wives, their children, his work, the family had perhaps piled onto her shoulders and slowed her down, you know my dear Franz, she said pontifically, what threatens old age, and I often think about this, is our own indifference, no, no, no, he said, his elderly childlike eyes sparkling with mischief, that's all your own imagining, who could be more generous and welcoming than you are, and where would Julio, Jenny, and Marie-Sylvie be without you, oh we all have our human duties on this planet she replied firmly, thinking of Caroline, how indeed had she carried out her human duties which so often seemed alien to her own happiness, when she said the knife blade would now turn in towards her, was she referring to that deficient love and humanity that she'd often displayed even in her own judgement, here no one was equipped to judge her but Caroline herself, now the jurisprudence belonged to her alone, she was her own tribunal Mère noticed in the dream, I always wanted everything without ever lifting a finger, she had said, I was all envy and desire, all of it was owed to me don't we all live like that dear, I mean, wouldn't you do the same, if a painting or a dress or a piece of jewellery pleased me, I bought it without a thought, and Jean-Mathieu was all mine too, wasn't he, I knew that too, and now look how everything has left me, in this fireless room, but always remember Esther, if our lovers lie, so do our children, oh they do lie and we're blissfully unaware, thinking of her words, Mère was highly distressed at the thought of Mai's hidden actions, her behaviour so incomprehensible to her parents, and if she really had been in the car with that man, well, the Mercedes was gone now, and all she saw were two black kids playing ball on the sidewalk, but the smell persisted on the humid air, though the African lily smell from the yellow hanging corollas was so heady itself, and Franz's nostrils seemed so drunk with the delights of whisky that Mère no longer knew what to think, he just went on with his elitist chitchat about the orchestra, his friends, musicians, students, elitist she thought, it had no place for the world in upheaval inhabited by all those poor people, but just a handful of bright spirits who, like himself, had chosen art as their promised land, without ever wanting to know what was going on around them, and suddenly he said, I know what you'd like, Esther my dear, I am training some young women who will be greater conductors than I, for I really do prefer composing, for instance the opera I can't say anything about just yet, except that I am consumed by the

music I hear, isn't it about time, Mère interrupted, to bring
along even more women conductors, I do believe you've
waited too long my dear Franz, and some of them have been
able to do it without you, but not here, yes it is what is most
needed he said, but it is indeed sad that our musicians have
to go elsewhere, first hurricanes chased people away, then
the need for fairer pay, and now international celebrity, and
don't go thinking you can sleep with all those gifted female
musicians you teach, because that's what happened with that
young wife of yours, she nearly said, instead, realizing he was
beginning to sober up and wouldn't listen, she kept quiet and
turned her thoughts again to Mai whom she couldn't see any
more, and she felt herself tighten up inside, no car, no man,
no Mai, and even the kids in the street had fled, Caroline
wasn't the only one, we were all capable of deficient love, she
thought, when we carry out our feeble duty to humanity;
perhaps her grandson Augustino was right to judge that weakness so severely, having made an armour of our arrogance, a
presumptuousness that wormed its way into all our relations
with other people, wasn't that what he saw in us, she thought
knowing it was true, of course, to disguise cowardice, but she
still could agree with his sometimes irrational indignation, as
she chatted with Franz, Mère knew as he did from the morning paper that a boatload of Haitian refugees had been pushed
back to a beach in Miami, starving and worn out as they strove
to get back out to sea clinging to the cords of their boat, blinded
by the sun and the water, not only hungry and thirsty after ten
days' journey, but some needing medical attention, besides,
how had they ever survived on that makeshift boat, salt water
and no toothpaste, they said here on Hallandale Beach there
were always a few porous entry points, and perhaps the sym-
pathetic Coast Guard, offering blue-gloved hands to women
out of the deep water, and activists shouting, look at those
millionaire condos all along the beach, and you won't let
these people in, condos the twelve children of these refugees

saw when they jumped into the water playing and heard their parents say through their tears, we've risked our lives, are they going to put us back in the ocean, where to, and the Coast Guard removed the dead body of a man, the only one who didn't survive, go Marie-Sylvie de la Toussaint had cried, saying, they're going to have to go back to that misery, and from windows in skyscrapers, locals had watched the sad arrivals with binoculars, and why should they be deported, the activists asked, when others were accepted temporarily and even protected, why them, repeated Vénus from Little Haiti come to protest, Marie-Sylvie de la Toussaint had come to grieve for her people and was disconsolate until Mère told her they wouldn't all be sent back, some families would go to homes, not the usual detention centres, while they waited for legal procedures, homes scattered across the coast or in little Haiti, she remembered Mélanie, Daniel, and Mère's hospitality and regained hope that some might be saved as she herself had been with her brother, but what would a life be if you had no safe place of your own, no country, what was a scattered, torn life nowhere at all, then Ari remembered his promises, they had to get off the bus, because a little boy had drunk polluted water and was having an attack of colic and holding his stomach with both hands while his father undressed him by the side of the country road, when just then Ari saw snakes coiled in a scattering of dust, he was about to reach for a stick when Asoka said no, life had to be respected wherever it was, and these snakes have done us no harm, if they become aggressive, it's because we threaten them, reptiles are more nervous at mating time, but they're everywhere Ari said, they cross the street, you must have no fear, Asoka said, contemplate them and the wonders of nature, in fact Asoka was more troubled that the boy had been contaminated by bad water, which was frequent in these regions, like the rising infant mortality rate, we were on our way to the clinic the father said, I've already lost one son, I don't want to lose two, Asoka took the boy in

his arms, saying softly, we'll soon be at the clinic and you're
going to get better, the child wasn't crying any more, and
Asoka's voice seemed to calm him, looking back, Ari realized
he hadn't given a thought to the snakes darting their heads
towards him, crawling fast as lightning, and they all seemed to
be heading towards him in a supple attack of elongated bodies he could never have warded off without a stick or a branch,
which Asoka had already forbidden, but there are also monsters in nature Ari yelled, no there aren't, said Asoka, they aren't
treacherous, we are, Ari was close to the boy now as well and
touched his head as though calming his own fears, it'll be
allright, really, because we'll soon be at the clinic, he said to
the father in turn, but he was not so sure, what a handsome
little boy with dark eyes he said of this poor child, sick simply
because he's drunk some water in his parents' home, the same
unhealthy water drunk by all the most destitute in the mountains, living in whitewashed huts opening onto the highway
day and night, their animals as abandoned as themselves wandering around outside, Ari thought how much care he gave
his daughter, only filtered water, and wondering what he'd do
if she were afflicted like this boy by the plague of filthy water,
perhaps snakes were simply deprived of limbs and defenceless as Asoka said, vulnerable to almost anything, the lugubri-
ous denizens of a cursed country where children and animals
shrivelled up imperceptibly in stupefying numbers while Lou
just went on her way to school in Mummy's car, or took swimming lessons in Daddy's pool on Thursdays and Saturdays, or
drew on the computer; here small boys just died silently, one
after another, like this man's sons, a man to whom Asoka was
trying to bring a tiny bit of joy with simple words, here in the
utter mindless burning of thirst, the loss of countless children
and animals in cities bordering on huge, almost virgin forests
full of oranges, mangoes, papayas, and torrents of water among
the eucalyptus, lands soon to be debased and stripped by land-
owners, while nameless phantoms, sparser than phantoms,

would be unconscious somewhere at dawn light on their endless, stubborn, hopeless search, though for them everything
was visceral and vital, especially under this white-hot sun,
remember our history, Reverend Ézéchielle was saying in her
community church, remember Sandy Cornish; it was 1840,
and you may think that's a long time ago, but it was yesterday,
there's no date, no season, to the sorrow and humiliation of
men, no right time to feel pain, and you Petites Cendres, listen
to me, don't stare at your nails, and what have you been doing
in my church all this time anyway, someone's after you, aren't
they, maybe those cops on horseback I saw in town this morning, Sandy Cornish now, he paid for his freedom and more
than once, poor man, caught while working for the railroad
company in Tallahassee, had once been a slave but had no
papers to prove he'd been freed, hurricane washed them
away along with everything he owned, the great hurricane of
1843, and so he wound up in the slave auction in New Orleans,
it wouldn't be right if I wished all slave merchants to burn
in hell, but I sure can wish that they pay the debt they owe
us in troubled consciences for all eternity, but those slave
merchants didn't know this Sandy Cornish, no way, and they
didn't know what it was to be a man with just one desire in
his head, to be free, and do you know what he did, he took
a knife right there in a public place in front of Blacks and
Whites and he cut his hand, and if that's not enough for you,
he tells them, I'll just open up my guts right here, and you'll
understand once and for all I will not be sold on the slave
market in New Orleans, and I'll never be a slave again, well
that man was blessed by God, and his hand healed itself, after
that he moved to this island and became a member of our
community, and this venerable man got the Cornish African
Church built, our oldest, where we still venerate the holy
man's name, she said, for there is a time for remembering, and
that's the truth, thought Petites Cendres staring at his nails,
and he had really beautiful ones all polished scarlet and

smoothly finished, now if the rest of him was not so attractive, at least his nails, eyebrows, and hair could still do the trick, Timo his decadent and thieving little friend was the one he really should have been thinking about, because they were after him, but his nails were so beautiful he couldn't help getting distracted for a minute, if he went dancing tonight, they'd be shining like diamonds, he'd be sure to get a few customers if he strolled around the sauna at the Porte du Baiser Saloon, so that was the secret to being free, just cut off a finger, mutilate your hand, what a bloodbath, so what should I do with my hands while the Reverend's talking and glaring at me: tell me, do you ever get around to praying, oh in a while Reverend, I'm always praying, but where on earth can your friend Timo be hiding, she went on, probably somewhere in the archipelago hiding with lizards and deer . . . dunno he said, besides why would I turn in a brother, but this bit of dialogue was just in Petites Cendres' imagination, he was that obsessed with the idea that Timo might be surrounded and caught, and him too as a witness, he'd seen Timo swipe his customer's keys after a night of dancing on tables and skating with nothing but his jacket on around the bar's artificial rink, then flittering around his client like a moth to a candle and slipping his keys out of his pocket to take the Sonata for a spin, quick, on with his new jeans, it was always new clothes with him, pretty coquettish Petites Cendres thought, even when he hadn't a thing on, bracelets, necklaces; what would he do without a maximum-security prison around, he wasn't just anybody either, plenty of cocaine in the Sonata, credit cards, passports, quite a sneak, he wasn't going to be easy to catch, he may have had a lot of enemies, but he had quite few friends too, a regular little mafia of his own unless they sent him to one of the toughest jails in the county, the real thing: four by seven, the size of a closet, wash basin, toilet, thin mattress, and that's it, except for a solid metal door with no openings to talk to the other inmates, meals on a tray, just bare light-bulbs 24/7, twenty-three hours in lockup, one hour of exercise in the afternoon, sure he'd start thinking about escaping, what could be worse than this, he wasn't really a felon, but there he'd be with them all, no way out this time, wonder how he'd make out with all the gangs and the drug-dealing, even in there, hmm and what was he going to do in his cell, maximum-security under full surveillance, pretty rough, especially for someone used to perfumes and lotions, and those necklaces of his, well, one bite would put an end to those, yup, he might wind up killing himself in that killing college, too bad, rough on old Timo, oh I pray every day Reverend, Petites Cendres blurted out in a high voice, like you say, any time is the right time for prayer, so let's sing and dance to the glory of God she said, for it will soon be Christmas, and who says it can't be one of lightness and joy, we're going to have a feast for all of you who smoke your joints all day on the porches over on Bahama Street while your women are slaving away, couldn't you have a thought once in a while, I'll tell you lazybones, you let the women work for you while you get into fights and waste your time jawing like nobody's business in front of that dice-table, cocks pecking at the grass, and one day you're gonna have to explain that to the Lord I tell you, yes, oh yes, Petites Cendres repeated with the others as they danced and rolled their shoulders, he had eyes only for his polished nails spread out there before him, telling himself perhaps tonight he'd have them on the hook, with that and his arched eyebrows, meanwhile Timo would be on the run in the Sonata with the sheriff right behind him, God help him, Petites Cendres his accomplice as well perhaps, though he was really innocent, Timo, he was the one who always had these bad ideas, and look where that got them both, straight to the bottom, and Alphonso thought the Reverend was right, even if she was a bit too liberal, still she was just a woman after all, though she was imposing in that white surplice, just a woman, and women often were more liberal than men, influenced by all kinds of things, not always the right things, too much bleeding heart, no she was right this time though when she said he'd be unhappy in his new parish, anyway what was he doing there in this huge, freezing presbytery far from his Haitians, Cubans, and this place, New England wasn't for him, and so far he hadn't seen a single ·parishioner, I mean who was going to go out of his way to meet the successor to a disgraced priest mysteriously sent off by the Bishop to some seminary or other, there would be children there too, Alphonso thought, and this man shouldn't be sent to jail, he told the Franciscan bishop, only to be rebuked that he had no authority, nor the place, to judge such things, but we're talking about the sexual abuse of children Alphonso said, calm yourself my friend, said the Bishop, you're not in this parish to judge anybody, that is for the Church to decide, not you, you, like your predecessor, owe obedience to your superiors, remember that, and Alphonso, who had never obeyed anyone, kept quiet, although the Bishop seemed a gentle enough man in his sandals and grey beard, only the red mitre on his ascetic head showed his position of authority, utter discretion my friend, you must not forget that the things we've been so violently criticized for go back a long way, and a wound open for so long cannot be healed, especially when the victims waited a long time before coming to us, and as far as your predecessor is concerned, surely an excess of solitude can lead who-knows-where, and in this case it was disastrous indeed, and of course we are distraught, and we'll make restitution for the assaults on these children, material first, and that includes the entire diocese, and our bishops will repent these abuses you mention, and there will also be atonement when the time comes, you know, of course, this represents millions of dollars to the clergy, an enormous loss, and we face accusations in every direction, now we can't just lock up everyone who is inclined to do evil, in any event, it often only happens once, now should one be punished a whole lifetime for that? Living or dying depends on just one chance too, Alphonso replied, one only needs to kill once, there is no second chance, our duty, said the Franciscan bishop, is to restore the faith of our New England parishioners, you see what is happening in Boston, hundreds of victims have filed complaints, and that has got to hurt us, even with the best lawyers, the accusations of misconduct by our priests are so very serious that we have no way of dealing with them altogether, we do have to restore faith in our innocent priests too, priests like yourself Alphonso, though your superiors have reproached you for being too protective of illegal immigrants in your church, I merely obey the commandments of God, replied the latter, charity towards my brothers, standing before the frosted window looking out on the snowy landscape and grey clouds, he thought of his archipelago, of giant palms by the sea, doves flying to the heights at evening when the sun shimmered on the water, come, come, the Bishop said, courage my friend, you'll have your work cut out for you here getting the children ready for catechism and first communions, and the red canoes and joyous paddlers streaking across the water now calmed after the waves, six in the evening always, before nightfall, the strident notes of birds in the high palms, the song of doves drunk from singing too much, getting staccato and intermittent, down there in my humble little church, Alphonso actually preferred greeting his parishioners outside, the church was really more of a refuge where he hid families arriving clandestinely on makeshift boats, his people, his friends, his children, then all at once he'd seen this priest guilty of corrupting all those souls entrusted to him in the seminary for boys where the Bishop had just exiled him, between stone walls in a poor seminary in some out-of-the-way place, and how was this man to fulfill his moral obligations, Alphonso was seized with a powerless sense of sadness, the Bishop had talked mostly of consolation and financial reparation for the victims when what they needed was more urgent help, love, hope, a hundred million, that's what we owe them, over a hundred million the Bishop said crestfallen, and apparently the enormity of the sum seemed to wound him even more than the pain inflicted on all those children, already relegated to a distant time, after all, for him all this was from a different era, most of the abuse happened in the '80s and '90s, why carry on and have trials for acts, rapes, let's not exaggerate thoughtless acts, with a few children, was it even true, how could one know for sure when it all went so far back in outdated convents and boarding schools that no longer even existed, this ascetic bishop who reportedly refused to live in the bishop's residence did penance by walking barefoot in the snow, was close to the people and loved by them, but, considered Alphonso, if he tortured his feet or slept in the street like a vagabond, he could never redeem the tears and shame of even one of these betrayed and brutalized children, no he thought as he watched the snow fall on the trees, there won't be any rafts washing up here on the waves, oh Lord, what to do, courage my friend, the Bishop had replied, you'll have plenty to do here, first get everyone to pardon and forget your predecessor, to err is human, and who would say that we are all of us saints, we are only men, we aspire to perfection, but we cannot reach it, Alphonso looked bored listening to all this formulaic repetition and pretext to cover up scandalous, inadmissible acts, while huge snowflakes fell onto the glass, whatever was going to happen to him in this place of frozen shadows, then Ari saw Asoka, the father, and his little boy get back on the bus with a bizarre person who said his name was Tigli and who was on his way to celebrate his thirtieth birthday in town, a jovial, likeable man with a felt hat pulled down low over his eyes, jumping from seat to seat like an animal and making the kids laugh, even the boy with colic stopped crying in fascination and watched with a smile as though magnetized, occasionally Tigli would cough into the beach blanket he carried just for that purpose, he was on his way to rejoin his friends

at a student rooming house where they'd spend all night
drinking and dancing the salsa he loved listening to, knowing
that the trembling in his legs from AIDS would prevent him
from ever dancing again, oh yes, salsa, he repeated gently, all
night drinking and dancing, and the wild-looking Tigli imitated
the movements with his moribund body, and do you know
why I have to drink and dance he'd say, I've got three days'
holiday, and do you know what I do in Guatemala, I'm a fireman and firemen do every kind of job, delivering babies,
babies like you he says, pointing to the little colicky boy, oh
I've brought dozens of babies into this world, would you
believe it, because we firemen are ready for anything, putting
out fires, opening up birth canals, and that's the way it should
be, but sometimes you just gotta dance the salsa, you know I
almost left the last one in there, he just wouldn't come out, as
if he didn't like the heat and sunlight, too much for him obviously, and I said to myself just pull him out of there, otherwise
he'll be in the dark night of his mother's belly forever, geez
was I scared, but he was the most beautiful of all my babies,
what a crier though, boy I never saw a newborn cry so much,
firemen have nimble hands, but I've never had three days'
holiday before, quite a career for just one guy, fireman, midwife, I still get the sweats when I think of that one, yep, quite
a job, believe me, and I'm gonna celebrate till I can't walk any
more, I mean, either your on the Earth or you aren't, quite a
difference, believe me, oh yes, I know all about birth and
birthing, the mothers all say I'm the best fireman there is, Ari
realized how enthralled Lou would be to meet him weaving
all sorts of subtle magic under the brim of his felt hat with his
slanted eyes and pointed teeth, got be some sort of affable
sorcerer or devil-dancer who just turned back all the pity Ari
might have for himself, as though Tigli danced him into happiness, and that had to be the true serenity of innocence,
accepting the present as Asoka said, Tigli was the vibrant
incarnation of it like a tree or a flower caressed by the wind

and cool rain, was this grace in living, Ari wondered? As Petites Cendres listened to the Reverend's words, his mind wandered to the street funeral of Cornélius the musician, the Korean War hero with his medals sewn right onto his suit, honorary ones were all he got along with his injuries, a life lived poor and alone in his trailer full of cats and brilliantly coloured chattering parrots on a dune by the sea, happily sipping his rum and sniffing the salt dawn, either when he got up early or came staggering home very late, mildly drunk, head still humming with jazz, the veteran blues man didn't take care of his health, all that rum every night, pancreas problems, Uncle Cornélius the father of soul as they called him, is buried and that's it, thought Petites Cendres, quite a while ago with all his family around him, in the streets dancing and singing, his niece Vénus who had sung as he played piano at Club Mix, all his descendants and all his records since the war still being listened to, his heart let go unable to hold on any longer, and buried here on the island, and all those Blacks from Harlem here in the joyful turmoil of music and dance, and there I was moving my legs and feet with the rest of them, around this time, just before Christmas, theatre-in-life, ah how he would have loved all this noisy celebration of his glory, our dance steps like we were all in a trance back in the old days of Club Mix when you could hear the wailing of the tunes in the hot smoky halls in the night with the smell of acacias rising from the bushes, boy did we drink and smoke for a long time, and Uncle Cornélius, man and musician, incandescent, and his fifteen-year-old niece singing to the blues rhythm, they said he had no parents, just an orphan in the streets, but where did he get that music, well, once in the bordellos of New Orleans, that's where he started playing, but the music, he'd always had that, more than the poverty-stricken parents who'd abandoned him, better than a foster home where he would have been bored, in the streets and the theatre, too poor for school, no one wanted him but the music, the mother that rocked his cradle, not a down-and-out, no, because he'd become rich, though he spent it as fast as it came in, never in prison like his nephew Carlos, who knows how long, too much cocaine as well, uncle and nephew both carried aloft on the wave, then going without, the emptiness, gospel songs in the night, I felt such release dancing and singing, then wondering where to get some powder, easy in that crowd, no not to hit rock-bottom afterwards, and Cornélius just did one tour after another, that was before rap when he felt alone in his triumph onstage, light-headed, but the drugs were sometimes terrifying, arrested at night in his car once but no prison, a red-hot night for him that turned into music, always music, even rap, the new generations scared him too, then all at once his heart just let go, couldn't go any further thought Petites Cendres, Cornélius the father of soul and his music still seemed to fill the Community Church with the delirious notes Petites Cendres sang and danced to, Mère trembled on Franz's arm in the cool and humid garden when she heard him say — had she really heard his whisky-fuelled confession, yes — he'd said in a brief confession that he'd never been fair or loving enough to the women in his life, the ones I thought I loved were often younger than me and I didn't love them well, and they still are, they approach you like a fly to a spider, exclaimed Mère, at least she thought she did, but her lips were sealed, and she listened to him reproaching nothing, even the strongest one, Renata, was a wonderful sparring partner with masculine qualities, oh I know you two don't have much in common, well she took my daughter away from me, Mère felt like saying, she used to have just one friend and mother, and the moment she met Renata, there was such a bond between them, kindred spirits, it's like a puzzle I can't explain, a link thicker than blood that shut me out, a determination to change the world that they still share, a common obstinacy I suppose, that I found impenetrable, and Mère listened to Franz in silence, the very thought of Renata

reopening secret wounds, a sort of humiliation at not being
up to her daughter's standards, Renata's even less with her
reputation as a judge, perhaps succeeding where Mère had
failed in public life, sad thoughts, and what on earth was
Franz doing here in the garden anyway, my garden, relighting
the embers of past loves, no flames any more, no she was
likely mistaken, for Franz was a man of passion, not her, realizing as she listened to him how much tepidness replaced
passion in her life, was it that or was it moderation, Renata's
sensuality with men was unmistakeable, a proud woman as
well whose age could never be pinned down, too proud for
a woman, and she should not be seductive and triumphant
anywhere and everywhere, oh she stood up to me alright
Franz said, so unsubmissive was she that I thought she wanted
to break me, those are masculine qualities, obstinacy and
rebelliousness like that, you know that a man cannot tolerate
that degree of resistance, dear friend, Mère again saw Renata
coming through the main door on a summer night, bare shoulders under a satin vest and the ugly jealous thoughts before
that tanned body under the pale clothes, Renata's magnifi-
cence irritated her, and now here she was taking her daughter
away, like Samuel with Vénus, with Samuel since they began
singing together with musicians walking before them and
flowers in their hair, yet still she was irritated that Franz deni-
grated Renata by calling her masculine in some ways, so she
started in, one has to be invincible like her and refuse all forms
of subjugation, those are simply the qualities of an exceptional woman, without that evident invincibility she would
never have provoked a worldwide debate on capital punishment, but she had done just that a few months ago when a
thirty-eight-year-old woman was executed for the first time
in the county since the Civil War, and the governor had not
spared her, saying with pious disdain, go to your punishment,
and may God be with you and your victims, Renata had even
managed to elicit compassion from the Christian Coalition,

and demonstrators came from everywhere to that dark dawn for several days of vigil outside the prison, to convince others of simple humanitarian ideas Mère said, give in to no one, and that's just what Renata did, and my daughter Mélanie sprang to her side, said Mère suddenly lost in thought, but Franz just then was thinking of Renata and all the other women he had held in his arms, a woman of desires he said, I worked hard and long in those days, and I was often exhausted when I got back from concert tours in Vienna, ah what a woman that no man dared let down, if one loved her a little less one day, it was as though she had been struck down, and she quickly fled to someone else, and that I think is very unfortunate in a woman, that effrontery and audacity which men usually have, don't misunderstand me Esther, that sort of thing upset me a lot, still it's something you do yourself quite often Mère said staring at him, ah yes, but a woman can't permit herself that, you know my dear, now you Esther, I see you as a perfect wife and mother, she said nothing, thinking still of the fresh and painful image of Renata coming through the door, we're distant cousins she said, feigning aloofness, but I've followed every one of her trials closely, and I think she's had a very positive influence on my daughter, I've always felt the need for women to admire, she nearly said but cut herself short, thinking suddenly of Mai and the Mercedes that carried her away, she'd have a talk with Daniel about it tonight, since Mélanie had left on the five-o'clock flight, she couldn't smell the cannabis a little way from the garden any more, and even wondered if she hadn't dreamt the whole thing, like the apparition of Renata in the doorway, the immensity of time sometimes seemed to mix and confuse different times of life, suddenly combining what was fragmentary and separating what was connected into one long and elastic tableau, as though one longed to drink all of life in one long draught, sweet or bitter, it was one's own, thirst must be allowed as a sign of enduring and of recognition of the time allotted, no more, no less, like Caroline, and when it was too short, she simply adjusted her thought to some form of personal growth, the prodigy of an internal resurrection like no other, Caroline had always been struck with the knowledge that there were permanent and palpable links between her and Désirée, the black servant she also called Miss Harriet, fusing her identity with that of the governess in her parents' house, bonds woven over and over again by anguish and sickness and the ties of friendship and support between two women, it was the name Désirée that she blotted out, we do have to keep hold of the alterations we have made, all the way to the brink, for if it ever happened that we were reborn with just a little more majesty, at least in the ordering of all these puzzle pieces that come down to us with our genes, and whose complexity left us agape and incredulous at the destiny of every being, what a fearsome thing, and one way or another, what would we do with it all, the responsibility reaching to blind panic, if on the very last day of her life Caroline had resisted the abject racism of running the two names together, as though she'd mouthed *love*, it would have been not only hers but her parents' and grandparents' from the southern plantations where their lives had been designed, the decadence the result of long, slow decay, Mère thought, and in that last moment of purification when the soul finally dissolves its veil, Caroline surely would have earned one last chance akin to seeing herself reborn with a crystalline spirit, this Mère asked herself as she recalled she'd be speaking to Daniel tonight while Mai was studying in her room as always, Franz went on talking, though what he had said about Renata bore a striking resemblance to the disdain with which Bernard told Valérie there were no women philosophers, she'd be quick to strike back of course, but in a more delicate tone that was so characteristically hers, My dear Bernard your words betray how very unsure you are of yourself, for as a woman and a very harmonious writer, she made sure they understood one another very well, thus her constant foresight with him, Franz resembled Nietzsche when he wrote that it was in bad taste for a woman to pretend to become a *savant*, what a word, it originally meant *Wissenschaftlich*: the exclusive property of the Emperor, a royal man, or existing for the monarchic imagination of Nietzsche in all naive goodwill and implacable candour, thus denaturing the spirit of every single woman to come, this was the spirit in which Franz admitted not having loved Renata well enough, she could possess beauty but not the knowledge or humanity of great men, nor their penetrating judicial awareness, thus she had no right to express herself, was this then how he would greet his revolutionary female musicians tomorrow, denying forever that they might be more than his equals, innovators, men must then stay together alone as Nietzsche said, the calling having gone out only to them, this was the immovable rock against which Caroline had struggled too, thought Mère: photographer, military pilot, she had been fully united with men in command and by their side still, often even more virile than they in her decisions, and so subtle and imperceptible was the denaturing effect that she had felt nothing, except perhaps that day when she had confronted Charly harshly, before that, Mère thought, Caroline had known only the gentleness of Jean-Mathieu, a sweetness respectful of everything she did and was, above all when she illustrated his books with her photos, the haunted and poignant portraits of English poets, and never did they quarrel, like the singers of one common poetry, rugged and lovely, Caroline appreciated the fact that Jean-Mathieu, born to poverty, provided her with an exotic and bohemian connection, forever seeing him as a kid on a boat, oldest of his Halifax family at eleven, the working child, an emblem of courage and determination, and the man he became, poet and sage of a unique kind, and she couldn't even understand how she had lost him, it was a well-deserved second chance to plan her life as she wished, especially now she was cleansed of the poison of drugs that Charly had overloaded her with till she lost her way between ambition and pleasure, what remained now was the distilled essence of her pictures, Mère realized that the little she really knew of Caroline she'd learned listening to her whisper next to her from under her wide straw hat in the catamaran to The-Island-Nobody-Owns, her lost voice asking Mère, tell me Jean-Mathieu is still at his rooming house in Italy, he is, isn't he, now do you know exactly when he's going to come back, never able to imagine that day that would never be, his ashes soon to be in the ocean forever, that would have been an outrage, especially with Jean-Mathieu on the point of writing one more book, she said on that burning hot day on the water, first they'd searched for Mai all over the island, in the pine forests and banks amid the bird and animal tracks in the sand, where on earth could she be, later, carrying her on his shoulders, her father would be saying where on earth were you, but mute and fierce, she'd just roll her sparkling eyes to heaven from beneath her dark shades, nothing to say except maybe to Caroline later on when she'd slide languidly onto her lap half asleep, always the same little secrets between the elderly lady and the little girl, oh if only you knew how much like her I was at this age, I too felt I knew everything about life already but couldn't say a thing, Mère remembered saying to Caroline, but what's the point of knowing the secrets of life so soon and not being able to define the feeling it gave rise to, conceding the point to Caroline who would never see Jean-Mathieu again as she thought, sad really, isn't it, Mai being so young, and what exactly did she mean by that, Mère wondered as the catamaran sliced through the waves in a roiling mix of water and engine sounds and Caroline dozed beneath her hat, forehead leaned into the hair of the child sleeping on her knees, at least she's not about to take off again said her father, she won't get into trouble while she's asleep, the sun roasted them still, and Mère knew Caroline's pretending not to know that Jean-Mathieu would never come back from Italy was just part of her painful madness. Lazaro's motorcycle circled Olivier and Chuan's house, their son, the kid with gold punk spikes on his head was still away at university he thought, kid from a good family he'd seen with his friends by the pool when he'd waited on the parents in his apron with fresh oysters and seafood, and his mother Caridad begged him to come home with his brothers and sisters instead of disowning her for abandoning the Islamic faith of his father, as well as his uncles and cousins still in Egypt, Cuban-style house with a red-tiled roof that overheated in the sun, walls that were ochre, orange, and sometimes brilliant yellow with roses, bougainvilleas, and frangipanis more outlandishly yellow than the sun everywhere, Lazaro was blinded in muffled fury, barely able to keep to the seat of his motorbike, his bubbling rage threatening to overflow, so was he there this Jermaine or was he home for Christmas, playing with his father's dogs, shining with care and affection, all the joy in this house, receptions, parties, friends at all hours, and late dinners, Lazaro's motorcycle could have ploughed a line straight through their carefully placed tables and chairs, and a grin pushed up his lips, yeah, that would fix them, bang, a long time ago the kamikazes on that grey November of 1944 and a dozen pilots standing by their bombers waiting for instructions before their final takeoff, white scarf of honour of airborne martyrs around their necks, my age all of them, maybe even younger, ritual letters left for their parents in a tent by candlelight, at least they didn't have to hate or renounce their mothers, not a Caridad with a flourishing craft, dealing with the enemy in her decadence, an enemy that despises us and all our race, at least they had parents to write to: I shall be the spring flowers in a cherry tree radiant with blossoms, goodbye dear parents, then followed sake from the admiral for his warrior pilots before their departure and it burned his throat as the dead air did the throats of doves, all is fulfilled dear Mother and Father, and I shall be cherry-tree-in-spring blooms, like

black doves they flocked skyward soon to dive on cities and
bridges one behind the other, hurled into the wind and clouds
all the way to the assembly-line carnage of their steel wings,
twelve Japanese kamikazes, a trickle of sake under the tongue
still, jaw tight even during the fall, thus Admiral Onishi initi-
ated his men into naval battle, counting them off one at a time
as he offered them sake, all present and accounted for, the
ritual, the letter to their parents, off you go to torpedo the skies,
kill them all, yet one had the astonishing thought, our country's future must indeed be dark if all the best pilots must be
sacrificed, a thought that shook the Emperor and his parents
when they read it, watch the cherry trees in spring and I will
be its flowers, but how could it be otherwise, no sentiment or
nostalgia, perhaps their son Jermaine is back, loafing by the
pool with a cocktail in his hand, a very grey November day,
a drop of sake still on the half-open mouth of the first kamikaze, so quickly gone and in goes the second clearing a path
through the fog, pilot-bombardiers glowing in the sky pur-
posefully exploding onto their targets so very precisely like
typhoons, the deadliest of storms, well-ordered squadrons,
surely feeling their own divinity like a wind sweeping over
the earth, thunder torn from the sky, this they felt for a few
brief seconds, then nothing, no heaven, no earth, no adver-
sary under a carpet of bombs, redeemed in honour like those
heroes of ancient Rome, and even if the war were lost, their
people would still be preserved victorious by their heroism
consecrated and without barbarism except towards themselves, I thought if we choose the path of vengeance, better to
be faultless like them and like my own people with the sword
and such thoughts set me on fire, perhaps a moment of sus-
pense or hesitation among these youths, one even writing to
his wife, but I do love you and the children, but the wife's
honour reduced his to shame when she committed seppuku
and drowned their three children, writing to him, you are free
now to die for the Emperor, five thousand others with him, a

mere beginning to the cherry blossoms, each one yielding to a sweet fruit cut down in a harvest like today's, and the wheels of the cycle cut across the circle from where my roaring engine can reach their Cuban-style house, or else up the white stone path lined with potted roses, past the pavilion where the father wrote day and night — I hate him the way I hated Carlos who nearly killed me, deliberately or not, gun loaded or not, still negligent homicide and he'll pay for it in prison, soon it'll be an adult one, his sister and her lawyer friend Perdue Baltimore and all those other bleeding hearts weren't going to get him out of there fast enough, and if they do, I'll shorten his life for him, I've always got something on me I can use, all those flowering cherry trees and all the letters to fiancées and parents, all those fireworks in the sky, the arms and legs festooned with garlands, and stars shining even on a cloudy night for all to see, and for me knowing the branches would always be in flower on the kamikaze trees, raised on high for me in their valorous forever, saying come join us, hear our song, the song in our branches every spring and summer, I saw them, those girls at the university in Pakistan, you used to be able to walk the campus almost forever without seeing many, the few decent and distant, or in confinement when they weren't out, the way I like them, not like here with concerts and everything, no meetings in refectories, monastic silence everywhere, no talking, no dancing, nothing, gender segregation in cafeterias, study halls, and the rector hated the arts, he would have none of it there, that, that is the place where my mother refused to obey our traditions, no music anywhere in the university, I was a religious student, no way I'd be corrupted, and it was the students themselves, not the administration, who set the limits: no music or literature, nothing pernicious, a moral code we all dodged a bit, and before the fast at Ramadan the women prayed in their dormitories separated from one another the way they were supposed to be in any house, what did he do anyway that kid Jermaine, studied film in California eh, I can just hear that rap music he used to play, what could he know about kamikazes and drums of heaven and their falling on villages, bridges, and roads, on people without morals, just look how they live, lavish in their immorality and abusing everything, the students used to say our moral code will be so rigorous we'll be entitled to pun- ish anything we consider wrong in public, stone them when necessary, boys and girls avoided talking to one another in libraries and parks so no one would see them, that was the law, a chastity belt for knowledge, political discussions fre- quently censored, otherwise every possible analysis might be tolerated, the chastity belt of religion to preserve us from all external threats, special rooms for provocateurs with women weeping beneath their veils whenever anyone came in, some- times their sons or fathers, and they would show photographs without any chance of success, a neck is easily cut and it's all over, it was common knowledge that anyone who went into the windowless room with dark-coloured walls knew what to expect, a glass of water, a moment to pray, then confession of one's indiscretions, one student cried Allah save me, Allah save me, for a long time, surrounded by the astounded wit- nesses and guards, sometimes it wasn't just one prisoner but as many as fifteen or twenty, all of it legal and recommended, this room was in a fortress built by a foreign engineer, and who knows if the young man calling on Allah to save him was ever heard or if he ever noticed the presence of women passing by in black scarves waiting and crying before their sen- tencing, one no longer knew if this was just or not, such a time of lethargy and running into stone walls, so what's this Jermaine doing, the birds on the roofs and the wires are sing- ing so loud it bursts my eardrums, the stridency is maddening, at sea I used to love birds, but now their screeching drives me so crazy I sweat through my black clothes, in fact the engineer from America no longer even thought about the fortress or of the rooms where a student implored Allah, he just went on building more of them, more fortresses and prisons, and buckled under the load of all the money he made, so he had other things to think about, not all this stuff about religion, he was spared ever having to think about it, he had men under contract and nothing to worry about, his conscience was clear, and the only concern he had was those prisoners' rights groups, oh those studies could study all they liked, it was nothing to do with him, he just did what they told him to do, he wasn't part of the killing choir, just an engineer with blueprints, Allah save me, why would he have heard such a thing as this far from those thick walls, why indeed, and Chuan thought the decorating style for this hotel in Bali should be all air and lightness, suggesting at the outset a kind of idyll, she was also thinking about her Christmas dinner, the table and crystal chandeliers, oh her son would have liked filet mignon with wild mushrooms and whipped potatoes, now why couldn't he be vegetarian, there would be bright balls in the tree by the pool, and the sparkle of crystal everywhere, a chilled olive soup to begin, almonds covered with strawberry jelly, and those good old pistachio wafers for dessert, and joy in everyone's heart, this hotel in Hong Kong would be a subtle meeting of East and West, pavilions like cells for a Buddhist retreat, light, breezy, and only slightly warm, oh the dessert was for Jermaine of course because Olivier didn't eat much, in fact he hadn't slept for several nights and here he was phoning for the third time since this morning, Chuan-Chuan where are you, you know I'm in my study working at my computer on the Bali hotel design, remember, I'm not far and I've got the preparations for Christmas dinner underway, now do stop worrying dear, why so many guests again, why not just a quiet family Christmas and where's Jermaine, he asked, he's anxious again she thought, even with the meds, it's that bad dream again, the worried voice came back, stop now dear Chuan began again patiently, so I can finish this work tonight, joy in the hearts of all, have you forgotten it'll soon be

Christmas, this article I'm writing is garbage, he repeated, really, I love you my darling, but where is Jermaine, she clung to his voice, if only he could get over this and not be so depressed thought Chuan, my poor dear, what a sad way to be, said Chuan, joy in the hearts of all, and in our family dear God, so what about dessert Olivier, tell me, then silence in the house and within the study walls she'd painted purple, how was she ever going to leave him alone like this when she went to Bali, of course Jermaine would be there with him, caring as always, a child to be proud of, even if Chuan wasn't always enthusiastic about the films he produced, virtual violence, why not something a bit more tranquil and hopeful, like an image under a magnifying glass thought Lazaro, Jermaine's mother moving from room to room with her white blouse untucked over her jeans, barefoot the way these women were, a strand of black hair over her forehead, way too much like her son, thin too, even the eyes a little bit slanted, a bustling woman in a hurry, always so much to do, work, family, just like Caridad plying her craft, a mother dissolved into the crowd of modern mothers just like her, one born in Egypt and one in Japan, but they'd both adopted the shame of an unscrupulous lifestyle, he thought, all in sad lockstep, and woe to them, at home girls and boys didn't talk to one another, not on the campuses or in the parks, always separate bodies unattainable, modesty beyond reproach and woe, yes, woe on them, the courting birds played lightly on the wires and long-fingered palm leaves in the wind, on masts, gulls, pigeons, plovers, and doves quick to attach themselves, a wealth of sound that amazed Lazaro while he sweated under his motorcycle helmet and black outfit, what kind of a mother is that he's got running around the house doing all sorts of silly things, my mother doesn't know I've come back for a mission and she wouldn't recognize me now, ah those bird sounds and those stupid kids parading in the street before Christmas all that noise gives me the sweats, Olivier still felt shaken by his nightmare, scratching the earth with his hands as though he'd helped Chuan in her garden, though she'd really never put up with his clumsy interference in her flowers and bushes, then suddenly seeing Jermaine's head pop out of a pile of grass and earth, then his whole body, then Olivier's fingers running over him like a blind man's, was their son still alive under his shroud, and Olivier immediately woke up wondering where his son was, gone, already up surfing first thing in the morning! Why wasn't he right here by his side, he called him, Jermaine, calm down it's all right, and Chuan quickly brought a glass of water and a sedative to his bedside, dreams don't mean a thing she said, now which friends would you like to invite to dinner dear, come on my love, get up, look at that brilliant sunshine on the water, Olivier gradually got over his disturbed sleep as the light sliced through the blinds into the room, I'm sinking into night he thought, but my wife is as joyous and full of charm as ever, I don't control these dreams, yet they persecute me as soon as I want to fall asleep, Jermaine, where's my son, Olivier got up and had several cups of coffee, then his huge silhouette slid along the walls to his study and there lay the unfinished article in front of him with themes he'd rather not touch on, the rebirth of an epidemic of cruelty among students in schools and colleges, it is written on fences, on gates to lawns where tulips and roses now grow, here it was in the beautiful month of May there were riots, then in October 1997 a brief truce of light before winter, ammunition in cafeterias and residences, knives under mattresses, and so we discover children with the faces of tortured angels, semi-automatic weapons. 22s under school sweaters blazoning "The Science of Tomorrow" at thirteen, first just joking, torture contests, small animals, then weapons collections, amused and amusing clowns, so like one another, no answers for us or for their parents, Lazaro was convinced he was seeing them under a magnifying glass these parents of Jermaine's, the retired Afro-American senator and his vigorous Asian wife full of health, too bad, it was the son Jermaine that obsessed Lazaro, so that was it, out on his surfboard already at this hour, never mind, he'd be there for their big fat Christmas dinner with all the hangers-on, vain painters, writers, and pompous intellectuals around the table, while Lazaro washed dishes in restaurants or worked at fishing on the shrimp-boats, down-and-out jobs, they didn't know who he was, did they, no notion of his piety and faith, most of all his mission, banished from their midst, their learned excellence, their fine manners and fortune, a well-known designer for a mother, his father in his cabin with his dogs could write all the memoirs he wanted about being a rebel, an agitator with posters of Martin Luther King covering his walls, yes epidemics of it in the schools and colleges, Olivier thought to himself, still too much noise to think, Jermaine's head as though he actually had touched it in the night, they were all he had, Jermaine and Chuan, not a thing else to sustain him in the coming vertigo, what did analysts know about it, this gaping void, the abomination of days and nights losing one's footing on the earth, Chuan was right there was a lot of light coming off the Gulf, almost as though it were already summer, maybe it wasn't a good thing for the heat to come on so quickly, Olivier had been wrong to get so upset about a dream, of course he was, he thought to himself, after all Chuan was there, radiant and undisturbed by his fanciful vagaries, yes wrong with Christmas approaching, Tigli bounced along on the bus, his wizard eyes peering out from under his felt hat, Ari meanwhile thinking about Lou, maybe he should have used those words he heard from the boy in the station singing into the phone as though it were his lover's ear, "you have my heart . . . you know what baby, you have my heart," lilting for Ari as though from far off, across the jumbled distance separating them, words he would entrust to her ear every single hour, "I give you my heart," like the boy into the steel ear, a direct conduit to his beloved, erasing worlds of distance between them, just fold it

up afterwards and slip the magic thing into his pocket knowing he'd scooped a heart out of the air the way a swallow did
a blade of grass, so it was Lou came to Ari saying I love you
Papa, he dreamed of selling his sculptures for a good price in
New York and having a cloudless future, but still, what would
all that really be to her if the earth held nothing good for her,
why the dreams of riches for his little girl surrounded by such
barren misery, shaming perhaps, thus he thought, surround
her with all the luxury and luxuriance he could, nothing that
was not beautiful, for she was his princess and he the prince
of consumption, no point in running from it, a gorgeous boat,
why not, an eye-catching house he'd designed himself, it was
all like that, try as he might to be like Asoka and not own
anything, the love of his daughter and before that his wife
Ingrid, all of it urged him on to the joys of materialism, living
was having, like the heart of the boy on the phone given away
to an abstract and heart-rending love so suddenly familiar to
everyone in the station: "I give you my heart" told them all
exactly what it was to love and made them feel it as well, Ari
thought, for discretion no longer existed any more, nor intimacy, it had been globalized as though everyone were on
everybody else's TV in their living room and in complete
confidence, deciding that the other would be oneself behind
another curtain of skin, and that must be all right, a widening
of perspective to infinity, the oasis of a too-introverted, self-
critical solitude was no more than a memory, still feverish, Ari
found these thoughts to be numbing, only one's children can
make one better, that was the only riches, he thought, anything else was satiety, vice, and a trap, and yet, and yet, the
thought of a New York buyer for his sculptures did buoy him
up, and that would be Lou's university, I'll put it away, an
artist's life had to be worth something for future progeny,
above all if one had a daughter, no point in saying anything
to Asoka, he'd simply scold him for such vain and prideful
thoughts, but if it came down to him as her godfather how

would this poor pilgrim create a future for her, by begging God, all spirit in a chaste ethereal body, good at meditation and prayer, no, that wasn't right, Asoka did act tirelessly for the poor and the sick, here they were on their way to yet another overlooked mountain clinic for which he had spotted new doctors and nurses unobtrusively wherever he went, orange robe flying in the wind, rehabilitating, healing, and consoling, though barely noticed, never allowing himself the kind of debilitating thoughts on the fate of men that Ari entertained, yes a fine godfather to Lou who had never been educated to the moral need to do good so natural to this monk, whereas he had taught her to read and draw and worship his art, no more than that, never having told her it was her duty to save the Earth, oh he had shown her the local newspaper with a photo of students underwater unfurling a banner that read "The sea is hot, and we're burning," if the ocean bottom, glaciers, and rivers were all headed for irremediable calcination, what conditions would she live in soon, would she even have a living space, thoughts like this ate away at him, yes, of course he would talk to her and the urgent obligation of her generation to . . . but what really would they understand, possibly it was already too late, calcination already blanketing them, suffocating them, skyless and waterless, Lou drew and painted, look Papa, it's you, and that's Mummy, blotches, colours, bodies and faces of her parents never together, dissolved in the breakup, not like the English painter David Hockney's touching portrait of his parents together in one small and innocent picture, his father an amateur painter himself laboriously bent over his palette, his mother sitting straight-backed on a wooden chair, mother of several children, hands joined over her blue dress, parents united as he'd always known them growing up in a modest home bare of books and even the comforts, but not of love sustained between them and immortalized in a painting of extreme candour, inspired perhaps in the smoky air of pubs, but ever present before his eyes, whereas Lou, from a family dissected in pieces, her parents who never mixed, this is for you Papa and this is for you Mum, her pictures were spirited and mischievous but still lucid, tomorrow night at her place she'd say, as he observed the too-realistic drawings and the refusal to blend splashes and shapes, sometimes he wondered if she'd forget him while she was at her mother's, and what would her mother say about him, they had always mistrusted one another, of course Lou had detected the advantages she could get from their egotism, she could stay up later at her mother's and not eat her fruit and vegetables like at her father's, something harder on the system instead, her mother being so busy at work she didn't have the time for the fine art of eating or sailboat rides with her father which she slept through gently rocked by the afternoon waves on a windless afternoon, the closeness to her father of which she'd been robbed for a few days, still hesitating to be won over easily by this man who let her off once a week in front of her mother's place as though she'd have to beg to get her place back with her taunting half-brother Julien, her mother and father kissed her and held her exactly the same way, but sometimes the causeway between them seemed about to break, yet still she was less fragile than they were, fighting for the same child, she was alone, but they were united in confronting one another, and she had only herself to think of when it came to presents, her mother would give her chocolate, hot dogs, and all the junk food her father wouldn't, and he gave her bikinis and tutus, seeing in her already the slender girl she was, no longer a child, nearly a teenager and woman, as though he'd watched Ingrid herself growing before his eyes, and of course her senseless loving father just had to give her a real scooter to replace the kiddy one she'd had before, weaving in and out on the cycle paths, able to brake with just one foot, and what freedom it was, that stubborn little blonde head for all to see, adventurous and parentless, depending only on tide and stars, just as her father saw her, a goddess of innocence, Mère was recalling what Mélanie would be reading out tonight in Washington, she'd consulted her mother and they'd discussed it, the things a woman elected president had to endure, always the same grilling, often from other women anxious to stand in their way, mistrust and enmity, always needing the stamina and inspiration that men did not, being the leader of a country must obviously make them too ambitious, not as important for men, but a woman always had too much, especially when allowed to turn around the declining economy of a whole country, but ill-advised to give too firm a voice to their ambitions, always watched for and criticized if they showed their overall determination, their desire for changing the laws, depolluting, countered and protested against at every turn like a window display with unacceptably wholesome ideas, when would combativity be allowed, even slightly, and perhaps a little world mastery, Mai probably was alone too much, though she did write to Augustino every day, Mère thought, she'd have a word with Daniel at dinner tonight, she was distracted by the arrival of some young people in her garden, oh said Franz, my wife and grandson have come for me, but the wife seemed as young as Mai standing there in her ragged shorts holding Yehudi by the hand, the child had the same dark mop of hair as Franz did once upon a time, and the clarity of his lively eyes, in a sailing boat, they'll take me home to Havana the way I used to go back, he said, forever a boat, and he spread his long arms towards his family in jubilant enthusiasm, we have news for you Esther, and Rachel's come to tell you wonderful news, she heard them whispering together, a baby, that's right, we're going to have a baby Esther, she said, I'm pregnant, isn't that wonderful, it had to be, the ageing musician and his young wife did make a moving couple thought Mère, who had seen him on the arms of many women, and off they went laughing in his antique convertible, she could see the circle of lively faces, already into the bubbles of champagne that Franz wouldn't lose any time popping open, yes, she really would have to talk to Daniel tonight, and if Mélanie was right, and there was still that mistrust and hostility, when on earth would women reach that masterly plateau where they could govern for women or halt inhumanity and war, just when was that miracle going to happen, was it really so denatured and abnormal to so many men? During a raid, Petites Cendres thought, the pillaging police had searched the islands and a few shopkeepers on Bahama, but Timo had been on the run for a long time, and they couldn't catch him, just a few grass-sellers caught with heroin, like in Chicago or New York from the age of ten, kids just starting out and barely ready for it who dabbled in cheese, the stuff that melts in our mouth, just slip it into a thick cold medicine and it gets you to seventh heaven cheap they said, you can get it anywhere, school kids drool for it, what they don't know about the slum-pillagers on Bahama Street, once you get into it there's no stopping, that wasn't enough for Timo, he always had to have the purest stuff, so what if his guts exploded then he fell into a deep hole without it, so now where could he be, if he was a sexual predator, they'd sniff out his trail, but just a car and cocaine thief, he could very well get away with it again, yeah, sure I gave him the client's car keys while Timo, all hot and dancing towards him on the table with that cute little butt under his leather jacket, distracted the guy, quickly I pocket the keys and Timo's off, Reverend Ézéchielle asked what was going to become of him and said God in all his bounty had enough of him and his scams, and today for once He wasn't going to forgive Petites Cendres for all his wrongdoings, she wasn't actually saying this, but it is what he heard, now what else did she say, remember, oh yes! how incredibly smart the Declaration of Independence was, a memorable document that said from now on all men were equal, um, except those that weren't, right? It was worth it, such an important document that said so little, in 1619 a Dutch captain and his cargo laid anchor off these shores what was that cargo again, about a hundred humans chained together all the way across the Atlantic, imagine the conditions, then the Dutch captain wound up in the Caribbean and said, here I'll sell you these, they're all healthy, there were 250 of the same fine quality on board the *Bance-land*, had to sell them before they all got smallpox, them and the bags of rice, sugar, and tobacco, men and bodies, now remember this or another declaration will be signed and you'll be banished all over again, a calamity they all took part in: Dutch, English, French, Portuguese navigators promptly delivering their cargoes of men, women, and children, it has to be said, a universal institution, a universal conspiracy, a traffic of souls for pennies, a bag of rice over the shoulder and a man in irons next to it, fine merchandise, watch out for germs though, infection, smallpox, careful, send them to work the cotton fields in sweat and blood, Petites Cendres said he had enough fears of his own without the Reverend dragging up the awful past, Timo, he was thinking of Timo, everybody dancing and singing the praises of the Lord with the Reverend, the musicians bringing their fingers down hard on the pianos, getting out their guitars and hoarse voices in the smoky air of the Porte du Baiser, that was the key to not hearing the slap-slap of waves against the cargo ships at low tide, nowadays the White Riders tossed burning crosses into Birmingham churches in an unleashing of treachery, at the scene of these hideous dramas Petites Cendres dissolved into the crowd of tourists ogling in the bars where the musicians and transvestites got ready for the evening's business way in advance, you could already hear Eric Clapton, the Doobie Brothers, Laydown Sally, Blackwater, and the blues groups out by the water, seas and oceans had transported human cattle to be sold at auction, their backs striped with whips and leather lashes of the Dutch, English, and French masters, the music of Blackwater could already be heard, and where was Timo hiding out at this point, in his presbytery, Alphonso reflected on the Franciscan bishop, certainly a virtuous man to all appearances, who must have heard his wayward predecessor's confession possibly a long time ago now, and if not this worthy bishop, then another in the clerical hierarchy had heard the criminal priest confess, never to be punished, lips sealed, filthy water never to be stirred up, the guilty party would simply be sidetracked for a few months, nothing more, let us never speak of this again, not even his name, the confessional means silence, but the silence of the Vatican is not sacred, this poor sinner must be prayed for they said, thrown out of isolated seminaries and provinces, the banished pedophile, though he was never called that, but rather an erroneous priest of questionable behaviour, practically a convalescing tuberculosis patient forced to withdraw to the mountains to recover, for whatever the deviation of his lechery, a priest was still a messenger of God, and Alphonso saw the same understanding and conspiracy spreading over all who came near it, all perfidious and sly, the confessor, the Franciscan bishop who knew all along and said nothing, an institution built on lies, a conspiracy against innocent children, women whose trust and money had been stolen, and Alphonso was possessed with anger, could he write well enough to denounce this, could it even be done in words, pacing up and down in the cold room, a woman approached him timidly, the housekeeper, my room is down there at the end of the corridor, she said, in case you need me for anything, do not hesitate, she was about to bow to him, but Alphonso raised her quickly, no, I am used to living alone, I am a demanding bachelor but very independent, you would have to endure my bad temper, he asked her name, Constanza she said as timidly as before, he was about to brush her aside then realized she might be an ex-nun and that he ought to show her respect, so he said more softly, very well, I shall knock on your door, but we will share the cooking, you'll see I can manage very well, later he thought she might know all about the evil priest as well, or was she simply too innocent to stand up

as a witness to daily reality, devotedly simple and perhaps
she'd not seen anything anyway, then Alphonso wondered if
he should soften his accusations, take on only the Church
aristocrats, forever multiplying in his mind, and his fury resur-
faced, of course they had heard it all, moist confessions of
confessions, and still said nothing, girls and boys raped, nothing at all, all other kinds of predators were punished with the
severest sentences, some of them even killed in prison by
their cellmates or neighbours, pariahs like that got the worst
payback and even summary execution by those who saw
themselves as less depraved, the instinct to punish others
being still very much alive in us, these prisoner executions
were hardly prevented and almost useful thought Alphonso,
no, these priests never faced a court and would never be
punished like the outcast predators who, even after their sentences, would be continually persecuted wherever they went,
nowhere to live without sinking to the lowest depths, no more
rights, in the scattered brotherhood under bridges, in tents with
the rats, under metal arcades, more threatening in this new
dissolution and misery than they'd been in prison, while these
rapists of young boys and girls just went on with their work
in parishes and churches, knowing full well they would always
be protected by their superiors, never to be accused of what
they had done, a virtual massacre, thought Alphonso, a massacre approved by the Church, because the seal of the confessional must never be broken, Mère smiled thinking about
Franz and this new child, like Yehudi he'd be bathed in music
with this many musicians around, he'd hear Britten's *War
Requiem* conducted by his own father in notes of universal
chaos for his very first steps, perhaps a child prodigy playing
the piano for his mother before he could talk, at thirteen playing the same Brahms and Schumann that Franz remembered
playing in concert at his age, a little more dreamlike, no, melodious, the master already butting heads with the student, he'd
say, listen son, the way he already did with Yehudi, you need

a more ample tone here, he would upset the child, even ter-
rify him with his knowledge, and yet teach him everything,
his large hands guiding the little fingers, now be bolder here,
you've got to, and little by little the child would be crushed,
no, not like that, no, his childhood would be immersed in
music, Britten and Berg, Franz would teach him everything
and then gradually disappear like fog on the water, the image
of a genial grandfather, he'd seem more like that than a father,
wouldn't he, the man would leave only a brilliant memory for
the child, like Mère with her children and grandchildren, a
picture on the fog like a boat leaving the wharf, drifting ever
farther away under a stormy sky, surely that's how it would
be, yes bathed in music, so Rachel was pregnant and they were
confident and happy, so let it be she thought, for now it was
as Franz showed Yehudi on the piano, careful, tenderly, it's a
gentler movement, listen to the sweetness of this note and let
it last a little longer, this delicate approach was how they would
all be won over, one after the other in this family expecting
its next child, Mai followed the cycle path with the dogs strain-
ing at their leashes, sometimes letting them go and watching
them run towards the water among the birds they'd send flying off as they went by, she would be in time for dinner now
that her grandmother stepped out less and less from the pavilion where she read and wrote and received her friends to
come and have supper with them at the house, tonight she
would be there, and Dad had said to get dressed for dinner,
white jeans, clean top the same colour, is that all right, no,
cover your shoulders if you're eating with Grandmother he
said, she'd be hearing his car horn and they'd run towards him,
tell me Dad how your conference on ecology went, tell me,
but at the wheel Daniel would say nothing as though assailed
by thoughts, you're not forgetting it's supper with Grandmother,
so no bathing suit, and wash your hair, she's not here every
evening, he might say that while the black labs, descendants
of their very first dog, licked his face, how's your book coming

Dad, still he didn't respond, in any case, she still had her ear-buds in, and though it was often better not to hear anything they were saying there would be no Discman at the table, absolutely not, oh you never like anything I do, Mai would answer, it's just normal politeness he would say, I want my children to be polite to adults, were you polite too, she would ask rebelliously, I admit I don't remember he would say, see you never remember anything Mai would shoot back, you're just getting old and you put all your memory in your books, that sort of banter and meaningless reproach Mai thought, but at least her father wasn't as taciturn as her brother Augustino, still he was often thoughtful after one of these conferences probably because they didn't listen to him enough or called him alarmist, of course he believed deeply in what he said, kids were throwing balls over the net, but neither Emilio nor his father were with them, people were walking along the water's edge with their dogs, like Mai headed towards more and more winding paths, it was as though leaving them behind meant they were no longer there, the setting sun glittered on the water and under the pink sky the sea smell reached her nostrils, and sand gathered under the leather straps of her san-dals, why this supper with Grandmother, just a little farther on there were a succession of more isolated beaches, who were those sloppily dressed young people sitting at a table off to the side under the pines by themselves, not eating, just drink-ing from bottles in paper bags, vulgar laughs as she brushed by them with the dogs, hey look at that cutie, said one man, a hand touched her hip, take a look, what's your name he winked at her, dirty laughs, if you hear the pigs we'll move off a ways said one, them and their sirens, gaaaah said one ruined-looking woman, they don't even notice us, curfew's at seven, after that it's like they don't see us, long live freedom, so chicky what are you doing around here, that's the moment when Mai heard her father honk the first time, must be quite near, he'll do it a few more times, usually he'd stop and make

a few notes while he waited for her or take a turn on the
beach, still thinking about his conference, well he could wait
a bit more, these weird people were interesting, no grandmother waiting dinner for them, not that worried about how
they looked either, there was always the sea or a nice cold
shower in a wooden beach cabin, probably not that concerned about hygiene for days at a time anyway, judging by
the dirt on their legs and faces, or were those wounds — injuries or clumps of dirt, they seemed to be wearing their own
stigmata but they did seem to have been beaten judging by
the marks underneath their sunburn, and she was revolted by
their smell, still some sort of obscure curiosity pushed her to
take a closer look as long as the dogs were pulling on the
leashes anyway, then she suddenly recognized a tall girl she'd
seen wearing a white dress at an afternoon wedding on the
beach, the bride or her sister, white dress and a bouquet of
white roses against the young bride's waist, whichever one
she was, all that was debris underfoot now the girl was here
before her as if to say, okay, this is what I really am, and I'll
never be the ravishing bride they wanted me to be, so go tell
them how much I despise them, tell them about my ravaged
face, my lovely mouth going fast, my black clothes, my foot
all cut up from stepping on glass while I was hanging out
homeless at night on the beach, and drunk, very drunk, coke
maybe, I don't know, tell them their June bride has taken off
and here she is right in front of you, those beautiful June-bride
eyes staring at her, for at least they were still intact and luminous as their gaze riveted Mai, hello said the bride with a stifled
laugh, want to join us, what are you doing here with your fine
dogs, see can't walk too well, hey guys, come give me a hand
and some vodka please, my foot's bleeding and we don't
know any doctors, hey yeah that's her, thought Mai, the June
bride or her sister in the magnificent white dress looking at
me like she knows me, then Mai noticed some battered bikes
in the sand and remembered she'd seen the tall girl on one in

town, upright on the seat with feathers in her hair and zigzagging through the streets, you can tell them I'm not going back said the June bride, to them and their stupid prancing, married to just the right guy, the limo, the flowers, goodbye, you can tell them goodbye for me, and they can keep their inheritance too, I don't want it, these guys here are my friends right here at this table and I'm sticking with them, we live here all the time, and when the bulls chase us out, we meet at the table under the trees in the park, we don't bother the people playing tennis, and the pigs don't bother us there, tell them no way I'm going back, I've got all the husbands I need right here, just don't know which one to choose, though none of them are too clean like you can see, her voice broken like the rest of her, thought Mai, the car horn came across the humid air again, come on she said to the dogs, Dad's waiting for us, don't forget what I told you now said the June bride, Mai heard her laughing as she ran with her dogs as agile as them on her long legs, she thought she heard her own heartbeat inside, as though she'd been caught up in a spell like the dead wedding day, dead who knows how, yes caught up in the froth of the white dress and white rose petals, as though she were the younger sister or her friend for a day in June and the suffocating embrace could not be broken, she ran towards her father, familiar and exuberant, though he was always a bit grouchy after his conferences in the library where he always had small audiences, too few he said, that this was him, Daniel, her father, her rock and her strength against the June bride and her ragged bunch on the skids, still she was enchanted, bewitched though, as though these creatures had her in some dark magic web without air or pink sky, Dad, she cried, my Daddy, and the labs licked both their faces, while Mai luxuriated in eau de cologne on her father's chest, still not certain the June bride couldn't hook her with one of the raised fingers when she said, you'll see, later on you'll see, which still echoed in the air with her horrible laugh, Ari saw the ten-year-old hitchhiker from the bus window, right thumb out to the passing drivers, he belonged to whoever stopped amid the uninterrupted roar of traffic through the folds between hills and mountains, there wasn't time for Ari to see who stopped, but he was sure the kid would be grabbed and robbed of his Sunday best in seconds if not by now, already out of sight, and he wondered if it was just a dream like those other kids from the bush under the cypress trees of over-heated cities at night, their Sunday pants and shirts lit up by headlights amid the scattering of lights and hot dust, smiling, broad foreheads under thick hair like masks, busy but peace-ful in the squares ogled by passing drivers with an eye to the looks and charm from behind tinted windows in the parade of cars clicking by, one by one, then disappearing and noth-ing you could do about it, Ari thought, or the ten-year-old hitchhiker, just devoured childhoods, chewed up by ogres, lost or dead, fragile stuff this stretched skin and constantly available from destitution, at least it wouldn't be Lou's ado-lescence, yet how did he know that, the world could just as easily play one of its crazy tricks and make Lou the ludicrous plaything of all, kids bought and sold wholesale for retail, hit on the head with a stick or wiped out by a handgun, kids wholesale like rags, waste paper in the streets and on the sidewalks with skeletal dogs, no that was not for Lou, the ten-year-old hitchhiker had parents too, parents he had to feed and give his pay to, or had they just up and sold him dressed in white as driven snow, a ready offering by the roadside till the lord of the slaughterhouses passed and collected it, Ari was pained that Asoka had not seen the boy in their flight, not a thing, as if he never existed, eyes closed, praying and meditating while Ari tormented himself with the vision, the monk's profile as impenetrable and secretive as ever, would his prayers save the boy from danger, him and all his brothers and sisters in the bushes and squares wearing their snow-white Sunday best, would Asoka in his piety save them? Ari

saw the affable Tigli in his felt hat slide past to an empty seat
near a young girl crying and holding her hands over her cotton dress and the child in her belly, he dried her tears with
his handkerchief, smiled and said they'd go to the clinic
together, he'd have time to do that before he went out with
his friends for the evening for some salsa and margaritas with
salt around the rims, then more salsa under the stars, the glit-
ter of alcohol in the eyes of the women he'd dance with till
dawn oh! Angelina you mustn't cry he said, putting his hands
on her breasts, see there's life here little Angelina, boyfriend's
gone back to Barcelona and doesn't want to see you any
more, what a bad one, filthy beast, ah men, won't marry you,
won't even see you again, but I still love him she kept saying
between sobs, don't worry about me said Tigli taking her
hand, no really, I'm a fireman, delivery boy and fireman, all
kinds of talents, all kinds of jobs, eh, but most of all there's
no one who can dance the salsa like me, you'll see, we're
bound to stop sometime before the clinic and I'll show you,
he's in there, she said, breathing, I can hear him breathing,
she said, ah bad boy, bad mean boy, I need to have a duel
with that thankless father, traitorous seed, good-for-nothing,
what were you doing in Barcelona anyway, studying she said,
see what happens, I was at my aunt's and here you see what
can happen, oh life, it just never stops, Tigli said, there's no
other way for it to be, good thing too, like the fish and the
plants, that's the way the Creator wants it, believe me, I know,
sometimes these little things give us a hard time as if they
don't want to come out, they dawdle, but I'm stubborn too
and I push them every which way and pull on them by the
head or the feet to get them out of that tiny nest they're stuck
in, and their mothers complain I'm not fast enough just the
same, I mean that's asking too much, but don't you worry
Angelina, little girl, how old are you, not yet fifteen I'll bet,
now don't sniffle like that, smile, I'm sure we'll find a guy selling cookies and ice cream, I'll get you some, but stop sniffling,

when they get here it's not your ordinary yell, it'll bust your eardrums guaranteed, I never get used to it, once they're out they've got to let you know about it, boy! Wait Angelina, you'll see, you're going to forget this so-and-so, please stop sniffling like that, a cold's not worth having for a good-for-nothing, be reasonable, Angelina, here we're stopping, and here's the cookies-and-ice-cream guy, I'll get you some, but only if you stop sniffling, you want a slice of melon too, it's the best, so juicy it runs all down your fingers, you're going to have a sweet chubby baby, I can tell, let me see, an angel, an angel like you Angelina, I can feel his shape, he's moving, he's coming soon, well on the way, wait and see, no advance warning like his dad, just like him, expect anything with this one, actually I think it'll be a girl, here's the ice cream and cookies, slice of melon, good for both of you, we're not in any hurry, but he sure is, all of a sudden, oops here I am, and then screaming, screeching to blast your eardrums, Ari thought if we all had Tigli's gift of wonderment, life could trickle and flow again everywhere, no matter how wasted, it could be reclaimed everywhere, and Tigli's hand on Angelina's belly was the proof, right there under her cotton dress was the breath of life, the inexhaustible source of all flesh, Ari's throat-tightening despair was gone, and Mère thought about all the details that ornamented her days in the acquiescence of serene solitude, writing her diary while she waited for Augustino, perhaps they would all be together, Augustino, Samuel, Jermaine with Chuan and Olivier this Christmas night so soon, to think of the conversation with Mélanie perhaps a little too assured in the compassion of a woman president, for according to her ideology, such a woman would have to be beyond reproach, mother first, leader second, always pleading for clemency even in the most dogged protests and demands, not a woman to shut herself up loftily on her estate or in her opulent villa refusing to see the mother of a dead soldier, knowing that a mother had every right, this made all mothers a problem, for

they spared no one, presidents or ministers, from the cross of
their sons' sacrifice on their shoulders, breaking down ranch
fences, villa doors, and shouting Why have you killed my son,
I defy you to see me, hear me, his mother, I'm not leaving
here without talking to you, they couldn't just be arrested and
sent home, far too embarrassing, there they would be all
shouting together, what have you done with my son Jeremy,
what have you done to him, putting up white crosses in a
wheat field, never to forget, distraught brothers and sisters at
home, and she spoke for all of them, pickaxing the doors and
fences, a voice heard from afar saying it wasn't for nothing,
no it wasn't, this was really embarrassing, because these mothers with their sons on their shoulders like crosses would
listen to no one, it was a man's voice that said it was not in
vain, but a woman Mélanie said, a mother from those desperate ranks, who said yes it was, it was in vain, and she understood the distress was her own, Mère felt troubled that she
was so sure of what she said, the ebbs and flows of human
nature are in every one of us, aren't they, she also regretted
that Mélanie was not here enough with her and Mai, and
where was Mai, how awful to think that old people were good
only for keeping an eye on young people, and just as out-
moded and useless when they did it anyway, they would have
to humour Mai tonight, and knowing she loved to read, she'd
suggest a visit to the writer, a bit of a long car trip with her
father, they'd go to the farm in Georgia where she'd always
lived, born in the village of Andalusia, a recluse but still hos-
pitable to friends from the village with whom she discussed
Kierkegaard, a local writer as a matter of fact, and Mai would
be inspired by the story of this modest woman who could
discuss absolutely anything, but perhaps Mère would just go
on her own without Mai who was now dancing to rap with
Daniel, and it would be good for her, if he had time for this
little pilgrimage, the house of a male writer who died in his
youth, a house under enormous oak trees where books and

stories had been written, typed on an old-fashioned type-writer up against a wooden wardrobe in the nighttime glow from a yellow lampshade near a chair, long curtains in the windows where one could see the farm, simply called Mary Flannery's house in the village, once the lupus set in, she wrote three hours a day, then less and less until there was no time left for it, the typewriter now mute in the silence of the mornings and the afternoons, not a sound, not even the buzz-ing of a fly, the lawn still appearing green from the window, the building shared by the farm and plantation, students visit-ing by the thousands, Mère would take Mai to Andalusia, always provided she didn't have a dance class or a singing lesson with the school choir, and if, if, what was it exactly Mai was interested in, was it true she smoked now, that smell of cannabis in the garden after the rain, if it were true as Caroline said in Mère's dream, that our children lie to us, lie to us and flee from us, she said, my dear friend, we are from another time you and I, no it was just Mère's preoccupied and over-active imagination, and they would soon all be assembled at last around Chuan and Olivier for their traditional festive sup-per on Christmas night, her gaze, all those who had met her in this house said they would never forget the frankness of the gaze behind her glasses, its acuity, but lupus so soon, still at any hour in the late afternoon she'd welcome friends in this room, this writing-house, she'd rest her gaze in all its sharp-ness and thought on Mère, saying this is Andalusia, my king-dom, the home of a local author well hidden beneath the trees, like the title of one of my books, *I Am a Displaced Person*, displaced by lupus that eats away at my time, and now there is so little of it, it is 1964 and as my time shrinks in the afternoon and the light dies on the typewriter, on the varnished wooden wardrobe, on my deformed and clutching fingers on the keys, you see, and thus it will be that I shall die at the age of thirty-nine, and I shall be the Displaced Person, as you too will be one day in your own home Esther, a person displacing a great ill we know nothing about, as she got dressed for dinner, Mère thought of death as oversized clothing that is draped on us with folds we can no longer conceal and too many people beneath it, but she would go to Andalusia and see the house of the writer and the writings, she displaced now, and the old-fashioned typewriter, the rattling relic with a sound like hammered metal, from the window Mère would see the meadows, the stable where the family's old Chevrolet slept, and peacocks, maybe she'd see the peacocks on the lawn or some other sign of animal life reviving this over-quiet landscape, left by an author now in her own silent universe, oh! that's how it would be, with Mai or without her, Mère would visit the house in the village called Andalusia, Chuan was thinking about the design of a house in San Juan, the imperious architectural style of the Spanish Caribbean would have to be respected, and that meant elevated light-sources, the architects fashioned their designs around light, and like them, Chuan, purist and austere, chose a fragile substance such as glass so that nature could appear anywhere and be integrated into the walls and decorate the rooms with gardens and forests, the phosphorescence of glass linking with the blue water of the pool, interiors escaping from the white walls towards the changing colours of the sky, a transparent purity, aha she thought, perhaps a yellow corridor would add to the sunny aspect of the guest-room where one could see the cathedral looking out over the ocean, Olivier and Chuan could have been a couple like any other, relaxing with a drink, sitting in their deck chairs contemplating the beauty of twilight on the water, talking about their work, were Olivier not constantly in the depths of an excessively delicate consciousness of life, she thought, it would have been sheer ecstasy, rather than this slow collapse into night into which he was sliding, in fact, a conscientiously modern and ethical designer would likely do as many women have when they mastered the art, lightened the fabrics and tones and flowered motifs of any macabre outside influence, but the wool carpets woven by child slaves in Nepal weren't right, yes, they could have been a couple like any other, façades painted white, so why, why was it so with Olivier a vase of green apples and roses in a vase in the bathroom, ascending, a flood of light in every room, of course, there they'd sit vivacious and facing the ocean every evening, him in his books, her fascinated by the herons meticulously lifting themselves onto the wharf, a couple like any other, their life spinning itself out without incident or harm, days and evenings flowing together, nothing too complex or cruel, like these things that haunted Olivier, Chuan loved her husband, and was it her fault or her son's, really, she heard the the accelerating rumble of a motorcycle out in front, she'd just close the door, all this noise was unbearable after the silence they were used to, but this mood Olivier surrounded himself in had to be cleared up, sometimes the silence led them into a wordless understanding, like when Olivier left off what he was doing and stretched out his hand to his wife's cheek, and she said well, how about if we go and sit out by the ocean, not say or think anything, what about it Olivier, the gesture supported a common understanding more tender and more closely linked that she could not resist, those moments when all restraints were put aside, then Chuan could have surmounted the sadness of all those days when he went entirely without speaking to her or anyone else, for even in dreams he slid away from her and she'd awaken and feel him beside her, a suddenly carnal presence, like when they made love, but she dreamed of his no longer being there, just like everyday life, draped in her bathrobe, walking the hallways of strange hotels calling her husband, and he never answering, up and down watery corridors dark as craters at the bottom of the ocean afraid he'd drowned and calling out his name, Olivier, Olivier, but he never heard her, where was he, the pavilion door had been closed for hours and Daniel thought about what Augustino had written in his book *Letter to the Young with No Future,*

that the greatest misfortunes came from the failure of the old
to repair their own mistakes, Mai was exciting the dogs on
the back seat of the car, and her father saw her slender face
in the mirror under a veil of blowing hair, maybe Augustino
was right, but these were not thoughts for a boy his age he
thought, people now eighty-six years old who once seemed
so charming and straightforward were dying peacefully without ever having to go to trial in a rural Idaho county, white
supremacists who had run indoctrination camps on a twenty-
acre property without anyone noticing were the old travelling
salesmen of racial hatred, Long Live the Aryan Race they pro-
claimed along with all the hush-hush neo-Nazi networks, and
they were growing without drawing attention to themselves,
former aeronautical engineers with no past worthy of note
while they operated in complete impunity with their extreme-
right colleagues, and hatred, always hatred, lately Indians had
been their targets even more than Blacks, then when these
creatures finally died, what did one find but camps, forever
camps, in Idaho and elsewhere, but they'd been so crafty in
their attacks that they'd never been seen and caught, dead at
eighty-six like any nice old men going about their business
the same as anyone else in the streets, ties and beige rain-
coats, what were the consequences of their disappearance
from the face of the Earth wrote Augustino, human offal,
might not the germs of their actions cling to the flesh of every
newborn child, perhaps the blood of hate flowed back into
our veins, surely this could not just disappear unpunished, no
indeed it must not, these were not thoughts for someone of
Augustino's age thought Daniel, with characteristic distraction
when he was in the car, he asked Mai if she liked singing in
the school choir, and what would they be singing at the
Christmas concert he stared at her in the rear-view mirror as
she shrugged with her usual nonchalance that those things at
school didn't interest her, Daniel noticed the pearl encrusted
on her lower lip and her left earlobe sparkling with another

just like it, she wasn't really a child any more, how on earth
had that happened so fast, Petites Cendres came out of the
Community Church and pulled his cap down over his eyes so
as not to be seen, Reverend Ézéchielle had asked him, what
have you done, and where's your brother Timo, what have
you done with him, nothing Reverend, I'm just a humble sinner come to pray here in your church, the Church of Hope
they call it because for you everyone's a sinner, but everyone's
a man, I can appreciate sinners she replied, but not their sins,
those can stay outside, you understand me Petites Cendres,
and as for your friend Timo that little so-and-so, I'm afraid for
him, I really am, I can feel a rumbling in the sky, so pray for
your friend Timo, that the thunder may not fall on him, for all
sin in this world will be punished, and there are laws even for
the worst of us, Petites Cendres loved this time of day when
the sky pinked and the birds in the coconut palms and down
by the sea got agitated, a crazy time in the trees just like in
the bars, thought Petites Cendres everyone running every
which way, the boys with their hair drawn back or cut short
wading into the Porte du Baiser in their white vests and shorts
with cargo pockets and a cigarette, bad boys, said one man
when he saw them and took off his straw hat before them,
here's to you bad boys, long time I ain't been a student like
you, not going to get any degree in two years, here's to you
and freedom tomorrow, wouldn't have a cigarette for me
would you, one of them said he'd been drinking martinis non-
stop since the vacation began, he even put his morning eggs
in one, he laughed, young folks said the man with the straw
hat, wild partying, then lazy carelessness, then not wanting
anything, you think that's any way to be, the boys were all red
from sunbathing, open-throated laughter and cigarette smoke
everywhere, even into the face of Petites Cendres who liked
the company of strangers, these boys knew nothing about
Timo nor that the sheriff was looking for him, and as for himself, well he wasn't above reproach, Reverend Ézéchielle had

something to say about that, she told him, it isn't because I
welcome sinners that I welcome their sins, make no mistake,
Petites Cendres, I can read in your soul and the terror's going
to get you, what do you think of that, nothing Reverend, nothing at all, you know I think I'll just go out and take a little
walk, midnight, by midnight the terror's going to get you,
little by little as you think about your friend Timo you gave
those stolen car keys to, the Reverend Ézéchiellé never actually said these words because she was in the middle of her
prayers and songs, he heard them clearly enough like the
waves on the sea, the pinking sky and the screeching birds
were all warning him, they'll get him and they'll get you too,
grateful for the presence of the kids around him, Petites
Cendres admired their attractive simplicity, if only he could
be one of them, tanned, white shorts, or him, the man in the
straw hat with his hand on the shoulder of a boy named
Sluttie, telling her he couldn't live without her, that lightened
Petites Cendres' heart, hey I could go out to the dressing room
and slip on my black dress with flowers and just be a girl on
the dance floor tonight, they're all so drunk on cocktails no
one will notice a girl anyway, unless she's called Sluttie and
built like a boxer, Sluttie my little drunk bitch, come over here
said the man in the straw hat, but Sluttie just shot back, beat
it Grandpa, this place has got way better stuff than you in it,
but I gotta have you, the man said, maybe later Sluttie replied,
wanna buy me that coffee martini, sure thing my little bitch
he said, anything for you, and Sluttie said, yeah now if you
were twenty years younger that would be a different story, ah
that's youth for you said the man, you're all just merciless
brutes, believe me, I know Sluttie my love, ah you're a sight
for sore eyes, classic perfection, you gonna scratch me if I say
I'm crazy about you, I'll rip your heart to shreds she shot back,
that's just the way I am, well, Petites Cendres would love to
touch that classically perfect body the man talked about, hold
that masculine arrogance real close, but Sluttie was gone out

onto the terrace and was dancing glass in hand, lots of friends no doubt, under the black dress with purple flowers, Petites Cendres' sex would be flattened and barely visible, better hide his face with the peak of the cap that let his voluminous hair flow like a girl's, the straw-hat man said, Petites Cendres, I've got everything I need here, bad company's got nothing on Sluttie, sure it's a vulgar name, but that's the way I like it, love it in fact, a hymn to sex thought Petites Cendres, see what it does for us even on days when all we can get is a bit of ecstasy, a worn-down and sleazy hymn, but it keeps me going whatever Reverend Ézéchielle says, you've got to know how to get by with what the Creator has given you and no complaining, a hymn to all of creation, Petites Cendres said to the man in the straw hat, that which the Lord made is good and we are all children of his kingdom, he repeated the words of Reverend Ézéchielle's sermons and draw strength and respite from them, Timo was in for a long hard time he thought, all this noise and the balloons of every colour out on the terrace, you just had to feel like dancing and having fun till nightfall with all these boys and men in a sensual stupor, where the hell's that Sluttie the straw-hat man was asking, where's she got to, ain't even had her drink, if he tells you he's graduating in a couple of years, it's a lie, I picked him up in the street, and there's no way I can get him to go back to school, got to study these days, right, just a little street-whore, that's all, forget him, but I can't said the man, what do you think he asked Petites Cendres, that which the Lord made is good, he said thinking about Sluttie's classic perfection, if only he were Sluttie, I don't know what to say the man replied, I'm a total atheist, believe me, it's better that way, it just makes the Earth even more beautiful, and that's why we're here, to taste every fruit of temptation, there you are he said, no other reason, he mopped his brow beneath the hat, but where the hell is that Sluttie, my flowered dress thought Petites Cendres as he worked his way through the dancers to get it and cool off

under the breeze from the fans while he slipped it on, maybe
the passionate old man with the straw hat in love with Sluttie
was right, who knows, Samuel reviewed the ballet he'd cho-
reographed in a style close to the work of Matthew Bourne,
so convincing a new version of *Swan Lake*, in Samuel's version all the swans were danced by black youths like an urban
drama of street fights between gangs in Chicago or New York,
it was late and Samuel could hear the scratching of wind and
hail on his window, weird he thought, it only hails in December
and it was springtime in New York, tulips and daffodils open
to a lunatic sun all of a sudden, now dead under the hail, and
black swans were dancing with swords and knives, that wasn't
how he first saw it, not like that at all, woken by hail falling
on his window, the swans still seemed to be there fluttering
their wings next to him, and he would be the next victim, yes
he had imagined it so differently, little by little he remembered
the warmth of Veronica's arms around his waist, she'd had to
get up early while he was still asleep, it was a rehearsal morning and he was stunned with sleepiness, the swans would
return, it wasn't a dream, a presage, or a presentiment, just a
dream he'd soon forget, and in a few days he'd be with Mélanie,
his mother, Daniel, Augustino, all of them, for their Christmas
dinner, Chuan and Olivier, their parents' friends, would be
there too, dreaming of walks on the beach, not remembering,
all the better, that's the way it would be, he missed the warmth
of Veronica's body close to him against the cold, and now this
hail outside instead of the wraith-like few days of spring fool-
ing no one with its flimsy display, the family again, air, water,
and ocean, freedom to brave the waves, the dogs, first kiss for
his grandmother opening her arms in the pavilion, Samuel,
my dear, dear Samuel, what a man you've become, quite a
change, a bit intimidating after the little boy I still have in my
mind, remember when you helped Julio at the bar on holiday
evenings, and you scared us all by going up there and diving
straight into the pool, so this is what happens, our children

become unrecognizable to us, and Samuel thought of other mothers who would not recognize their children, in fact not ever see them again, unlike this one who was with them once more at Christmas, sons of workers in Mexico and El Salvador, recently arrived here and working on the harvest, while Samuel's social standing protected him better, gave him the exclusive right to return home alive and not as a picture in uniform pored over on the red tablecloth by an impoverished Mexican family of believers, and poring over them the picture of Christ and His bleeding heart, halo and hair amplifying one another's golden lustre among the balloons and flags, nothing more known about Josué than this ceremony of the missing, philosophy, that's what he was going to study, play the saxophone, fall, just fall, Bible in hand, that was all, said his mother, he'd long looked for a spiritual direction to his life, dead now under enemy fire, why had he so begged his parents to let him go, and why had they let him, remember the tattoo under his right arm: goodbye don't wait for me, honoured son, his tomb zealously watched by an honour guard and borne by trumpets to his grave, his father laments, what is all that morbid symphony when you have nothing left, just a framed photo, so far away it was in the Afghan mountains, we shouldn't ever ever have, you know what he liked most, comics and cartoons, when he was a kid we never heard him laugh so much, it rang all through the house, our unlucky lieutenant, our son, he wanted nothing more than to be a hero, Bible in hand amid the explosions, one mine he didn't see and where is he now our hero, life ebbed and flowed like that, Samuel was not a face immobilized in a frame, living, breathing, there to embrace his mother and grandmother, brothers and sister, just one of those normal exchanges, his exclusive right by nature, hail mixed with snow beating against the window, the caricatured portrait of Jesus above Josué's head in his parents' house, why him and not Samuel, and what would Mélanie have done if he'd been her fate, tears

running down a face intact, even feeling the sudden sensation
of being wounded like Josué and a river of so many others
like him, in their pools of blood, Samuel opened the door,
went down into the street, one had to live life even more for
those who couldn't any more, would he always suffer like this
for the extra days he was allotted over those who had none,
dance and art were his to soothe his wounds, consolation, no
more than that, not reparation for the perverse manoeuvres
of men, maybe the elfin Nijinsky had triumphed over the evil
of his time, putting on his scenic disguise with all the languor
and lethargy covering the animality, fleeing with leaps like
flight, whether a tiger, a snake, or a bird, flight far from this
world and this theatre, for here below there were only viola-
tions and dishonesty, he knew that, all around greedy expectations, be he the flying moujik as he held on to a flying
ladder where birds perched, his mysticism, the voice of God
he believed he heard calling him to mount ever higher, to
etherealize himself still more, some sort of disequilibrium of
body or spirit thrusting outward with that frail body, the shipwrecked soul, a flight as material as it was transparent towards
the azure he'd discovered, transfixed, as though passing through
a hole in the sun, when suddenly it was over, he fell offstage
like a block, the miracle of a few seconds had so weakened
him that his socks were stained with sweat, not getting up
again, he was suddenly transformed into that poor compacted
creature, brought to ground, pale under the makeup, almost
a child on the point of crying, the art and the dance belonged
to him, thought Samuel, Mère felt a sharp pang at Caroline's
absence, for to her alone had she confided her disquiet about
ageing and death, she could not have decently done so with
Daniel or Mélanie who were still quite young, Suzanne though
showed an imperturbable serenity and talked about a stay in
Switzerland she would go for with Adrien and from which he
would return alone, did they even realize her leukemia was
fatal, why be afraid of physical decline, the ravages of the

body when this wife of a great poet and critic was still radiant and brilliant, perhaps there was a certain cowardice in denying how fleeting life was, come let's talk about it Caroline said in a dream in which she invited Mère to follow her into a monastic room, you see, I have a garden too, a winter garden, no vegetables or anything like that, I couldn't, it was something my adored Harriet, Miss Désirée loved doing, dear Harriet, Caroline kissed Mère, and though dignified she was as coquettish as ever, in a dark dress, don't resist Suzanne's wish she said, like me she's always been very free, and to consent to being free you must also consent to being lost when the moment comes for dignity to collapse, Mère listened to Caroline and suppressed the trembling of her right hand, you do understand what I mean dear friend, quite wise from here on, something of an omnipresent wisdom Mère thought, and how do you deal with the long slow procession of hours she asked, just like you, I go out to my garden Caroline replied, I might see what I don't wish to, the gazelles I've shot in the flanks at point-blank from my husband's convertible in the desert, and here are my antelopes in the savannas of Africa, capable of impaling my chest with their arching horns, but instead they just circle me at a fast gallop, and I cannot stop them, no reproaches in their liquid brown eyes, no, just a sweet gravity that strikes me like an arrow, now when I was free what was it I did, where did all my actions lead me, all these gaping wounds in the creatures I loved, you know we are what we wound with a thousand blows and a thousand spears, this is my conviction and I don't repent of it, here in this winter garden my dear, dear friend, and in the evening when I think I'm alone under a sky full of stars, the trained falcons I once saw with my husband ready to attack the buzzard, they're after me, just as the falconers of old trained them to hunt their prey, please oh please Esther, you must let Suzanne go, this will be their last honeymoon, such a golden couple, but how will their daughters and sons take this, asked

Mère, don't think about them Caroline answered, the antelopes on the African plain, ah! that round afflicts me, the one
shot taken from my convertible after standing for so long, it
can't be undone, yes, let Suzanne go to the winter garden, I
beg you, the trembling of her right hand woke Mère, and
Caroline's words disturbed her still, as she thought Caroline's
winter garden was also the garden of numbing and sleepiness,
though Caroline seemed so very alert and attentive to details
that wouldn't have impressed her alive, such as the trembling
in Mère's right hand which she missed through distraction or
possibly apathy for other people's pain, her combative energy
was matched by her ability to quell the heart so often dormant
in her, in times when action was her life and commandment,
when she was entirely taken up with her role as woman-
leader capable in so many areas, don't believe, my dear friend,
that a woman of Suzanne's grandeur will bow before the ill-
ness eating away at her, oh no, out of the question, that acute
proliferation of white globules in her marrow is just the beginning of the invasion, believe me, but she'll know how to stop
it, you'll see, and one day many countries will recognize it as
the only genuine right we each have — the right to leave this
Earth, it is a personal decision, I know Suzanne well, she has
always been a groundbreaker, the garden of sleep thought
Mère, no this was surely not the way to describe what she had
seen in her dream with Caroline as her guide, what troubled
her most was the amazing plan Suzanne had so joyously con-
cocted, this stay in Switzerland from which Adrien, the "poet
of certitudes" as Daniel dubbed him after being offended so
often by the venerated critic, would return by himself, a wid-
ower, how irreducible and implacable could one be towards
oneself, Mère thought, then she remembered Franz and his
child-to-be, like his music-to-be, his tireless life of pleasure,
the operas he'd compose or direct in Germany this autumn,
he said, whose activities, family life, and loves could be reconciled only with his music, a man born without borders,

never needing to get his breath, likely happy in this chaotic freedom that suited him so well and added to his voluminous experience, this surely must be why Suzanne's ideas about life and death scandalized him so much, dwelling in the zone of dissatisfaction at being the national poet's wife, which must be hard to grasp, he told, from the age of thirty Suzanne had written a number of books, then suddenly, a very fulfilled woman, they whispered, she never wrote another line, we're all guilty of not having understood this hiatus, blinded by the golden couple and their brilliant success, who exactly was the Suzanne in Suzanne-Adrien during that silent period, how did she live, did we even know, but then we all knew so little about the mystery of any of us, said Franz, Suzanne's joyous-ness had deluded them all Mère reflected, these continuing dreams of Caroline, her distant reaching out, surely they were proof that the dead are always with us, for no dream was without its reasons, a single dream being perceptible and understandable everywhere, the life of those we love inhabit-ing us, growing inside us even when we think them gone, art and dance, thought Samuel as he unrolled his woollen collar against the cold and hail in the streets of New York, Nijinsky, the sylph struck down perhaps had a foreboding when he danced Petrushka in *Le Spectre de la Rose* and fell into reli-gious ecstasy, his enduring power to fly from a scene which then disappeared with him, forgotten in those miserable asy-lums, like Mozart in a common grave, did he sense the com-ing of this lost choreographer who now danced only for the angels, to what destiny was the world steering itself, Samuel's world, a world without fairy magic where a dancer could not but dance the onrush of melting glaciers, emptying rivers and oceans, the drying up of Asia, huge shortages on overheated and burning continents, children crying as polar bears drowned under shattered, ragged icebergs, the hybrid dance of his Petrushka in *Le Spectre de la Rose*, did he have a premonition of where Samuel was to find himself, an era set against life and survival, a planet destroyed, an eternity stretching like an ocean, or was he consumed by glory, the summer of thunder to which he would succumb, what purpose this glory that would drag him down later on, or was he like Samuel, delivering himself up to the counted hours of us all, delivered up also to the sentimental attachments, dancing on a shredded map of the world ripped by revolution and war, what did his hallucinating brain already envision so quickly to be compromised, in the bouncing of the bus Tigli put one hand on Angelina's belly, better not be in too much of a hurry to be born, no, I mean what are we going to do with him here in these mountains, okay, calm down, you too, Angelina, so this boy from Barcelona broke your heart, you know, sometimes I think men just shouldn't be allowed to live, I'm afraid they hurt women, and it's almost like that's all they're here for, God forgive them, I'm going to go there and join him, murmured Angelina, really, he's waiting for me and the child, oh! he's jiggling and moving, what am I going to do Tigli, you're the one that's moving too much, now you've gone and got the kid all upset, mind you these bumps aren't helping, cursed be the guy who dumped a girl like you and left you so sad, Angelina, oh we're getting married, she repeated, as soon as I take the baby there, want some almond cookies and ice cream, Angelina, Tigli asked again, his eye glinting under the felt hat like a satyr getting ready for the celebrations in town, I'm gonna dance the salsa till dawn, unless you make me a fireman-midwife, Angelina, and wreck my three-day holiday, three days, that's all, nothing gets done in Guatemala if I don't tend to it, really, I mean, a fireman's a jack-of-all-trades, did you know that, Angelina, yeah well! Let me tell you, they need men like me, especially with all these punks around here, take your S.O.B. for example, it's a crying shame, and I hope your kid's going to be better than his old man, sometimes crap just produces more crap, they're not even men, he's moving, can you feel him moving Tigli, hell no, he's just trembling a little bit, that's nothing, you're not going to tell me I've got to give up my three days' holiday now, are you Angelina, no, no, you've got to hold him in, that's all, I'm gonna slosh back those margaritas, hey, either you're on vacation or you aren't, wow, look at those two wild horses galloping down the hill, they're not even looking one way or the other, where are they going like that with no riders, hey, and a donkey all by himself at the side of the road, wow, we've got the whole of creation on the march here Angelina, all by itself without anyone telling it what to do, can you imagine how it will be, one kid more, one horse more, one donkey more, all of you on the march with no one to tell you what to do or where to go, alone at night, hungry and thirsty, have you thought about that Angelina, the whole of creation on the march with nowhere to beg a crust of bread or a cup of water, no oats, no corn, I get dizzy just thinking about it, I'd better just stick to the salsa, oh for a time when I don't have to deliver babies or put out fires, fires are no fun either you know, all that smoke in your lungs, gaaak, oh if only you knew, Angelina, yep, I do it all, a well-rounded man, that's me, but it isn't always fun, you know, nope, see what happens to me being around you Angelina, but I've got no choice, have I, just gotta do it, in a perpetuity beyond the serene profile of Asoka, Ari saw in a lightning-flash a horse galloping alongside the bus, its mane flared to the calcinating sun, the loaded donkey labouring as well, many babies playing in the grass in front of corrugated metal huts, where, all of them, where are they going, he thought, how he'd love to have the fast-growing Lou here on his lap, she'd already have changed when he got back, with her lashes curved towards her cheek, now gangly, he'd probably still carry her as though she were smaller when they came out of restaurants, cafés, and expositions, all the places he took her to where she fell asleep at the end, or even in the middle of a meal after running on the beach all out of breath, restaurants, cafés, her weight now would be stretched out but no

less, surely as big as Ingrid by now, as though the stem, growing too fast, had of itself become a little of its mother and
taken on some of the seductive power over him, already a
little feminine, victorious over him, lording it over him, what
did he care, she was his flower, his treasure, and an artistic
extension with the added subtlety he didn't have, his sculpture retrospective was coming up after all these years of being
only a father, now steel would have to become less abstract,
the lines more supply elongated, and two of his giant pieces
would be exhibited outside in a flowered courtyard park, a
green space with no sense of confinement, people could just
sit nearby and meditate, the vast spirals under the heavens
whose movements they would translate day and night, *Open
Corridor 1 and 2*, intersections in the greenery, variations on
a single spiral, steel walls that buckled and straightened again
almost without weight or volume, his sculptures always took
him on untrodden ways, suddenly to hold him prisoner like
someone at vertiginous heights, undulating matter, that was
it, like an oriental bronze or Chinese sculpture, if not more
like *Suspended Mural* than *Open Corridor 1 and 2*, a con-
tained aggression as in all forms of art, he thought, at the next
visit he might get an e-mail from Ingrid or a word, a thought
from Lou, some acknowledgement of his love for her, in a few
hours perhaps, her name tacked onto her mother's, she'd won
a medal for reading, just seeing those names on the screen,
disappointed by their greediness, where was Lou, she didn't
like to read Dear Dad, I love you, a mist of inaccessible tenderness, Lou, Ingrid, a conjunction of syllables, no hugs or
kisses from Lou, what had he done for them to write with so
much coldness, he was proud of her medal, he suddenly felt
his little girl was no more, and during the night Alphonso saw
the images of his predecessor's parishioners parade before
him, those who'd complained about the things done to their
daughters and sons, many of them a long time ago, molested
children all, but now the mothers no longer kept quiet, we

are a good Catholic family and look what's been done to us, the betrayals and the affronts, our children raped when we send them to confession or to choir or to communion, nothing is holy for us any more, the Bishop must have known when all he did was send the priest into the countryside, some place quiet and out-of-the-way, both of them keeping quiet about it, the arrogant silence of an ecclesiastical conspiracy, what can a child do faced with this, but we, we won't keep quiet any longer said the mothers, yes, Alphonso saw them in his nightmares, rushing towards him and forming a circle of righteous fury, and what exactly do these corrupt priests say when questioned at their trials, that they haven't done any such thing, and why would they, it's not something that interests them, such contempt from on high began to obsess the mothers, oh, they weren't interested in that sort of thing, penetrating their little girls' vaginas, no, why of course not, and the obscenities these mothers raised before them left them simply disgusted and above all indifferent, the indifference itself was a crime, wasn't it, such impassiveness to their own demonstration of opprobrium, maybe even this very presbytery that was now where Alphonso awoke and prayed every morning, who knows how many victims it had seen abused and mentally tortured, virginities harvested and murdered one after another, he could no longer sleep at all, then in the grey landscape of dawn, he fell to recalling the illegals seeking refuge with him right now, sometimes entire families had nowhere to stay, given his room or the church to live in, and in the knowledge that the housekeeper would be his ally in this, virginities harvested and murdered one after another, all children of my parishioners, and what do they care, they remain unmoved, indifferent when asked about what they've done, old dried-up priests under the sign of Venus, no remorse or even memory of their past acts, Alphonso thought, just indifferent and fetid executioners, Mai went running into her room and took off the skimpy swimsuit, determined to put everything away and leave nothing lying on a chair, for the stern silhouette of Marie-Sylvie against the striped light from the blinds would be saying, I'm not always going to be here to pick up after you, 'fraid not, your hair's wet, so you'd better brush it before you meet your grandmother, here, I've ironed your jean outfit, and put on a clean shirt underneath, not the one with the hearts, the other more serious one, and stand up straight so I can at least comb your hair, you know Vincent's going to be here for Christmas, your dad's going to pick him up at the airport, then he's going to study medicine in a while and go work with Jenny, so soon poor baby, but he's never going to be strong enough, I just won't let him, said Marie-Sylvie de la Toussaint, Mai was afraid she'd be there looking over her shoulder and scolding as always, and will Mum be back soon too, Mai asked, suddenly she wanted her near and would have gladly shut the two of them up together in her room or her parents' or even Augustino's which was so often empty, yes, shut her in so she'd forget about her job so far from home and all her political interests and her devotion to social causes; it would be just like before when Vincent was convalescing in Vermont, a winter of coughs and fevers he'd come through with difficulty, she'd broken her leg skiing with Mélanie, then all of a sudden her mother had been so caring she never left her alone for a moment till her leg was better, the way Mum looked at me, oh how I remember that, even telling the stewardesses on the plane to be careful lifting me, oh when she gets back I'm going to lock all the doors so she'll never go away again, no more Washington, just us together, no Washington, no Marie-Sylvie de la Toussaint either, I hid my cigarettes in a metal box, but where is it, I've got to smoke now, because later I won't be able to. Grandmother notices everything, maybe she even saw us in the Mercedes, the smell, oh yes the smell, I'll say it's a perfume that just won't go away, we were in each other's arms, no I'm sure she didn't see us, I've got to have a cigarette, just a taste in my mouth, then I'll butt it out and nobody will see a thing, that's it, I'll lock her in and tie her to my bed so she'll never go away, even if she did see us, she'd never say anything, ah the cigarettes are there, I'll hide the box under the bed, Marie-Sylvie will never look there, she doesn't like my cats, in fact she doesn't like anything that's mine, one smoke and I'll be more relaxed for Grandmother, and nothing will show, I'll say, Mélanie, Mum, you're not going anywhere any more, I've got you prisoner, Dad says each one of us has a special destiny, a special law for each life, even an abandoned cat like Lola found by a homeless person in his sleeping bag in Las Vegas has a destiny and a life-law that's just his, and the homeless man adopted her just like you adopted me, Mum, I mean I was born to you but you adopted me anyway, just like the kitten Lola snuggled in with the fleas in the filthy sleeping bag, Mum took me along with her, that's the individual destiny Dad meant, and so Mum said to the stewardesses, her leg is broken, be careful when you lift her, she's my daughter, you wonder what we're doing on this planet even if we each have a different fate, invisible stars in the sky at night, ants working under a pile of stones, Lola in a sleeping bag in Las Vegas, and Dad seems quite sure of that, whoa, just a toke and I'm stoned already, ummm, Marie-Sylvie said shoes, the white ones with straps, not the sandy sandals slimy with sea-water, let's see, I can borrow Vincent's iPod, he won't mind if I don't ask, why do you have to explain everything to people all the time, he won't notice anyway, he's got tennis and Dad said he had to dress up too, so maybe Dad's right about the invisible night stars when it's black out with no moon (for the ants and the cat that had a long life and a home), everyone does contain their own destiny, at least a beginning and an end, a higher law he said, a future all predestined for us, nothing to do with Mum or Dad or us, Marie-Sylvie de la Toussaint would still be out there on her raft but with a fate far beyond her home shores, and her destiny was called Vincent, and it bought her to us like a magnet or the sun, she'll tell me that something smells bad of course, what is that, smells like smoke, so you're smoking now, and who with, why, your mother told you not to speak to strangers, who are these grownups you hang around with, there's always at least one or two of them, I'm telling you you're what they call a troubled youth, I'm going to have to talk to your parents about it, and I'm not having any of that cannabis in this house either, God knows what else, and your mother can take you to see the psychologist all she wants, you are what I said, I'll tell him just what Dad said, I am the custodian of my special destiny every bit as much as Lola is, the big girl on the beach who was supposed to get married, who said do you want to come with us sweetie, free as the air and even the pigs can't chase us away, they got William and David with their tricky business stuff yesterday, but they'll never get me and the others, c'mon Mai, in her dreams she remembered following them away from the beach, and it was night when she tried to find her father's garage, but he wasn't there any more, the car closed up all by itself seemed like a hearse, and the young people on the beach had forgotten their pup, and it ran hungrily along behind her and ran a way off whenever she tried to grab him, where was Dad anyway, just don't think about those dreams where she'd keep on seeing the dog on the edge of her consciousness, she was going to have to get dressed up for supper with her grandmother tonight, dreams that really made you feel bad like that were better off not being thought about, especially the dog not getting fed tonight or even tomorrow, no, forget about it. And Petites Cendres wondered where Timo could be, there were swamps and snakes down there and pools where the alligators barely broke the surface and submerged again, unscrupulous vigilantes watching for poachers like Timo gun in hand, and well, one snap of those jaws and a twirl under the boats, just a mouthful and it was all over, where was his head anyway with the fog of his cocaine addiction, nerve cells overloaded with chemical treasure seeing the water so ample and beautiful under a cobalt sky, the world really was melodious and fine, the spasms of pain were gone now, and the empty hollow of want Petites Cendres felt, still unable to find a john, maybe there just wouldn't be one tonight, after a hundred days you can't help but need it and hear your brain cells scream for it and lie low and compulsively wait for it, the reward, yes, it would need to be a grave in Paris with fresh flowers every day like Jim Morrison, tumbling onto a toilet seat in a nightclub wasn't sordid because the flowers would just keep coming every day, lilies for all the gods in the sanctuary, Kurt Cobain, Jim Morrison, and more, all with haloes of stars elevated to sacred idols by acid and art, prayed to and venerated as though singled out by fire from heaven, the unknown flower-bearer comes with lilies for you every day, just like Jesus in the Community Church, and now in their healing sleep beneath all the flowers and homages, they want nothing more, nor miss what they craved, no need when they're heroes, right, heroes for nothing, internally combusted, heroes to Petites Cendres: Jim Morrison, Kurt Cobain, Samuel felt the crowd swelling and flowing around him more and more, forgetting that today was the demonstration, a day of voiceless cries and revolt like a rising black tide of men and women, some with empty baby carriages, boots, everywhere boots, mud-caked laces, damp soles, they might just have been worn, others with carts all filled with boots, pairs and odd ones, all worn and torn, mismatched, leather worn away and soft, laces dangling, and the boots seeming to move with the tearful men and women, yet tears invisible as though strapped inside their clothes with cold, these women marching, bent double under the weight of all those feet no longer shod but seemingly there still, no one speaking, not a word, a black wave, shoes marching as if on their own, footless, bodiless, an endless cohort of misery, disabused to silence, mute in saturation, sometimes a stop with roses thrown, a colourless flag waved, nothing but leftovers of the day's bouquets, thought Samuel, and when would it be over, and how would he dance tonight with frozen hands and feet, and if this was a foretaste of spring in the winter, why were the sun's rays so sickly amid the long shadows of this afternoon in anger where none dared speak, not even what they felt, it must have been this row of boots from the trenches that imposed such funereal respect, such austere wordless tenderness, there was art and dance Samuel thought, he'd have to run for the subway, firmly melt a way through this crowded silence of resignation or desolation, baby carriages with no babies, carts without men, just the imprint of their feet in these boots and the pale stain of their blood on the soles would be art and dance he thought, yes, Tigli repeated, I've got to deal with this, you're really telling me Angelina you're about to propel this new creature into this whole mess we're in, okay, okay, just relax and don't tighten up like that, you've got to relax and concentrate on that, oh boy, what am I going to do, usually I get the head free then the shoulders, I'd really like to spare you any pain, honestly, how about I tell you a story, okay, here's one that'll relax you, this birthing business isn't as much fun as they say it is, I'm gonna go to the chapel in San Andrés Itzapa, light a candle and pray before the altar for you and your baby, Angelina, from my village you can see the volcanoes all reddish under the clouds, I'll go right up to the Madonna and Child and place orchids and orange bougainvilleas in front of them, my heart pounds when I see those mountains again, but you know they're actually here all around us, Antigua my open valley, three volcanoes, forests that enthrall me, these busloads of tourist invaders, what are they going to do to you, bring the city's overpopulation and pollution, the shantytowns' poverty, our sky's still blue and the air is pure, without our majestic jungles and forests, with their helicopters flying over our ravines and bean or coffee plantations, without our past, what have we got, TV towers and ugly buildings, without our seabirds and the orchids in our gardens, our iridescent butterflies and medicinal plants, and our sea serpent, what if they destroy that, the spearhead killer, whatever will we have left, tell me Angelina, so their search for paradise will destroy our Indian huts and the people in them on the way, the grottoes in the wildest parts of the mountains, will they finally really be emptied, no more murmuring of water or parrot calls, just the noise from machines and power generators, no more chapel of San Andrés Itzapa burned along with our huts and our vegetation, and our freedom from agony, oh yes, how my heart leaps when I see these mountains again, and my mother, that woman who does laundry alone on rocks and against trees in the immense rainforest surrounded by plaintive birdsong, beating it against rocks, proud and dignified, with a skinny dog sniffing the moss-covered ground beside her, she gave me life same as you'll do Angelina, for better or worse, yeah well, now I can feel him move too, he's fidgeting in there Angelina, what are you going to do with him if you haven't got a man, no father for him and us in the middle of all this turbulence and chaos, she paled as she listened to him, she said suddenly lost and listless, no it's not true, my child does have a daddy and he's waiting for us in Spain, oh he is, and he loves us and he's waiting for us in Barcelona, and that's where we'll go, the baby and me, I've got my passport and I'm all ready, ah! he's pushing every which way trying to come, what am I going to do Tigli, what, sing to him, Tigli, that's the only thing that works, sleep, sleep, she sang low while Tigli stroked her to soothe the pain, first her head, then her shoulders, I'm a birthing pro, you know that, right, as he leaned towards the window and saw a second horse galloping alone, frenzied in the heat, foaming at the nostrils, won't be long before there's another little one he said, I'll pray for you in the holy chapel, Angelina, and I'll light a candle for the Madonna and Child to watch over you, soon I'm going to do some salsa, and women will send me a river of kisses, the dizziness of dancing till

dawn and right into the next day and the day after or until my
friends drag me home drunk with them, still laughing, when
they drag me all the way upstairs with my feet trailing along,
then I'll laugh some more, I mean you've got to laugh Angelina,
why come into the world and never stop crying, tell me that,
Olivier wondered who still remembered 1964 and what they
called Freedom Summer, ours to make our demands heard,
Fannie Lee Chaney remembered a long time, that summer the
Ku Klux Klan killed her son and she had to flee the county
because of death threats, that summer when the Mississippi
turned into a river of burning coals, Chaney and two of his
rebel friends killed, oh his mother remembered, and in the
chapel the prayers for him were joined by prayers for her as
well, later on when she was buried with him after fighting
long and hard for him and for justice and for the murderers
to be put on trial, as they were so much later, what did it mean
forty years later, their justice was never our justice, 1964,
Freedom Summer, I knew those kids who were killed, Chaney,
all of them, thought Olivier, we all fought together with the
same fierceness, and of the few who survived that summer
was the murderer, he alone spared and scot-free, he and all
of them went on hunting Blacks for a long time after that, and
the idea haunted Olivier, this was the article he was working
on this week, forgetting nothing of the summer of 1964, Fanny
Lee Chaney's son, friends assassinated, nothing forgotten, and
short sleepless nights, freighted down with nightmares heavy
on his spirit, when Lazaro went home to his sleeping wife
and son, yelling wildly arise, arise, eye for eye, tooth for tooth,
arise, you're going to pay now, Chuan with her cool hand on
Olivier's forehead said, one of your nightmares again, what is
it this time poor darling, hear that, it sounds like the same
motorcycle again, Olivier said, I don't hear anything she
replied, go back to sleep now dear, I've finally got my menu
planned for Christmas dinner, good night Olivier, they're just
dreams, that Lazaro, I don't think you should let him hang

around here, have you seen the hate on that man's face when he looks at us, I never noticed anything, Chuan said, and now you really must go to sleep, Olivier, we'll talk about it tomorrow, good night Olivier, forget nothing of 1964, he thought, Ari bounced around on the bus and dreamt of his home and his daughter, then all of a sudden it seemed as peaceful as an Edward Hopper painting, at this distance probably just as impersonal too as those houses on the New England coast he'd depicted, equally impenetrable, their inhabitants equally anonymous, whether inside or out, sitting on their high balconies or going about their daily activities like reading a newspaper in the living room or tinkling on the piano keys, secret defences that protected their intimacy, as though Lou herself and her mother were in one of these houses, shut away forever in secrecy, faces turned inward on a secret that obsessed the painter always, the icy light and the ennui of life was simply that melancholic to experience sometimes, casting its gloom over everything, perhaps the aura of mystery here seemed to root all of life to the spot beyond anything Ari could comprehend, still he felt certain that despite all appearances, the painter was by no means detached, the essence of his emotion being to describe country houses or city rooms peopled by passive and unflappable beings in reflected lamplight under half-open blinds, as pale profiles inclined towards a book or magazine, this stifling feeling of restraint emerged from the contrasting white of the walls against a violet sky, in the rigorous interiors it might come from the blinding splash of a man's shirt stained by a contrasting tie or the slash of a streak in his hair, this paralyzing mystery was the feeling behind the paintings, stamped with the numbness of repeated gestures, banality masking the passage of time, from our first breath to our last, had Asoka told Ari with such certitude that being born in human shape was the highest of honours, for thus it was expected we would know how to make the best use of this gift, dubious though our conduct really was, the

inhabitants of these houses were then every bit as guilty as
Ari, the worst behaviour, under cover of reading a paper or
playing scales on a piano, each in his own way and in pro-
found isolation was capable of anything, often more in the
thought than the act, no, he thought, if being born human as
Ari was now was a quality, there was no guarantee we'd be
honourable, and many would be the regressions to lower forms
in our future lives, invertebrates of all sorts, even the scummy
membranes of still other lives awaited us, Asoka alone might
deserve the term honourable human, Ari reflected under the
morose silence in Hopper's paintings, the docility of North
American comfort, the rectitude of his landscapes, his myriad
nameless beings ceaselessly harried by their existence, unsta-
ble, dissatisfied, cocooned in an apparently benevolent tran-
quility, each labouring under the weight of the struggle, yet
out of touch with others in his own private round of shadow
and shouting light, whether chilly morning half-light like a
winter moon multiplying in the shadows, Lou and her mother
so far away from him wandered through this countryside with
them, green trees and vast spaces where the painter had
shown what he believed he saw and felt, as he'd used to do,
Ari got up and drew in a single stroke Ingrid sitting on the
edge of the bed and showing him a back as solitary as Hopper's
women in their Brooklyn bedrooms at dawn, putting a stock-
ing back on, motionless as statues perhaps, the solitude
unconquerable he thought, Vincent said the important thing
was to have good models, but I think he's wrong thought Mai,
his models are all the sports heroes he has on his wall, why
have models when you know yourself what you want, Vincent
swam for long periods, but he'd never swim or ski as far as
them, he's no immortal like them, the only thing that gets
them is accidents, they don't just die, that's what he doesn't
understand, he's mortal the way his skiers and swimmers and
mountain-climbers aren't, they can do it all, but not him,
Marie-Sylvie is always looking out for him, that's why he never

does more than he's able, she just won't let him go that far, and she's there with him in his thoughts even when he's far away writing his college essays and says how good Dad is to him, imagining he's with a guide on the ice-faces of Chamonix, just like Everest, breathing that uncorrupted air and the guide is pointing his pole and saying, come on, just a little higher, you'll breathe even better up there, and it's so beautiful, geometric even, up and up Vincent goes along the snowy trails, a single rope holding them together, behind his hood and his glasses he knows that up there you cease being mortal, the glazed rocks and ice sheets are translucent, one of the climbers on his wall, handsome and blond, was swept away by a wave as he sat on a rock, just one of those accidents, and now here he is forever scaling the wall in Vincent's room, the Irish coast, any rocky place, an avalanche or a wave and you are gone, not even a pointed cap or a cape to be found, immortal he isn't going to need them any more, not like the rest of us, Vincent and me, it's about not being afraid, that's all, Vincent repeated what his idol had said in Ireland and then disappeared just like anyone going to another place, carried by a wave licking you from the rocks while you wait to go higher, the praise Vincent lavishes on his father in his essays comes from the sense of alarm Dad's seminars and radio and TV appearances raise in all of us, alarm for the disappearing seas and oceans, for the animals and the Coral Coast, the Pacific Ocean and all of them from Thailand to Australia, the cod, both types of salmon, species disappearing in South Korea and Japan, even the sharks unable to produce anything but soup and other delicacies, Vincent wants to be a doctor and biologist, he says, but Marie-Sylvie, his old watchdog, says he can't, his health won't let him, in a quarter-century there won't be anything left to fish Dad says, then someone tells him he's an alarmist, worse yet a poet, and he should zip it because he doesn't know what he's talking about because he's no scientist, but Dad goes on describing the sharks and whales

wounded with harpoons and arrows, crashing to the ocean
floor, we're just getting started Dad says, it's our future he's
thinking about and we're lucky to have one Vincent says, lots
of Chinese won't have one at all, this isn't happening on the
moon, Dad says, but it seems like it when people live in veg-
etable cellars on cold camp cots with just a wooden ladder to
a hole in the ceiling that bathes them in a grey light that seems
to come from another planet, a beggar-child with skeletal,
twisted legs, unable to get up off the wheeled plank he uses
as a stretcher, waits with his tin cup on the sidewalk for hand-
outs that don't come, they say the Chinese economy's doing
better, they say things are getting better all over, but not for
those living in moon craters or sub-basements without air or
water or bread, Vincent's not into video games, he just wants
to be a doctor like Jenny in Doctors Without Borders, she's in
China right now, he says, and she writes to Dad to say, if they
have no future, then neither do we, and the same storms will
reach us too, so we have to have models Vincent says, people
ready to deal with anything, immortals like the sportsmen and
climbers on his wall, just because they die in accidents or falls,
that doesn't mean it's all over, for they're always there, what
an idea to go sit on a rock like that and just wait for the roaring waves to calm down on that bleak Irish coast, how naive
to think it would just wash around them, well they just don't
know fear the way we do was Vincent's reply, and that's why
they'll always escape in a way, in faith not in fear, it isn't way
off on some lunar landscape Dad says, but right here in front
of us, okay, now to get dressed for supper, I'll check with my
grandmother who's still able to play and who isn't, the stooped
ones like Uncle Isaac or Grandpa Joseph are to old to play
violin at Christmas any more, Dad says we should venerate
all these old people for their stories and their history, like
Great-Uncle Isaac and Great-Uncle Samuel, he's always talking about who got shot in Poland with all the rabbis, but I
don't want to listen to him, and all I see around the table at

Christmas are old people, I'm always afraid their hair will fall out and their teeth will turn black so one day I won't even recognize them, it makes me think of Caroline, the lovely old lady we don't see any more, not immortal either says Vincent, but she was still young the day she lost her bag, and it was so awful to think the dead could suddenly not have anything to say, drop out of sight, or if not they act as though they don't see us, somehow shunted off to the side on parallel tracks, Caroline, whom Mère called sometimes, went off on her own road, a farm with cows and horses in the field, Mère never knew what caused a city-dweller like that to leave her and go off to the country where she seemed utterly at ease as always under her wide cotton hat, her eyes hidden by it, this seemed a voluntary retreat to Mère, a few nights earlier she had been so warm and welcoming, and embraced Mère as such a dear friend, saying dear Esther, at last here you are, her trip to this limbo might be a short one, but why did it have to come at the same time as Suzanne's departure for Switzerland . . . for good, anesthetized into sleep, now what was it called, oh how Mère hated the word, that irreversible definition, that self-immolation, when Suzanne had never before been predisposed to it, the thing Mère refused to say out loud, killing oneself, that wasn't Suzanne at all, Suzanne, in love with her husband, Suzanne the writer, Suzanne of imperturbable serenity, that wasn't her at all, in any case they'd make her drop the idea once she got there, all kinds of effective treatments for leukemia were available now, even the most virulent and aggressive, as she said, Suzanne, I don't want reasonable, Suzanne said, I am a reasonable woman she laughed, nonchalantly sipping cocktails with friends, who would have thought you'd torment my heart like this, taking both hands in hers, Mère wanted to say, why are you doing this — think of your friends and your children, all of us who love you and dearest Adrien, without you, but no, Mère said none of this, unable even to open her lips, not to speak or scream, as though in the most cavernous dream, knowing only that Suzanne, like Caroline, was taking a wrong turn into a desolate landscape, another inevitability she could do nothing about, this year she was comforted that her sons would be there at Chuan and Olivier's for Christmas dinner, for them to come at the same time of a common accord might mean they were afraid their mother was declining, had Mélanie passed on what should not be said about her trembling right hand or some other indisposition, Suzanne was right to avoid all this shame, if one has known dignity in happiness, why give it up, it was most disturbing and perverse that the living or the dead could plant in us this terror of being monitored down to the least of our hiding-places, you have to admire Franz's way of living only for the moment, the moment of life, of grace, look, he said, at how the works of Brahms and Beethoven transform the acceptance of life's end into grandiose consent to the angel's victory over us and the last veiled smile with which he banishes our breath, that indeed is what he said to Mère as they walked side by side down the garden path filled with deep perfume after the rains, isn't it? An eye for an eye thought Lazaro amid the dry stuttering of his motorcycle, I've seen my mother Caridad, merchant and woman without honour, selling her woven cloth, her rugs and tablecloths to Jermaine's mother, her fingers touched those threads interwoven with gold and silk, red-painted fingers, I saw the whole thing, heard her wonder at my mother's work, Caridad has renounced us for them, and they talk about getting together for Christmas all of them, the links of friendship between them and my mother's subservience, and now my mother's crying, saying she hasn't seen her son for so long, he left on a boat and never returned, and now this woman, Chuan, the mother of Jermaine, is consoling her, oh how sorry I am for your anguish, and they just say whatever they want, all of it lies, violence — sectarian or not — and bombardment coming at us from every direction, so easy to get into a house when the garage door's left open, two young thugs did just that, I'm no thug though, I hate them for being without religion, they raped and strangled the girls before taking off with the money, no matter, they were girls from private schools, despicable and without religion, vegetarian as well, molested by disgusting men, while ours are held indefinitely behind barbed wire in the beating sun, no chance of a trial, I wonder why they never remember to close that garage door, and so it was the armed man who lived day and night with his munitions, raging and howling when he couldn't be heard, I wouldn't be invited to their table, nor my apostate mother, the painted nails, the threads woven together, an image that drives me mad, we haven't seen Lazaro for months, I am so sorry; my son Jermaine will only be with us a few days, and what a blessed confusion it all will be, the faithless thugs tied the girls to their beds, and it was all so easy after that, fit for the scaffold and nothing else, degenerate perverts, violence like ours now must be pure, for holy is our anger, and he who said we are multiplying everywhere in profusion will be punished, for Allah alone is master of the world, and whoever mocks him will be crushed, my mother deserves only to be stoned for abandoning my father's faith, yes, see, the garage door is open, I can hear the kid's music, and they don't know I'm here, can't even hear me shouting, no echo, nothing, they're born deaf to us, everything we are or I am makes no impression on them at all. I never know what's going to happen, thought Mai, that's why I want to keep Mum with me always, she could be attacked like those journalists who go to countries at war and never come back, Olivier, my parents' friend, says she's not nearly careful enough, women activists never think something terrible could happen to them, like that Afghan journalist sleeping beside her twenty-month-old son, they came in and killed her but left her children alive, a few days before that another journalist, guilty of what exactly, except believing in freedom of speech and the press in times of terror, and Olivier says it too, they've got closer to heads of state and tried to make the incomprehensible language of power clearer and easier to understand, and they've been killed for it, interviewing Yassar Arafat, Golda Meir, and Ayatollah Khomeini from a moderate viewpoint, modestly sharing what they knew, always on the lookout for the transparency and authenticity that move the humble more than the powerful, then, all of a sudden neither seen nor heard from, erased, walled up, sleeping next to her infant son, unscrupulous killers, disappearing one by one, Olivier says, and for so many women, says Mum, just being born a woman is a curse in itself, oh at Christmas, I'll have them all near me, brothers, uncles, and Mum too, sometimes she's tired and doesn't even look at me or she's preoccupied with Vincent, but still she's there, and all I have to do is break my leg again and then she'll love me more, saying to the air stewardesses, be careful, please lift her gently, she's my daughter, I'm too lucky, that's what Marie-Sylvie de la Toussaint says, with parents like these, it's not right to have everything, she says when I'm too happy that I cause her suffering, when I run along the beach or laugh with my friends or run crazy with my dogs, I pour sadness on her head she says, she can't love me the way Mum does because I'm not hers, she says when she thinks no one hears, never mind the colour of her skin, Vincent is her son, sometimes when she hugs him with his frail head on her breast, she moans the words, oh my child, just you, yes darling, oh yes, I hear those words when Mum's not home, and what I want to say is your meanness pours sadness on my head too, and I think of the bobbing and broken raft out on the ocean from Haiti, all those drowned and Marie-Sylvie grabbing hold of the side in fear and nausea when she swallowed salt water, and I feel shame for us both, that we know one another, what have I done to deserve her hatred except to be Mum and Dad's daughter born in a place that isn't miserable, Mum says they'll explain it to me later, actually there are very few people on this Earth who do live a decent life, and I tell myself they're my good fortune and my happiness in this garden with papayas, animals lying around on the steps or in my lap or in the trees, my lizards, my white butterflies, but girls always have to be rebellious Mum says, not docile before the fate of Marie-Sylvie on the broken-down raft, and her fingers would have been cut off to keep her out of the men's boat, the eighteenth century called itself egalitarian, but women all knew it wasn't true, and the lower classes even more so being below them, the air of independence was breathed by whom exactly, a few maybe, girls of my age and even younger worked in factories and textile plants like Lowell from dawn to night on their looms, supervised by men with whips and all was well under the first democratic government, young country-girls from all over New England, revolting against servitude to their fathers and brothers at home, fled to these shops and the day-and-night communal living that prevented them from fleeing again, but in the dormitories and refectories, pretending to pray, they began a rebellion that would soon be heard rumbling louder and louder till the girls staged their first strike at the the factories in Lowell, so much noise that all anyone could hear was the silence of the looms, they were paid and then fled to freedom, strange the glimmer of money, a handful of dollars or cents for the first time ever, nevertheless paid for their servitude to the machines in the stinking shops, they couldn't believe they had this right, even if they couldn't vote with the men, pushed aside and humiliated, they had counted their miserable pennies in their cracked and crumbling homes, and now girls their age do the same thing in Indian cotton mills, destroying their eyes and hearts at the task, the smallest boys and girls dyeing cotton in sulphurous basins and swamps of ammonia and detergent that leave their feet chapped with open sores, that is the indecency in which nearly all live, even children, Mum says, not us though, and I'm ashamed if what Mum says is true, art and dance will always be there, thought

Samuel as the demonstrators pressed around him with their ever-present boots, and one of them suddenly cried out, what will our children say tomorrow, how will we explain what we have done, and Samuel felt the silence around him melt over them like lead, a few steps more and there was one of the towers again, reality or illusion, just as Daniel Libeskind, the Polish-American architect had designed it anew, a stupefying summit rising 1,776 feet to the sky, what he hadn't foreseen were the long ribbons of pink smoke coming from every window along with white flags that no hand or arm appeared to wave, Samuel was afraid the crowd would pour itself into that putrid-smelling smoke that stuck to his face and clothes as he yelled, be careful, the fire's spreading everywhere, yet not so much as a single flame, get out, get away from here, but where, he was afraid he'd be crushed by all those boots that no soldiers wore, asphyxiated by air that no longer inflated his lungs, where did he think he was going, to what rehearsal hall of waiting students, he'd heard Arnie Graal's words in his ear repeating as he had before, march on babe, the world lies before you, the gift of dance is the gift of God, march on, infidel, onward and listen only to the music that directs your steps, you white men, men of no faith, and Petites Cendres thought the warmth from the bodies was rising, the evangelist Larry would surely come to see him wading in the sauna at the Porte du Baiser, saying, I'd love to hear how you spend your nights, Petites Cendres, it's for your own good, because I've come here specially to convert gigolos like you, I would see the obsequious man in his grey suit, the zealot, feasting on him with his eyes, your Creator will first ask why you have spilled your seed, then He'll throw you down to the depths of Gehenna if I cannot save your soul perverted by evil, which is my duty, come closer and let me see, now don't run away, black serpent, one may look on you without laying hands on you, looking is not taking or doing anything one wants, say those words thought Petites Cendres, all you can think about is sucking and buggering, you're the pervert, now us at the Porte du Baiser, we're just hanging out and waiting, that's all, splashing around a little, sighing maybe, grooming our eyebrows with our fingers, tired, it's tiring waiting for someone to buy us drinks tonight and coke tomorrow morning, waiting, always waiting, all those genitals squished up in those swimsuits is definitely making the temperature rise in here, especially the tanned torsos here and there, drops of sweat, and the man with the hat dying for his Sluttie, everybody's panting, in the bars and in the saunas when Sundays get so boring, they aren't bored at least, so succulent and adorable, the evangelist Larry knows what he likes, so tell me what you do at night, Petites Cendres, who with, c'mon Petites Cendres, I just want to convert you, that's all, and Petites Cendres just couldn't pretend with this virtuous man in the grey suit, whatever repugnance he felt, he'd just have to follow the man with the hat who was so frank and likeable, though his age was, well, still he was never alone, sure he'd come to the sauna tonight, the detestable hypocrite, paying tribute to Petites Cendres and the boys, all you who have sinned, Larry would say, he'd come and treat them to the spectacle of his wife and kids, a Christian family, getting more and more from Petites Cendres in that water steaming like hell as the evangelist would say, the sauna water at the Porte du Baiser, peel away just a little more, that's what he'd do as he slipped his dagger into the dark body, God preserve Petites Cendres from the advances of this white man, on his way out of the bar, into the street still bathed in waves of warm light, and by the sea glimmering far off, Petites Cendres saw a dove drinking fresh rainwater from a puddle, dipping its white head into the trickling rivulets along the sidewalks, all that cooing he thought, and you're going to drink where the parade of cars and young people in the backs of red trucks go by singing and shouting with tattooed arms held high, flying low towards one another, when all of a sudden one of them wings you and here you are bathed in light

and able to see nothing of that glittering line that drew you
from afar, is that what death is, the open wound is my own,
falling, spiralling as I do in my frenzy, onto the dangerous
ground, not flying any more, your torn wings are my own,
your plumage mine too, and so it was as he watched the dove
drinking that Petites Cendres felt a pressure, a contraction of
the heart and soul he thought was connected to all that God
created, the sea, the doves, and the sun, but also this frantic
accident that cut short all the beauty of this creation, that ren-
dered it hostile by this one senseless accident, the laughing
drunk at the wheel had done irreparable harm without knowing it, and the wondrous bird, marvelling at being alive for
an instant, was no more, drink, black-banded turtledove, a
sharper eye than men's, drink, thought Petites Cendres, aware
that his own life was just as wondrous and fleeting as the
bird's, where would this dead little thing go now, or himself
one day, or the little girl he met at a party who thought she'd
been cured of cancer, it was even written on her T-shirt over
a flourishing breast — cancer's not going to get me — then
suddenly somehow she learned she had only six months to
live, what are you going to do with that time, Petites Cendres
asked her, and she ingenuously replied, dance and laugh and
dance, Petites Cendres, then he watched her dance all day and
night with that same tightness of heart and soul, like the bird
flying too low, tomorrow she won't be able to any more,
wings, plumage, the stabbing pain in his heart, then a client
tugged at his shoulder and said, hey, what're you thinking
about, no matter if it was Larry the evangelist or someone else,
what I need, he thought, is the hurt that God gives us when
we're born, forget, forget it, let me tell you a funny story said
the customer, I knew a guy from Argentina who hid kilos of
cocaine under his mattress then got deported, so we going to
the sauna or not, yes or no, hey, said Petites Cendres, hear
that, thunder, to be just that, flying crazily then hitting the
ground, he thought, one fall and a second, coming, he said,

walking nonchalantly to the door, still thinking about Timo, the weighty ties that bound them together, Timo about to be captured at any moment by the cops or the patrols in plain clothes wherever he went by road or water, they'd pose as johns or marijuana-cocaine pushers, ready to trip him when he least expected it, Petites Cendres had given him the keys to the client's Sonata with the kilos of coke, and he'd been taken away for deportation by two officers, did he even hear the man who'd grabbed him by the shoulder as if he were just a flour sack, c'mon, let's go, he said again, what's up, it's the sun at this time of day said Petites Cendres, the sun and the open wound of the bird bouncing into the air, his too he thought, the cancelled hope inside the flourishing breast of the girl dead from cancer six months later, his too, hanging by the thread of one breath, all the while dancing and laughing. If this kid decides to be born now, we're screwed and my three-day holiday's washed up, 'cause I'm not letting you down, Angelina, at least I'm a man, Tigli told her as she got more and more agitated, they call it coming into the world and living, and it's really something, he went on, you never thought about that, did you, bursting out of the maternal cavern, then, bang, here he is, and the crying and living begins, their own organisms, independent beings, I've seen double, even triple my share, believe me Angelina, a fireman-midwife knows all about life, and it's all a mystery people know practically nothing about, whether it's a good or a bad thing, the jury's still out on that, no expert has ever weighed in on it, okay, so no three days of salsa for me with girls hanging off me everywhere, I'm a big hit with them you know, and they all love to dance with me, I buy them rounds of margaritas see, first we're going to have to get the head clear, then the shoulders, after that you'll gradually find it easier, Angelina, you'll need to push and don't hold back, okay, because by then he isn't yours any more, he's his own organism, so you've got to let him go, you hear me, listen, we're never going to

make it to the clinic on time, no holiday for me, but I know
about premature deliveries, don't you worry, Angelina, hey,
turn and face me, okay, you need to calm down, feel the
strength in my arms, getting born's a complicated business,
kind of like a flower, petals, corollas, and all that, then he'll
go off and join billions of others in the same bouquet if he
wants to, and open wide among all those other coloured
plants, cherry blossom, orange blossom, what will he be,
man, woman, who will he look like, one day he'll start talking
and walking like them, running with the horses and donkeys
along the flooded muddy streets or winding mountain roads
with his little brown legs, sweating from hunger and thirst,
donkey, horse, and eagle somewhere behind him, and where's
this on-and-off race going to take him, probably won't even
know himself, then one day, the most dangerous, cruel, jealous, treacherous avenger . . . or the mostly saintly man cloaked
in invisible holiness, as unnoticed as certain stars, divinely
remote, vulnerable, and hurt, then hurting back at them, consuming those around him beyond his appetites, striking and
stabbing with hatred, he will be flowers and fruit, forever
ready to blossom, a conformist or an inveterate rebel, out of
place, impulsive, cursing or keeping quiet, even under torture,
praiseworthy and unworthy in the face of misfortune, he'll
have your eyes and graceful neck and your soul too, Angelina,
your sweet credulousness, he'll be your rose and your butterfly, four wings open to the day, don't you worry, Angelina,
first the head, then the shoulders, no, don't worry, I, Tigli, will
always be there by your side, and since that's the way it has
to be, goodbye to the salsa and girls and three days' holiday,
tomorrow's for dancing, Angelina, 'cause this one's got to be
born first, he's slept long enough in that liquid chamber of
his, time to turn his head and face our way, cut the ties tonight
and head for daylight, bright colours, being, no more hesitating, four butterfly wings in the wind, can you feel the strength
in these hands, Angelina? So much noise in this bus, thought

Ari, so little peace in our lives, so much clamour and clash from the voices of men and women, and the mocking laughter of children, all these voices, all this dust stirred up from the road, unstoppable wheels, suddenly here, anywhere, we no longer know where we're going, no wife, no little girl, body in a seat insulated from the multicoloured multitude in the window, nothing on their feet burnt in the sun, Ari's piece on art would be started over again when he got back, Picasso's picture was still in his mind's eye, he'd never grasped the nuances of the monumental tumult before, not seen it as though painted against the backdrop of the sky, the stifling blue of today's heat, now it was Picasso who cast his piercing eye on Ari, here is the savagery of any war, the painting said, women, horses, bulls, all of them brutalized, jaws open wide, hear the desolate cries of the women, the horse's cry of pain like any crushed creature, the dove in its distress, the dislocation and dismemberment of one and all, this is your battle, surely you see that, cities and countries you lounge in luxuriously now bombed, dark Spain once again, years of wrack and ruin, about to sink once again and you with it, just a painting by the master, oil on canvas, no, much, much more than that, an attack on Ari himself, his principles of pacifism, the nonchalance of a man more epicurean than ascetic, private dreams not permitted to disturb his happiness, the artist in him rebelling against the military caste denounced by Picasso, frightened for the wholeness of the planet he lived on, even more than for his dove, defeated in this masterpiece, he feared for his daughter, feared that the artist's struggle against the rule of unreason and madness was mere illusion, another of his dreams that he'd cultivated into hope, not any more, no, Ari saw the painting again and again ceaselessly and thought about the article he was going to write, Picasso's painting looking at him, observing and judging with its piercing gaze, thus it was; come let me untangle your hair, said Marie-Sylvie de la Toussaint as Mai felt the brush landing in

her hair and against the scalp that felt so tender like when she
was small, do I really have to do everything in this house, she
repeated with irritation as Mai thought about the student meeting in the fenced schoolyard where the principal solemnly
addressed them all in that peremptory manner that was Marie-
Sylvie de la Toussaint's with her, we have had to expel a
fourteen-year-old boy, the principal said . . . because of the
coma due to alcohol, hashish, and sex, thought Mai, though
the principal refrained from giving details of why his parents
had come to get him, though maybe it was the ecstasy, and if
this is how our students behave, girls letting fourteen-year-old
boys molest them, drug abuse, then very few of you are going
to live long enough to graduate, the brush pounded on Mai's
head as the nanny's strokes with the wooden implement continued, precious few of you, Mai knew you came out of a coma
a different person, another physical and mental envelope perhaps, but still, wasn't it strange that you could hang around
with eighteen-year-olds who came to school in their fathers'
Mercedes, and that would protect against abuse, coma, alcoholic stupor you never woke from, eighteen-year-old adults
now could do anything they liked without permission, they
were strong, armed with handguns and knives, Mai disliked
the garbage that older people drank, but she would like to
be protected by eighteen-year-olds with guns and knives,
although that was increasingly frowned upon in schools and
colleges, still, at least they knew how to use them and didn't
ask anyone's permission, it was common knowledge more
and more of them were armed, and Mai always felt safe with
them, with an attitude like that, very few of you will live long
enough to reach graduation, the principal's peremptory tone
said, have you given any thought to that, and those of you
who take advantage of the others will be outcasts and convicts, for some it was a coma from which they would emerge
forever changed, in a new physical and mental envelope Mai
thought, different because they were not themselves any more,

fractured somewhere inside themselves, but they didn't how or why or where, they went to a dance, that's all, then they emerged from the vortex somehow built differently from the day before, had they lost an arm or a leg at the dance, not one of you will attend university with such behaviour, but while the principal spoke, Mai noticed the the whole schoolyard was fenced in with chain-link, even the pine trees, palms, everything, yet someone had left the gate wide open, that must be where the predator got in when the girls weren't paying attention, better if it were wide open to the sky and the beach and the sea, and the predator got in, the one wandering on the beach from morning till night, better that he be there, then Mai could still feel free herself, free to leave by the open gate, free from the principal's brisk voice, free to follow whomever she liked, maybe it wasn't even a predator in the first place, and her mind was wandering far from the principal's voice over the loudspeaker, yes, with an attitude like that, very few of you will live long enough to reach graduation, Mai felt the brushstrokes through her hair, yes, she would get her diploma, and no, she would not listen to any of them, the principal or the grating voice of Marie-Sylvie, she would hear none of them, do you hear me, Tigli was saying to Angelina, this is your friend and midwife speaking, what do the silent heavens care about one more offering, Angelina, still a life's a life, believe me, a tiger-striped butterfly, the least grain of magic dust sprinkled among us, everything that lives gets to chatter and sing, hear me Angelina, sacred little pearl, don't think you can escape your liberator and delivery boy, even if the cyclone whistles round our ears, come on, you call this labour, Angelina, you've got a life to launch here, hey, wakey-wakey, Angelina, come on push, do something, what're we going to do in all this hustle and bustle, I'll get to see the crown, just think, the top of a human being, small as my fist, I'm the assistant here, Angelina, you're going to have to listen to me if you want this thing to be born, so tiny you can barely hear him, okay, you're off and running my filly, don't you stop now, a bit of curly hair, a moving shadow at my fingertips, can that really be his head, let's see those puffy eyes and old-man lids, so, what's a life, Angelina, then out spill the head and the neck, he's alive, Angelina, a butterfly, a pebble, a seed, tomorrow's hit man, or the target, arms folded on his chest, thus I deliver him from the trap and lift him into the air, a big, bouncing boy, Angelina, and Lazaro again pictured them being executed in the Tehran dawn, more than twenty of them today, tomorrow there would be even more, no counting them from here on, all of them hanged from behind steam shovels against the full, round azure sky, just like puppets waltzing at the end of their ropes he thought, gently inclining his forehead, necks broken, no longer able to support the weight of their heads, eyes shut or wide open in terror, there was no describing how the knots scraped their throats, one could not and should not try, the pettiest of criminals, not even rapists like the five black vultures whose defiance and rage Lazaro had admired yesterday among the crowd of ten thousand in Tehran, these were nothing, young racketeers, the steam shovel swallowed them in one mouthful, people would remember, good thing it was done, yes, people would remember, that would teach them obedience to the law, more than twenty in one day, against a sky so exuberantly blue, this was the morning shift, they set off in the same filthy rags they woke up in, no respect, clothes still wet from the sweat of dread for the knot that wouldn't hurt so much after all, there, done, just have to make do with that and say good job, otherwise it would soon be our turn, they were just poor people with no nobility, nobodies, nothings, no weeping for these ridiculous creatures losing a sock or a shoe swinging somewhere between heaven and earth, thought Lazaro as he considered picking up a sandal and burying it out of charity and respect in a moment of pity for its forlorn and desolate owner, artisan, worker, thief perhaps, man of nothing and yet still created by Allah, it would have taken someone in the bloodthirsty crowd to have a moment of pity for the shoe or the sock, any clothing snatched from the body when the discharging intestines ran their brown river and viscera, it would, he thought, but these dawn hangings would soon be forgotten along with the clamours and cries, he thought feeling relieved by the accelerating force of his motor-cycle as it circled the house with all blinds closed against the sun, the garden and the pool where they would celebrate Christmas night, he thought he heard the shrill laugh of Chuan through the walls, so where was Jermaine, probably having mindless fun out on the water with his sailboard or water skis, sure they'd have lots of fun, get drunk on booze and wine, right up until . . . until . . . without Lazaro they would just go right on procreating, both them and their vices, their faithless-ness, all at once Ari felt Asoka's presence beside him in the bus was a pretence, the pilgrim monk seemed to be praying, reciting some silent mantra, but wasn't there with him, Lou's godfather would never be there to embrace her, would his work in the clinics of Guatemala soon be over and he be off somewhere else, far from the thankless, repugnant sham of a civilization Ari and his daughter belonged to, Ari knew that, though Asoka was discreet and placid enough never to talk of it, in the cottony meditation with which he'd wrapped him-self and shut out Ari for the past few hours, like his sober orange robe, the monk, the exquisite creature in appearance so peaceful, with hands on knees, was actually battling with all his strength matters far removed from the instruction of Ari and his doubts about God and Man, about art and the felicities of this Earth, for he was already among his own in the temples and pagodas of the Far East, under a vault representing men at prayer, and beneath these sculpted monks real monks prayed on their knees against gilded columns, surrounded by crows and monkeys scratching the temple floor, and outside the gong of revolution sounded, penetrating their prayers, causing their faces to start atop their immobile bodies, the hour of silence had passed, now seized by jubilation bordering on euphoria, Asoka got up with them all and ran into the street, all of them spilling over with joy, the struggle now was outside among those being whipped and beaten, the walls of temples and pagodas soon would be aflame, while ash-covered crows and monkeys escaped the smoke, as soon as he returned, Asoka would be one of them, raising his arms in the circle of fire to be pursued at gunpoint like the others, shouting enough, enough, you have destroyed our people enough, we beg peace for them all and share their pain, enough, enough, it was to be with his own that Asoka had left Ari, for the ardour of revolutions to purify the world of its atrocities, but without his friend he was alone with his art, Ari thought, a wife who refused to live with him, his too-much-loved little girl likely manipulating him the way her mother had done, what a noise on the bus, like a woman's scream, while the horses went on alone, riderless and no mountain bridles, staying to the right of the sandy road as if they were about to graze the cars and buses on the highway, life itself in this thoughtless onrush, all of life, thought Ari dozing off with his head so near Asoka's placid shoulder, while he was so far away, with the temple and pagoda monks, did they even know there were healthy insurrections and angers, the crackle of fire very near the temples and pagoda where crows and monkeys took refuge next to men praying, the hammering of bodies, feet and footsteps, art and dance, thought Samuel, and six solos to create, but the act of choreography must always be transparent Arnie Graal used to say, the body movements must be resolute, the lighting close to twilight over the sea, no real dissolution of bodies, dancing or not, poorly defended, unprotected, no ornamentation, violins, cellos, drums, and a range of sounds extinguished, he thought while the demonstrators regrouped farther back along the streets of New York, a man's voice shouting tomorrow we will be so ashamed, very soft lighting Samuel thought, you had to admire the slightness of Franz, Mère reflected, his spritely temperament, the ease with which he travels far and wide conducting orchestras, today Germany, tomorrow California, concerts and compositions piling up for a musician impermeable to the changes of the times, and why not change or adapt, well he said, he was always in love, and although he was always stirred by it, and in his carnal dynamism rarely knew stability, even with this new young wife of his, that's just the way he is thought Mère, a rich instability that communicated what life is, nuances could be found in his art alone, a moral elegance absent from his daily life, no nuances when approaching a woman he wanted, or conservatory students training for his orchestras, dreaming all the while of seducing them, well, that was Franz's strength: he couldn't live without desiring, and he never stopped desiring, every bit as much as he embraced the ancient and modern repertoires, each interpreter bringing something new, something exotic, fresh nuances and reflections to the music that allowed it to survive from one tour to the next in tempos ever more delicious and vibrant, success from the incoherence of an artist's life, sometimes painful, festivals and concert halls one after another, Munich could be his as much as a work by Richard Strauss or a Mozart adagio, but his childhood wanderings in that same city, those same halls could dispirit him all at once, how could he live without a family, the family of musicians, women, children, how that eternal wanderer, no, Mère knew Franz restored his life with love, old or new, like his music, always different, with different interpreters using every one of his variations on love and desire, and of course there is no end to it, Franz said, one day, I fall for the music of George Gershwin, next day, well, you know me, Esther, on this damaged Earth I'm never the same man twice, of course the soaring notes of Mozart's loveliest airs had to be heard again, but for Franz it was above all Britten's *War Requiem* that was played lately, and he still hadn't finished composing his opera, and while you're listening to *The Art of the Fugue,* Augustino wrote to his grandmother, the habitats of rare species of animals are being burned by the very people supposed to protect them, these savages in Srinagar, India, "protectors" of the parks, forests, jungles, and savannas terrorizing them with burning lances, we are witnesses, my brothers and sister, to this solemn and macabre ceremony every single day, disappearing species, our own as well in the ovens of overpopulated cities, the crumbling arctic ice, soon there will be no polar bears left to drown, fifteen million species vanished, swallowed up in the deluge, rivers with no beds or directions, massacred by us, Earth, oh Earth will lay its disappearance on your shoulders, polar bears, gorillas, jungles all gone and only a world of water or murderous drought with cracked deserts of malnourished little children dying one by one at the drooping breasts of their mothers, hopelessly raising to the skies their empty eyes devoured by flies, and all this time dear Grandmother, you'll be listening to *The Art of the Fugue,* where will we go, what will become of us with nothing but dark dampness all around, the waste of an abused and putrid Earth right here on this carpet, no room left for any of us, tomorrow, tonight, where to go, what to do, Japanese school-kids having lunch in cafeterias in Taiji fishing villages taking a slice of forbidden and protected whale meat, slices of dolphin heart, though it too is prohibited, boats in Asian waters overflowing with protected fish whose intelligence sometimes outstrips ours, do these kids even know what they're eating, the last seafood in existence, the last whales and the last dolphins, do they see the blood-red sunrise, the scattering of red pearls all the way to distant shores, here it is late September and the whale-and-dolphin hunt is on, do they know they are communing on the last mortal remains of the seas, have they seen the red tide from this washing at the wharves where they will soon play barefoot while you're listening to *The Art of the*

Fugue dear Grandmother, Augustino wrote, and she thinking this child is all too genuine, he is too truthful, must I concede he is right or fall silent, I cannot allow myself so much discouragement, if I were twenty like him perhaps, sincerity is not always a virtue in a writer I'll tell him, I'll try and make him understand how different we are, although still Petites Cendres remembered his dream from the night he and Timo were in the Sonata, Timo must have been crazy to drive that fast, drunk or out of his head, any moment now they'd hit a tree or the concrete arches of a bridge, you don't know what you're doing Petites Cendres told him, but Timo just spat cigarette smoke in his face, so that's what you think, eh, I don't know what I'm doing, I'm getting the hell out of here, that's all, have you seen what's behind us, Petites Cendres, you think I'm going to let those stinkin' cops or rent-a-cops get their hands on me, hear that siren, they definitely want me, nope, I'd rather drown among the crocodiles, Petites Cendres, I'm takin' off, no way they're gettin' me, and Petites Cendres felt his chest tighten when he lived that dream again, the Sonata smashed against a wall, Timo covered in blood, the cigarette still between his purple lips, too fast my friend, too fast, but Timo wasn't listening, just hurtling along in that Sonata and head-over-heels it went, and, just a dream he told himself, as he felt with disgust the client pressing his lips to his in the Porte du Baiser Saloon, still that feeling of fear that Timo was in danger and needed him somewhere near the archipelago waters, couldn't go any farther without being captured, well-wrapped packets of cocaine in the Sonata, Timo, my friend, thought Petites Cendres, I know they won't get you, I'm the one who has crazy ideas, wonder if Sluttie's gone off with his sugar daddy, more groups of boys arriving, devils' horns glinting in the blinking red lights, and they bump and grind onto the dance floor, wonder if Sluttie will wind up winning them all with those jeans and the hole that lets his butt-skin shine through, sure he will, has no time for me though, Petites Cendres saw someone come into the Porte du Baiser in a rough woollen robe, a belt, and a face made up white as chalk plus large wraparound shades, he asked Petites Cendres when he'd be free, who's this grubby customer, he thought, so it's carnival time, said the man, I can dress up how I want, right, that set Petites Cendres to thinking about his dream and Timo again, who are you under that white makeup, he asked, the man started laughing and didn't answer, Petites Cendres sensed it was true, Timo must be in danger, his brother and friend, are we really as different as I'd like to think though, Augustino and I, Mère wondered, I just can't let myself get in touch with that much pain, especially at Christmas, I'll take him by the hand and talk to him, even though he tends to shy away from friendship, I'll tell him, this garden is rich in flowers because of you, you who not so long ago were saying, here, this is where we need a coconut tree Grandma, and hibiscus over here, and if we hear the doves cooing at night in the fountain, it's thanks to you, because it was you who landscaped this garden, it was your advice I followed, at night I hear the croaking of the frogs, and I think if only I saw my grandson more often, I'd say to him, you're wrong Augustino, there is generosity in every creature that lives, at least a little part that even you can't deny, what about the ones who go about quietly saving the world, ordinary men and women, think dear boy about the gratitude you must feel for your parents, to life, and to us all who have loved you ever since you were born, Mère would say all this, her un-trembling hand in her grandson's this Christmas night, even the most different could be reconciled and near to her, what about Jenny in China treating people with AIDS every day in unbearable conditions, would her words just bounce ineffectually off this stubborn child, now tall and thick-haired, they had so much to say in such a short time, Augustino, I want to tell you you're mistaken, I cannot take hold of thoughts as dark as these, you see the beauty of this garden at night, hear the modulations of the grasshoppers, look and listen, but perhaps he would hear and see none of all this, Mai thought of her during her Sunday outings on terraces and in restaurants by the sea, wearing a wide hat like Caroline, the old lady who'd befriended her, and asking the same questions Caroline had, it was only recently that Mai had seen her grandmother as an elderly lady in a wide hat like Caroline, and had the feeling that one day she might no longer be there, just a memory gradually erasing itself, not a person, just a vague shape like Caroline, the old lady she'd liked and never seen any more after their outing to The-Island-Nobody-Owns, the day the ashes of the poet Jean-Mathieu went into the calm and glittering sea, that day Mai herself wandered off, then came back only to disappear more and more, so secretively no one knew who she could be, little girl or delinquent, of course Marie-Sylvie de la Toussaint said she was a liar and a cheat, even while she brushed her hair, I mean we never know where you are or what you're doing, your parents and I, now do you call that normal, perhaps that's just the way it was she thought, and Mai would get used to seeing her grandmother's face get smaller and smaller under those wide hats, her hands getting so thin, suddenly as evanescent as the elderly Caroline, still Mai remembered perfectly Caroline's hat and gloves, the lofty tone of voice, I may once, she told Mai, have been a child rather like you, Mai, and I can tell you now, no one understood me, maybe she too had a nanny, wonder why she spoke in such confidence to little Mai when her own grandmother talked to young people from on high, it wasn't indifference, it was, well, an old-fashioned form of respect and politeness, Mai might be under the inquiring gaze of her grandmother, Mai where were you and what were you doing, they had no idea at all what went on in schools, some might not even make it to the end or go to university, they could never have guessed what she knew, maybe they didn't want to know, nothing you could say anyway, not about Manuel in his father's Mercedes or the others, and Manuel's little trades and gimmicks, no, not a word about those, especially not at breakfast with Grandma, just keep it zipped, he said when they were alone in the Mercedes, about all the money he had, schemes, but he didn't involve Mai in anything, just drove her home from school, better to hang out with adults like him than schoolboys who didn't know anything, much better, this wasn't the little Cuban Emilio she'd once shared ice cream with, no, this Manuel was something else, almost a man, and she wasn't a baby either like in the old days when she ran to play with Emilio on the beach, playing volleyball with his father like champions, that was all gone now, she would never get it back, Manuel had a father too, but he was involved in shady dealings too, commerce Manuel called it, what you have to know, Manuel said, was that business, however shady, would never die; in any city bombed and shattered to smithereens, there would still be some basement or hole in the ground with a nightclub or discotheque and electronic music, of course, he said, the new generation thinks of everything, there's actually a club called Abri, or Shelter, and no amount of bombing or trouble can reach it, the DJ can't be stopped, the kids and the rock called Youth or Basement invent their own music in the slums, hey, who says they can be shot with bullets or missiles, no way, the sub-basements and discotheques are safe as can be, he told Mai in that mournful voice of his, hey, know what, ganglylegs, those parents of yours have almost managed to make you just like everyone else, braces on your teeth are all you need to look just like the others, we're the descendants of post-punks, got to understand each other, that disco's got to exist, even in Beirut, my dad thinks it has to be a good shelter, really safe, yep, the East and the West are just going to have to get together right there in the Middle East, you'll see, my dad knows, he says sex, drugs, and fun will always catch up with us in the end, doesn't matter if countries are occupied, divided, or whatever, you'll always see commerce on our side, liberty through discos and music, nobody's ever going to stop us, drugs and sex are our revolution, we'll tell our rulers how much we hate them, doesn't matter what nationality they are, we curse them, Mai listened to Manuel's sad and blasé voice, and saw only the white cap pulled back over the nape of his neck, the boxers rising over his shorts, you've got to let all that crazy stuff go, he said, we're the insects who will never disappear, we'll always be right there in their dump, no matter what they do, and just you wait and see, our music will be there too, so when was he going to Beirut, oh, soon, he said, real soon, to open that discotheque Abri en Enfer — Shelter in Hell — too, oh you think it's funny eh, well, it's true, we've got plenty of imagination, knowledge too, you'll see, all that romance and cruelty, we'll get them and squash them into the ground: Mai's friend, this was Manuel, and Emilio was ancient history now, they were to be feared now, all of them, her protective father, her grandmother whose eyes drilled into all her secrets from under that wide-brimmed hat of hers, got to keep things to myself from now on, Mai thought, the times are changed, Vénus told Rebecca, we still sing the way we used to, pray and dance too, you have to use that way of singing in your recital Rebecca, the parade's at six Rebecca said, they'll go along the canal then Seventh Street, don't let go of Mamma's hand, I can't do everything at the same time, you know, working and studying, her mother replied, when I know someone like Perdue the lawyer, I've got to do everything I can to stop them from locking up my brother for twenty years in their filthy prisons, they're the ones that'll be chained hand and foot, then put on trial, even when they're only fifteen, I wonder if I'm doing the right thing bringing you up in Pastor Jérémy's faith, what's God ever done for us, was the speech that moved crowds on August 28, 1963, the sermon of a prophet or the dream of a brilliant politician: on these mountains of Georgia, he said, we would see the sons of slave merchants and sons of slaves seated together at the same table of brotherhood, oh yes, believe me, for I dreamed that my four children would one day not be known for the colour of their skin but for their strength of character, I had a dream that one day in this nation we would all of us sit down at this fraternal table, he repeated to the crowds, but more than fifty years later, the evils of segregation still exist, don't they, in those years we got governors, senators, everyone to back down in our desperate march, this is the heritage of Little Rock and Elizabeth Eckford walking alone through the horrific insults of a savage·crowd, like a delicate flower in her cotton dress, books in hand, on her way to high school, and all of them trying to stop her, teeth bared, but her step was firm and there was no looking back, everyone has a right to knowledge, you, me, all of us, all we had to lose was our chains of servitude and an ugly heritage, all, in the name of that speaker, a civil war, all, so many desperate efforts, the firm voice of the speaker, his dream and vision crossing the mountains of Georgia, and who knows, all sharing one dream that cannot be brought about, would they one day sit at one brotherly table, it was so long ago, I'm not sure I should bring you up·in the faith of your grandfather, Pastor Jérémy, if I do, it is so you can sing in the Temple of the City of Coral, all of the temples and churches, for what has God done for them and for Carlos, locked up and blotted out behind bars, and if he were free tomorrow, that Lazaro has only one thought, kill his friend and his brother, I wasn't around in those days of glory and infamy, Vénus told her daughter, no, I wasn't born yet, but Mama and Papa told me about it all, the glory of great speakers who wanted a better life for all, and the infamy of those days was overthrown, yes, they told me everything, and they had seen their smiles, heard their words while they were still able to smile and speak, getting out of a limo and holding out their hands, then suddenly the leather seats were spongy with purple liquid and bits of flesh, that's what Papa and Mama told me, red roses in their hands, and a woman felt blood soil her fine clothes and the roses she held, the warm drops of her husband's blood just after opening and stretching her hands out to the crowd, after the smiles and the words, they heard three shots, a warm sunny morning, someone said those must be shots, yes, gunshots, is that really what we're hearing, is it, yes, and the infamy of these times just never ever stops, whether the silencing of the voice from over the mountains of Georgia, for he too, smiling and opening his arms to the crowd, and Papa just cried when he told it, Pastor Jérémy cried, and yet it was not enough infamy, for there would be more, this one, the youngest, had danced, laughed, and hugged his friends in a ballroom to celebrate his victory the day before, he too wanted the good of all, or so he dreamed, for no one wanted the good of everyone, he too demanded the end of racial segregation, that day when he saw all his enemies lined up at the windows of houses and buildings, their noble dreams never to be satisfied, surrounded by an army of enemies, the young and glorious one saw it in the windows too, then barely emerging from the ballroom after speaking to 1,800, and why go through the hotel kitchen when it was just after noon, perhaps he wanted a little solitude, yet by some error of fate he headed straight for the Palestinian and his .22 revolver, by what impenetrable error did he approach, then arms wide apart on the floor trying to murmur something, but who knows what, his eyes searching for whoever was leaning towards him and softening his fall by holding his shoulder, a young Asian cook, but what was he trying to say, was he trying to see what was left of that day of infamy, this *Pietà* of cook and dying man, all of them lined up in windows of houses and buildings, they would all have waited, by what ludicrous destiny did they head straight for one another, the three names were pronounced that day, the prophet from across the mountains of Georgia and the two brothers, and everybody knew there would be no more dreams, those too had been killed, and it's there forever in the

archives of shame so none of it will be forgotten, Vénus said
to her daughter, their sermons and speeches for peace and
the faces of their enemies, hypocrite apparitions in the windows of houses and buildings, all of them conserved in the
three *Pietàs*, like the degrading image of a woman in Little
Rock showing her teeth to a black student, frail but bold in
her cotton dress walking alone on her way to high school,
that's the way you have to be when you sing and dance,
Rebecca, so you never lack courage, hear me Rebecca, no,
don't you ever give up the struggle, then Rebecca reminded
her mother they were getting to the boats, suddenly that night
they'd be seeing Trevor and her father's musicians, kayaks,
and canoes shaped like sleighs, right there that night, the musicians said Trevor was a prince of jazz, you'd see them coming
from Seventh Avenue, and Papa would be disguised for
Christmas night, and Rebecca said, no way I'm going to sleep,
sleighs sliding over the sea, not sleighs, boats really she said,
walking next to her mother whose anklets and bracelets made
a clinking sound, and I'll sing too with Trevor and the children's Bible Study Choir, your dad says he couldn't live without music, music and rum, Vénus said, says you've got to
warm up your veins when you play bass, crazy things like
that, and his fingers all yellow from the cigarettes he smokes
when he plays, kayaks, boats with flower-decked masts,
Rebecca said in a clear, staccato voice, nope, not sleeping,
no way, well maybe just for a minute on your lap or Trevor's,
why's he want to get dressed up like Santa Claus the way white
people do, did he do that when he lived in Jamaica, street-
singing on the sidewalk with dogs sitting beside him, no, he
was just a wandering street musician, then they go and call
him Prince Trevor, jazzman and lord of the bass, and he's
someone else, I'm going to sing with the Bible Study Choir,
Rebecca said, those musicians are all kind of strung out on
something, if I was like them I'd sing with Uncle Cornélius at
the Mix Club, then Mama and Papa wouldn't want me over at

the house, say I'd be a bad example for Deandra, Tiffany, Carlos, Le Toqué, not like Carlos, bicycle thief, they wanted to send him to a plantation in Atlanta, I used to sing on Sundays in the temple at Cité Soleil, Papa said I had a beautiful voice, Petites Cendres was thinking he shouldn't have left Timo and let him run off alone like that in the Sonata when the patrol cars and sheriff were after him, in the desolation of his spirit, he heard the voice of Reverend Ézéchielle in the Community Church, saying Petites Cendres, that lost child and plucked chicken, would always find an oasis of solace and rest with her, why be dragged down into the muck of life, she would have told him to raise his senses to Heaven, yes Heaven, but where was this Heaven while we were battling it out here on Earth, degraded more and more every day, that's because you wanted it that way, she'd have told him, with your finely drawn eyebrows, idle and busybody hands, yes, you went looking for it with your miserable withdrawals, sniffing coke around the clock, itchy nose, weeping eyes, you just went running after it, she'd have told him, in your weird outfits, almost naked, 'course you did, get on your knees and await the bestowing of grace upon you, to which he'd have shot back, what the hell are you talking about, you fat preacher, to a man like me a poor, fragile creature perhaps, but filled with desires and maybe not very recommendable excitements, and she'd have answered, I tell you son, good for you if you are fragile, my debauched son you don't eat, sweetheart, because you're stoned and never hungry, those corrosive desires are feeding on you, you're hungry, good, because the poor and thin like you will fit through the narrow gate of the House of God, the others, too heavy with pockets stuffed with gold, won't get in, the gate is made only for plucked chickens and sacrificial lambs, my son, hear well what I say, I'm not going to repeat it, this, my son, is your home and your family, come back to me you empty head, so I can set you straight, crooked plant and Petites Cendres heard the music spilling from the bars into the street, the Mississipi blues of Riley King, born in Itta Bena, rural Mississipi where poor Blacks counted themselves rich if they owned a mule, the music of cotton pickers, born of the forced labour of men, women, and children when the Great Depression swept the farms, the sweat of men composed it, thought Petites Cendres, *Three O'Clock Blues*, he thought, *Three O'Clock Blues*, when all of a sudden, nothing and no one seemed to want to pardon you for being alive in this hot and beating sun, of course he shouldn't have let Timo go off alone in the Sonata, Riley King's music battered his forehead with ancient stigmata, it was the music of thousands of howling voices, men, women, and children, listen to the whistling of the leather whiplash on their backs, you'd need two weeks in bed after treatment like that, with the pus oozing from the open wounds, the music of mass exodus over the water to the ports of flesh merchants, men leaving Africa chained to the inside of ships and stooping low, a master or captain in large boots and whip in hand saw them piled up in the holds, did those who committed these crimes know that this hateful spirit would leave its essence in us for so long, this distinguished master and captain, bearded beneath his hat and distinguished, imperious, sovereign, did he answer the question as he herded them below decks stooping below the lowest planks in the ship: unhappy man, how will you spend eternity, others were manhandled below by his accomplices, and when they met resistance, added a ball and chain and shouted get down there, get down, Riley King's music, thought Petites Cendres, said the men down there wore a symbol on the backs of their necks, an iron collar with a forked handle, an artistic-looking ornament designed by an aristocrat who thought it made a certain aesthetic impression, its weight had indeed made its impression around so many necks that it is still stared at with horror in museums today, archives of unpunished murders by the sons and daughters and their children descended from the masters, the woven scars of blows on

distended backs still as impressive as ever, something we'd
rather not see, in Virginia in 1619, before the voice of a man
cried out, though he owned these exiles working on his plantations, is it not self-evident that we are all equal, is it just that
even the law protects slave-owners, all arrived by sea in what
we call the Middle Passage, then on shore they were sorted
and separated from one another, even families, surely it is
evident that all men are equal in this country, is this not a truth
that we children of God should respect, bent low among the
thistles and thorns of the cotton fields heard the voice of that
white man, Riley King's music hammered at Petites Cendres'
temples, and Mère remembered something Caroline had confided to her amid the engine noise on the catamaran taking
them to The-Island-Nobody-Owns, the day Jean-Mathieu's
ashes were scattered, and Caroline talked about flying to Jean-
Mathieu in Italy that night or meeting him at the airport with
Charly her chauffeur, yes, right away tonight, and her mur-
murs were stifled by the sound of the waves, but I can tell
you Esther dear, a frivolous society mother placed me in the
arms of Harriet, our black governess, the day I was born, and
I can tell you, those same arms are where I shall die, in her
chagrin she appeared to confuse Harriet and Miss Désirée, the
nurse who took care of her, blending the two into a single
identity — Harriet, Miss Désirée — she said, these are the
strongest ties that can be, a husband, a string of lovers, these
are merely passing things, but Harriet, Miss Désirée, are testi-
mony to the eternal, mine, so small and fragile, I tell you
Esther dear, the black breast that welcomed me at the first will
also be there at the last, Mère didn't venture to mention her
closeness to Jean-Mathieu, her one great love, the grief of
having just lost him would be too hurtful, already it was affect-
ing her unquiet and wandering mind there on the boat while
she gently rambled in delirium to Mère, or delirium it seemed
coming from an elderly, senile woman, perhaps there was
truth in this story of beginning and ending her life on the same

black breast, for the tableau proved to Mère how real it could become, Miss Désirée never being away from Caroline, even when she ceased breathing in those arms, when they came to separate them, she said let me pray for Caroline, so she may finally rest, let me watch over her, thus what seemed a delirium was really not, and those bonds Caroline had talked about on the boat were true, that was why she had photographed so many black nurses in the South holding white babies, their faces, both nurses and babies, so often expressing dissatisfaction, mutual dissatisfaction in the type of bonds imposed on them all, benevolent tenderness in distrustful eyes for the nurses, and already the racial arrogance of the children in their arms, but perhaps those bonds emerged slowly and strengthen over time, as Caroline said, whether in love or in hate, yet for Caroline they had meant the enduring compassion of Miss Harriet and later, much later, of Miss Désirée, the young nanny or the nurse, witnesses to her coming and her going, to everything. This Caroline told Mère, in a moment of lucidity among the times on the boat when she couldn't even remember Jean-Mathieu's name and asked Mère, tell me dear friend, what are we going to do over there on that island, isn't it Isaac's island, what's the old architect building now in that wild place of iguanas, at least that's what they tell me, she was also telling the truth when she said, Miss Harriet, Désirée, that shining example of fidelity, will hold me in her arms right to the end, in that other *Pietà* Caroline imagined, the clash of races was over, peace and silence at last, the silence of all those reparations, this must be what Caroline meant in her photographs, an art that had often outstripped her in evoking the irreparable errors of the past, as if to say, is evil not always latent in us, the aberration of racism is not just a matter of epochs or nations, it is latent, and to say that, the full ugliness had to be laid before the petrified eyes of the present, Caroline added to her exhibitions photographs of her nannies and governesses with fieldworkers' arms carrying plump and pouting babies, the face of Miss Harriet, Miss Désirée printed in a night that gradually clouded her lively intelligence, two heads touching, the round child's hair just brushing the chin and cheek of a governess whose eyes seemed filled with tears, pictures of slaves at a market waiting to be sold, a man, almost an old man, standing draped in a blanket and wearing an iron collar with two long spikes pointing outward on either side like canes, a steel fork that held him tight, a long chain from head to foot and from his waist forward in a vise of misery, waiting to be bought and sold, his hands, perhaps the fine hands of a musician, resting on the metal prongs, the only place they could, as though lifting an umbrella, one had to look at him without turning away, one of her more acceptable pictures, thought Mère, her art often having gone beyond the woman herself in its meanness, for mean she was, often hesitant to pay for her friends' dinner, she herself with all the faults in the world, yet her art was magnanimous, not only flawless but exultant in its nobility, a grandeur that inspired her viewers to reflection, a delight they would never have felt without her, initiating them into this tragedy of hidden faces and bodies, this art would not disappear with her, thought Mère who found her photos so penetrating, her pairing of this black governess and the white child in her arms was so alive that Mère wondered if she could bear it, for the image of the comforting governess now merged with her about to die, in a few months, Mère would see her no more, except in dreams, as though there were a train with a joyous ghost always ready to go for a ride in the fog of special mornings that no longer belonged to us or ever would again, yes on the boat Caroline had sensed perfectly what would happen to her and to all of us, even if she sometimes appeared to forget Jean-Mathieu's name, calling him friend and poet, you know, the one I loved so much, is he still in Italy, and had an attack of vertigo on the catamaran as they approached The-Island-Nobody-Owns amid the noise of the waves, I don't want to go there she said, it's so far and they tell me it's uninhabited, full of snakes and iguanas and deer running free, that music, thought Petites Cendres with its plaintive guitars, Riley King's music with husky cries, it spoke of the slavery of poor whites too, also exploited in the cotton fields, barefoot in the burrs and thorns, they too with heavy packs on their backs, the injustice of the 1900s, all those faces stained with sweat and earth, thousands of little girls and boys in the fields and the factories, brought back to mind by the photo-investigator Lewis W. Hine, pretending to be a Bible salesman so he could find his way into huts and houses all across the country with his camera, faces of twelve-year-old miners smeared with coal dust, boys with arms lopped off in accidents, treacherous industry, invalids still at work with one arm or one leg inside their coveralls and cotton shirts, small faces, old and worn, all of them unforgettable yet forgotten whites, the fake Bible salesman going from hut to hut and across fields where kids had their feet pierced right through, had pulled this off and eternalized the disgrace of the exploiters, thanks to him, these pictures suddenly turned up in the Supreme Court, an agitator for reform without knowing it, he'd put an end to this type of slavery, though people had heard the laments of voices not even broken yet in the music which hammered at Petites Cendres' temples, the rumble of revolt was his too, three in the afternoon and Papa said I had a good voice, Vénus told Rebecca, Mama didn't like it when I sat out too late on the porch or in the swing with boys, I got slapped on both cheeks and they got hot, it really upset me, she was always tougher on me than Papa, mothers are jealous of their daughters, I won't be though, I have to say Mama was always very pious and upright, and she always had to be yelling names and hitting me every day, she said I hung out too much and rained slaps on me, and I don't know where those dresses came from, did I steal things like Carlos, I mean a real thief like him, then one day a saleslady in a store accused me, saying what's this scarlet stain of menstrual blood on my mousseline dress in the changing-room, what is this, and they were all around me, the manager, the salespeople, and I had to pay the full price, no, no I yelled, I'm Vénus and you're not going to get me, then I tried to get away, but the police, the bloodstain, was that me, me, I was devastated, and they were all on at me and insulting me, if it weren't for that woman, I'd never seen her before, but she stepped in and kept them from arresting me, she defended me, discrimination, she said, she was just visiting the island, and she probably won't ever be back, that dress was so clingy, and where would I be for a bit of stupid blood, Rebecca, someone passing through called Renata, a lawyer and later she became a judge, I've seen her trials, if I wanted to study for a long time, like Perdue Baltimore the lawyer, working at low-paying jobs in hotels to get by, I did it for you Rebecca, everything's for you, she might have been a bit snobbish or indifferent, but she told them all she needed to, proved my innocence, a lady from somewhere else, just passing through, for a menstrual stain, see, a big deal, then prison for young girls, Papa, till I fell on the floor in front of her, they got the blood off the dress, mousseline dress tight on the hips, it was over, so I didn't say anything to Papa and Mama, they'll never know, I told them, I'm Vénus and you aren't going to get me, I told them all, don't you lay one filthy hand on me, sometimes Rebecca, you need to know how to hate, really hate, not because you want to, but sometimes you just have to. Alphonso thought again of the men and women who were the docile, defenceless prey of the corrupt priest he had replaced in this New England parish, the man his superiors had protected with the seal of the confessional, and who would never be accused of his actions, a man of the Church after all, and that's how it was always, complacency, indulgence, the power of the strong over the weak, the insidious presence of a depraved priest, the memory of that man in the presbytery, the affliction of children whose innocence had been betrayed, how could

Alphonso put them out, even if his house, his church was now
the sanctuary of all the strangers coming to him with no papers
or documents, he had established a haven for them, he'd even
given it the same name as his church, the Sanctuary, a haven
to those threatened with deportation every day, and he was
afraid their number could only grow with the number of per-
secutions and spreading cruelties, in Spain, those who resisted
deportation were put in straitjackets, yet the Old Testament
said more than a hundred times that God was God without
country, love them and welcome them as you yourselves
would be, he who is without country is within my Kingdom,
or was Alphonso interpreting Scripture in his own way so no
one could be given up in handcuffs to savage customs officers, are they not all children of God, in fact, not one of them
ever set foot in Alphonso's Sanctuary, nor through the doors
of his church, they called him the activist priest, the Christian
theologian, and he thought, they aren't going to make martyrs
out of the people I keep here, that my housekeeper and I
feed, rather go to prison myself if I have to, we're all foreign-
ers on one Earth as it was written with regard to Egypt, each
every bit as much as the other, He Himself said, I am the God
of strangers in a country where all are strangers and wish to
drink from a single well, perhaps these images came from
Reverend Ézéchielle whose sermons in the Community Church
were one long metaphor, loving to tell stories as she did and
dancing from one foot to the other, girls had seen their mothers leave, and mothers their sons, on this Earth promised to
us all, in the Lutheran Church, priests, rabbis, and pastors followed Alphonso's lead, and all went to their sanctuaries for
refuge, they said it was because of Alphonso, the communist
priest, and what did he suppose was going to happen to him,
but Alphonso replied that man's Earth was also God's, and it
didn't matter if he went to prison, a shame though with all he
had to do for these families, blessing and consoling them, and
that he, Alphonso, could never be a bad priest, above all he

would be a man, Reverend Ézéchielle herself had told him
that he must act this way, first of all, be a man, Alphonso, and
it was with great sadness that she said goodbye to him, that
was when Alphonso was still in the archipelago, so moved by
the palms, the birdsong, and the summer breeze, friend of all
the neighbourhood kids, life was easier then, and he was perhaps something of a child himself, surely she was right to tell
him to be a man first and foremost, there were far too many
priests lacking in humanity already, she said, regretfully saying goodbye, so you're off up to the north my good Alphonso,
even if we never stopped arguing about your Catholic myths,
she'd been right to stand up to him, even give him a hard
time, how to admit, he wondered, that a woman so liberal
could be right? Petites Cendres was pushed away by his client
so violently that he fell on the piano, then he saw the carnival-
looking man in his belted robe walk towards him, and he got
up and said, hey plaster-boy in shades, what the hell do you
want, this is the time of madness, said the man, so why not
dress up as an impenitent monk looking for pearls in a saloon,
looks like you haven't heard the news about Timo, the man
laughed loudly, I bet you haven't a clue you coward, Timo,
whimpered Petites Cendres, I know he's gone and free with
his hair blowing in the wind, too heavy on the gas, faster and
faster, that's what I know said Petites Cendres, Ashley, Petites
Cendres, the man replied, don't you know the sheriff has
unleashed his whole pack on him, they even had to stop traffic to let them all through sirens wailing, he had ten packets
of cocaine hidden under the back seat of that Sonata, then do
you know what your friend Timo did, no, you don't know, do
you, when they approached him, he opened the car door and
made like he was going to run for it, guessed Petites Cendres,
he wanted to but he couldn't, and then, well, they reduced
his brain to mush, I'm telling you, and now you know, Petites
Cendres, while the man was talking, Petites Cendres saw the
blond kid with round cheeks again, would he be back with

his tailor, where are you and when are you going to come and clean up all this ugliness, sure it's carnival time, said the robed man, I'm allowed to have a little fun with you and not have you go all serious on me, aren't I, Ashley, Petites Cendres, come on over and let me give you a kiss, no, said Petites Cendres, get out of here, don't you worry about your friend Timo, he'll get out of this somehow, maybe a bullet in the back, but he's quick on his feet, so don't you worry about him, Timo's a slippery guy, he knows how to get his money's worth for a mashed-up brain, he was stupid enough to open the door, then Petites Cendres saw the strange personage go out into the street, someone else's hand was on his shoulder now, Dieudonné, his doctor, I knew you were here in the saloon, good thing I know I can always find you here, do you want to come over to my infirmary on Bahama tomorrow, I need to talk to you, with a name like that, Dieudonné, Doctor Dieudonné, you've got to be blessed by the heavens, do you think you've got some sort of cream for these pimples, nobody wants a guy with pimples, Petites Cendres said to him, see that's why I can't work anywhere but here at the Porte du Baiser, you, you're big and handsome, you impress your parents, and this dump isn't for you, right, but you're the one I came to see, Petites Cendres, said the man in a calm voice that assuaged Petites Cendres, he'd only go to the infirmary in a real emergency, he thought, but still Petites Cendres had been missing his appointments, all of them, this voice that would normally calm the deepest inner fears of Petites Cendres didn't pacify him at all, but just reawakened his anxiety at losing Timo, it was true, he had lost him, I'll go tomorrow he said, I'll expect you at two, Dieudonné, my Haitian friend, you know I'll be there, Petites Cendres lied, we're both black, both the same age, but look what you've done with your life, the doctor seemed to say but didn't, and your infirmary's overflowing with wretched creatures who aren't going to live long, Petites Cendres felt like saying but didn't, you impress them, all of

them, trembling at the truth you might be about to tell them,
even with your gentle approach, and the way you touch us,
they know they're not going to get better, Dieudonné my
friend, I'll be there at two, but you've got to promise you'll
get rid of all these spots, I will, he said, but I want to talk to
you as well, it won't be long, but I've told you to be careful
who you have relations with, I've always told you, Petites
Cendres wanted to cling to his friend's imposing frame, it was
time to dance, though they didn't see each other very often,
Dieudonné was still his friend, and such a handsome guy with
such a well-chosen name couldn't hurt, but Petites Cendres
wasn't that far into withdrawal, though he'd helped him out
of it before, but would he go on doing it, congratulations on
your success, Dieudonné, your infirmary's won the city's medal
of honour, really, congratulations, he shook him by the shoulders, though timidly, listen dance-time's beginning, I'd invite
you to dance, I really would, geez it's noisy in here, said the
doctor looking at his watch, I promised my wife I'd take the
kids to the movies tonight, so you've got that now, two o'clock
at the infirmary on Bahama, it won't take long, just one or two
things I have to say to you, and we've got to stop those pimples from spreading across your face, see you tomorrow, why
not make it an early night tonight, Dieudonné, my friend, said
Petites Cendres, may the heavens bless you for the good you
do, never doubt it, I'll be there tomorrow at two, right now,
there's Sluttie all alone for a change, think I'll go dance with
him. Christmas night, thought Mai, a night of elaborate fes-
tivities in the house of Chuan and Olivier, my parents' friends,
everyone's here, grandparents and bent-over great-uncles, I
feel a tremor of indecency, probably because I should be at
the beach or somewhere else with Manuel, she thought — a
slight tremor, that's all — oh right, maybe that's it, when
Grandmother and I were having breakfast together in town,
just the two of us, her with that wide hat and me with hair
freshly brushed by Marie-Sylvie, that I flipped with one finger

to cover my forehead, tell me Mai who is that much older boy, eh, I looked at Grandmother without answering, her gaze settled on me as though observing me for the first time, my pierced ears and the ring through the tip of my tongue, there was a blue shadow to her face, withdrawing as it did beneath the wide brim of the hat, and I thought of her friend Caroline, and that one day my grandmother too would . . . no, she took my hand, caressed and kissed it, my dear little Mai, she said with feeling, to think that at last your brothers are here with us, even if just for a few days, it's incredible my dear, I told her Augustino hadn't got handsomer with his curved nose and hair down to his shoulders when the fashion was short hair or a shaved head, of course, he was disagreeable too, a regular bear, Grandmother said, but you know he writes books, but at least he could tidy himself up, I told her, still, I was glad Vincent's health was better since he'd been playing tennis, maybe he will be an athlete after all, and Samuel, since he'd been home, he and Mum had been together the whole time, and I wanted her all for myself, maybe tonight of all nights, she said she was going to sit near me, but then there will be different tables, even outside by the pool, and she'll be talking a lot with Olivier, she hasn't come anywhere near me yet, Samuel said he'd dance to some electronic music, and Jermaine's fun too, maybe I'll dance as well, but Samuel's a dancer and choreographer in New York, and I don't want him to see me, maybe he's changed, maybe he doesn't even remember me, I'd be better off at the beach, candle holders glittering on the tables, stars in the sky, Augustino's eyes too, and Grandpa Joseph played a bit on the violin, then he said, my fingers are getting stiff, I'm sorry, please excuse me, it was supposed to be Sibelius, it'll be better tomorrow, I was so sad I wanted to run away, Augustino's eyes seemed to be reading my mind, tomorrow let's go for a walk on the beach you and I, it was true about Chuan, a fairy she was, as Grandmother says, it's all so festive around us, the African lilies perfuming the garden, lights shining around the pool, I might not have wanted to leave after all, but that sound I heard, and Olivier said he heard it too, noise but not noise, maybe near the house or the garden gate, hear that, Olivier asked his wife, but Chuan said, I beg you dear, don't start, I organized this party and I ordered fireworks, no, that detonation's from explosives or a fire, Olivier said apparently trembling with fear, and Mum came over and talked to him some more, what is that, he asked, what is that, I can see a red flame behind my cabin, no, said Chuan, it's just a mirage, those "flames" are just what I ordered, an ornamental fire, when they criticized my article, he said, you remember, I got threatening letters, even . . . no, she said, in pained patience, none of it's real, my dear, these are unfounded fears, hallucinations, we've already told you, no one's persecuting you Olivier, I got overenthusiastic about this party for your sake, that's all, and Jermaine, as well as our parents and friends, none of us would want to hurt you Olivier, look, here's Jermaine, this is a good moment for a heart-to-heart with your son, I'm sure you'll be a better listener than I am, you've got to calm down Olivier, Chuan may have said all this, but I heard the noise too, and it wasn't just the speeding tires of a motorcycle on the asphalt out in the street, something sharper, I heard it till Jermaine asked me to dance, I liked his hair dyed gold and his slanted eyes like his mother's, now it was time to laugh and have fun and stop being afraid, and since it's a holiday, maybe Mum will come and sit by me, the way she said she would, at the banquet table later on. And Daniel thought it very moving for a father to see all his children around him, quite an achievement when the book is never finished, like Franz's opera, unfinished, the frailest being Vincent, still, he was working hard at getting stronger, running on the beach with his dog for hours, Marie-Sylvie said, he doesn't listen to me at all any more, and he doesn't think about his heart rhythm at all, he's a very active teenager and tirelessly curious, he reminds me of Mélanie, same intensity,

same smile, at last my boy's got more robust, much less cough-
ing at night, he asks the old architect Isaac about his solar
house on The-Island-Nobody-Owns, an old man like me is
well on his way, said Isaac in his khaki shorts, leaning with
dignity on his cane, I thought I could complete it all by myself
without the help of younger architects, but alas, I've only got
as far as the stairs but not way up high between sea and sky
where the egrets and herons perch, and the ocean seemed
to go on forever when I climbed those rickety stairs with no
difficulty, oh yes, a liquid world, and the young folks said
what was I doing up there, I ought to come down, now why,
Vincent, would I not surmount that last obstacle, tell me, you
know as well as I do what's out there, more water, more
oceans we don't know, like you during your bouts of breathlessness, I wouldn't go that final distance high up there, they
said I might fall and break a hip, I planned this solar home
for you my boy, so you can have this space and air like in a
tree house, the island looks microscopic from up there, one of
these days, schools will be solar, water will be recycled so you
can drink it again, imagine schoolrooms with roof gardens,
everybody choosing his own plants and herbs, bamboo walls
like my house, old Isaac said, and we'll learn to keep these
fields green all the time, with rice, I see these kind architects,
too kind to me, who say, come down from that spiral stairway
to the sky, out over the ocean, what they don't understand,
no, really they don't, is what I saw up there Vincent, but you,
well, I know you can because the evil angel has brushed you
more than once with his wing, it really is quite an upset for a
father to see all his children at once this close, Daniel reflected,
to count them and not miss a single one, except the symbolic
one, the unfinished book, the imperfect book or Franz's opera,
the work he said would surprise everyone, it will come into
the world at the same time as Rachel's child, my young wife
who is the new beginning to my life, and what did Rachel
think, her youthfulness as untouched as Mai's, yes, what did

Franz's wife think of this, that Franz was a genial and candid man, but with a young son, as well as his grandson Yehudi who already played his scores for piano so well, his inspiration would be doubly renewed, and Rachel, the child transfigured by passion, had no way of knowing who the Franz of tomorrow would be in a very few years, a professor, musician, composer, directing his orchestra in increasingly rapid movements, keeping time with less precision, less regularity, getting upset, that enigmatic head under a thinning white crown, exalted in its conquest of so many women, no, thought Daniel, Franz, escorted by that dynasty of his, bubbling over with plans, would always be gifted with charisma and an infernal energy while others were giving way around him, a number of boats had been rented for the night, though you couldn't see or hear them from the garden, Vincent was telling Great-Uncle Isaac, but the dark water against the night sky was scattered with emerald lights, the boats not in the race were moving slowly and silently, polluting the fauna and the banks of the Coral Coast, that's what I don't want to see from up there in my tower and my house in the heavens, said Great-Uncle Isaac, boats as tiny as sharpened pencils, he told Vincent, even if you can't see or hear them at night, they do a lot of damage, but Vincent was preoccupied with the thought that tonight he'd be out in one of those light boats, *Southern Light*, nobody to see or hear them, a few hours from now at the marina, a Christmas gift from Samuel to him, and whatever you do, don't say a thing to Mum and Marie-Sylvie de la Toussaint, I mean, it's a holiday, and we can do whatever we want, if it got cold, Samuel would just wrap him in his captain's cape and there would be no problem, not like the time when Vincent couldn't get his oxygen and Dad was so frightened, nothing like that with Samuel, you think I'm dreaming, but it's really happening, Olivier said to Jermaine who was squeezing his hands in his own, those old cars and motorcycles always get caught at checkpoints or going onto the bridge, they get

the suspects, I'm not dreaming, Jermaine, what do they find
when they get them on their knees in the street, hands behind
their backs, this, my son, is ten pounds of explosives, each
one has a TNT charge, Daniel could see Jermaine leading his
father to sit in the red chair by the pool designed by a modern
sculptor, Jermaine said to his suffering father, Dad, what you're
telling me is the script for the movie I'm making in L.A., pure
imagination, Dad, well, you shouldn't write such things, his
father said, dear son of mine, I see you so rarely, do you still
love me as you used to, Jermaine wrapped his arms around
his father, saying nothing, Chuan was nearby with a pill, here,
take this, you'll feel better, Olivier, she asked, is it true our
son's written quite a sordid script, he writes, said Olivier,
what's going on, don't you hear that noise, it's right nearby;
Jermaine went over to little Mai, saying, you want me to teach
you to dance, Olivier could hear them laughing, though
Jermaine's music was so deafening, yeah, I'd better take this
pill, said Olivier, my agitation's spoiling everyone's fun, no
wind, such a beautiful night, Chuan said, soon they'll be unty-
ing the boats in the marina, Olivier, but I have to get back to
the kitchen, I'm afraid I can't always be after you, she said,
I'm fine here in this chair watching the dogs run around the
pool, you can leave me here, I know now why I got threatening letters, that's what I was explaining to Mélanie a few
moments ago, I reminded people what they wrote about us
in 1857, a man wrote that for over a century we've seen them
as an inferior race and ill-adapted to associate with the white
race politically or socially, and up till now they have no rights
that a white man can respect, as he finished his sentence, his
swift-footed wife in the pink dress was no longer there, the
dogs were barking joyously around the pool, and the stars
were shining on the sea, Olivier's pill seemed to bring him a
short spell of euphoria, Daniel, the brilliant novelist with no
more time to write but engaged in saving the unsaveable Coral
Coast, Olivier thought, might be right in saying that literature

was at the origin of changes in society and the ideological reconstruction of a country, Olivier hadn't yet read his books, there were so many writers to get through in town, Chuan would do it for him, if Daniel was to be believed, poets and thinkers had brought more impetus to the country than all the politicians put together, though their names were rarely mentioned, Ralph Waldo Emerson, Emily Dickinson, Herman Melville, Edgar Allan Poe, the real pillars of evolution, if we are to believe what he says, thought Olivier, while she was dancing, Mai saw her mother and grandmother chatting with some energy beneath the heavy branches of African lily, it wasn't the music that made Jermaine's body move in a cadence to which Mai set some awkward steps, was it the languor of ecstasy, Jermaine danced with his eyes raised to the sky, occasionally sighing, Dad, dear poor Dad, how can I help him, what do you think Mai, once in a while he would take her hand, then let it go, now she could see the faces of Mélanie and her mother better, brown hair framing the face of one, a white fringe over the forehead of the other, who for once was not wearing her broad-brimmed hat tonight, may you always keep your faith in women's success, her grandmother was saying, and may your children inherit it too, you know doubt is so deeply rooted, Marie Curie died sensing it, Mélanie said, ever since that day in 1964 when they included women in the Bill of Rights there's been so much progress, that's what I always say to young women at conferences, it was a woman who renewed the miracle, Betty Friedan, other avant-gardists, women writers and philosophers, the biologist Rachel Carson, with her eloquent and rigorous attacks on the use of pesticides, if Vincent wanted to become a biologist, it was because her efforts so stimulated the younger generations, all these women scientists were a treasure trove of rising stars, Mother, women governors and senators, yet in Iran young girls accused of murder cannot even avoid the death penalty, sometimes as young as fifteen, and why should that be when all they've done is repel an aggressor, what other solution would there be to rape anyway, implore the U.N. for help, women and girls, justice is now in our hands only, and what about women presidents Mother, isn't this finally a time of justice and victory for us, Mère surprised her daughter, replying that these words seemed illogical, what was Mère saying, it made no sense, had she even listened to Mélanie, was she nostalgic for the voices one no longer heard, Maria Callas, Elisabeth Schwarzkopf, who sang her to sleep at night in her garden pavilion, window open to the jasmine perfume, such luminous voices, how will we do without them now, Mère said, this nostalgic evocation was meant only to soften her daughter's expectations and lighten the impact of retreat and disappointment, for such was the world we live in, Mère then felt a chill silence come between them, better that way, Mère thought, thus her daughter would also suffer less later on from the end of their connection which was close, too close, yes, better that way, she thought to herself, Christiensen told Nora, we're going to be late at Chuan and Olivier's, tell me which you like best, she asked him, this dress with the white rose at the neckline like Greta's wedding dress, no, not that, he said imperiously, the simple white suit, I can't understand why you leave your painting outside when you know it'll rain tonight, I don't like the shading, she replied, already redressed, I don't like any of my paintings these days, Christiensen reminded her that she had an exhibition in a week, it was shameful she had so little respect for her own work, he'd carefully brought it back into the large library, tanned and wearing her white suit, Nora was already gone ahead of her husband into the warm night, so, she thought, he was leaving for the Niger Republic again in a few days, though he said it would be a short trip this time, an emergency, otherwise he'd never leave her, the children, or the grandchildren, no, there was no wish for this at all he told Nora, she walked quickly so he wouldn't be tempted to come closer and try to explain why he had to go, he'd miss the family dinner despite his promises, the lamps were lit in Chuan's garden, in a week there would be no more exhibitions Nora thought, I hate all these paintings, not enough light, I can't seem to capture the feeling of exile from my childhood in Africa, I just can't, and all this while, my children are marrying, their children are being born, perhaps my only happiness is with them nearby, the contentment of a life spent in benefiting others rather than myself, I suppose that's it, Mère, though, had told her she would return to Africa, her work there was not yet done, yes, go back to the orphans, the war-displaced, the popular neighbourhoods of Lubumbashi, in those diplomatic missions my husband tries to reconcile peoples, I guess what I have to do is more modest, all I want is my orphans and displaced in those neighbourhoods, but how can I say this to the kids, thought Nora, maybe I shouldn't say anything, Mélanie's mother, Esther told me I should go back, by the time he got to the beach, Christiensen could see the giant palms along the edge of the sea, glittering as though covered in silver lace, like trees filled with candles in a silent wind from over the waves, sad there was always this conflict over Nora's paintings and her insatiable appetite for artistic perfection, ah! And no matter how time swept through their lives, she was still nothing but a stubborn kid he'd never be able to convince of her artistic integrity or value, a waste of time, she just wouldn't listen, and Hans, it would be better if he didn't admire his father quite so much, if he understood he had many faults, and not see him as some mythic hero from the past, a great man of superior intelligence, in the here and now, it wasn't healthy for a boy to admire his father so much, it stood in the way of their relating to each other man to man, when he got back from Niger, Christiensen would talk to him unless Hans had to leave too as an airline steward for some unknown destination, he would have to talk with him, I'll tell him the same thing I told him once after I came back from Jordan, there are no heroes, every life has its dark spot, something we've done, a mistake we could have avoided, for me it happened when I was a little boy in Norway, a tough kid, the hero in me was blind, I remember the cruel joy I felt running after the trucks of crying women with shaved heads, and I can still hear that child's wicked laughter at seeing these humiliated women and the men who judged them, seeing them waiting in their ragged underwear, not knowing how to hide their breasts and lowering their eyes before us, so tell me son, why did I feel no pity for these pathetic women, you're wrong to see me as the father and man that you do, you must understand that I am just like any other, maybe a little more lucid than some, but that's all, Christiensen recalled a moment earlier that day when he was walking on the beach, his tennis racquet under his arm, when he saw three boys catching gulls in their shirts like nets, all Christiensen, used to commanding, had to do was order them to stop, perhaps with some suppleness, but still imperiously and angrily, and it would send them running, the youngest walked right up to him with an imaginary pistol in his hand, yelling, bang, bang, and Christiensen, still hounded by his thoughts, thought, well, that's how we're made, it seems like an innocent game, but it's really just torture, then he was distracted by the arrival of Bernard and Valérie as they came in the entrance, where there was a double row of red roses in vases, dear friends, Christiensen said, how good it is to see you before I leave, I hope I have time to meet Valérie, for breakfast tomorrow, I'd like to talk to her about Hans, here is a woman and a friend, he thought, who understands everything, she has grown children herself, she had them very young though, she's also seen many disasters that leave a stain of hurt and shame, still she resembled a Goya model, carnal and serene, here she was already kissing Christiensen, Bernard taking part in this overflow of sincere affection and embracing Christiensen himself, then promising to take care of Nora while he was away, you're the sunlight in this community, said the poet used to this kind of language, for a few days I've been looking for a special word in Hebrew, oh, it'll come to me at supper, the champagne will help of course, I used to have an exceptional memory, and now this blank all of a sudden, however exceptional Valérie is, it's only human, alas, Bernard laughed, and Chuan, with the little dog in her arms, was waiting for them so the fun could begin, Nora was quick to join Mère and was talking with lively enthusiasm, looking intent, Christiensen noticed how tanned Nora looked, and the white shell necklace stood out against her skin, always so changing and impenetrable, they all sat in their places at the banquet tables, each one designated with a card featuring a photo of two white herons against a setting sun, Jermaine liked the pictures he took and wanted to celebrate marine birds before their wings were paralyzed with spilled oil, such crimes were now known to happen daily he told his father, there were the instant pictures of the birds, so white on the white tablecloths, like the flashes of clarity in a last sea rescue before the sea was soiled, wings spread wide to show their splendour, Mai saw she was seated near her mother, too bad Olivier was on her left, because Mélanie was sure to turn his way; sitting next to Augustino, Daniel thought it was time to say something about his son's book, Bernard was already raising his glass to toast young Augustino's success, and the latter was blushing as he looked around at his writing mentors, Bernard, Valérie, Daniel, and all the others, Daniel felt a hint of jealousy, how awful to feel such a thing, more than just shocking, reprehensible, Valérie though was quite maternal towards the boy and said he was very courageous to write so honestly about what he felt, Augustino felt the sulphurous eyes of his father on him, how clumsy, the yellow glint in them seemed to say, yet perhaps it was really an indefinable hint of pride, the dark pride that linked a rebel father to an equally rebellious son, I've offended him by keeping quiet so long, thought Daniel, and now he's retreated behind that mass of hair and ridiculously intellectual-looking glasses, where does all this come from, he's so different from the others, or maybe too much like me, I never noticed that crooked tooth of Mai's, I'd better get her an appointment with the dentist, it's disturbing to see the eyes of all your children on you, how can one be fair to them all, those birds of the Coral Coast have to be saved before it's too late, said the scholarly Bernard, suddenly remembering the Hebrew word he wanted, *daleth*, that was it, it meant may the door to the greatest mysteries be opened wide, isn't that what Suzanne was saying, *daleth*, let the door open to the light, yes, that's what she meant said Mère, *daleth*, by the way, why aren't she and Adrien here with us asked Bernard, aren't they already back from Switzerland or are they leaving tonight, Mai heard all these voices but understood none of it, maybe Jermaine's music was about to bury them in sovereign chaos, Mum was smiling tenderly and talking to Mai, at least until Olivier began talking again about that noise he'd heard, like a detonation just out there in the street or maybe even here inside the walls, an explosion he said, didn't you hear it, so Mélanie turned to reassure him, but Mai said, Mum, I heard it too, and there was a smell of smoke and a young man, he had his hands tied behind his back, and he confessed, he said, yes, it was me, didn't you hear the explosion asked Olivier, look, they're all over there, Rebecca said to Vénus, the kayaks, the canoes, Papa and his musicians, they're all over there coming towards us, look, it's dark, but there's Papa Trevor, Prince of Jazz, sleighs sliding over the sea, Trevor who plays so well but already staggering, said Vénus, but he's my Papa, Trevor the Prince of Jazz, Rebecca said, hold my hand, I don't want to lose you in this crowd, Vénus told her, when dawn comes, said Vincent to Samuel, not a sound, and no motor, just oars, we'll hear the song of the waves, we'll take turns rowing said Samuel, *Southern Light, Southern Light*, said Vincent, breathing the sea air, everything for the precarious sweetness of living, all around him, looking at his parents and the friends of his parents, love, so much love.

Acknowledgements

Marie-Claire Blais wishes to thank Francine Dumouchel and Marie Couillard.

Nigel Spencer thanks his sons, Antoine and Olivier, with Pauline Karolewicz, for their great patience and support, as well as his mother, Phyllis Tester Spencer, recently deceased.